Happiness
Thru the Art of...
Penis Enlargement:
A 'Novel Guide' to Jelqing, The G-Spot,
How to Last Longer in Bed
& Other Sexual Secrets

Cristian YoungMiller

RateABull
Books

The characters and events in this book are fictitious. Any similarity to real persons, living or dead, is coincidental and not intended by the author.

Copyright © 2010 by Cristian YoungMiller

All rights reserved. No part of this book may be reproduced in any form or by any electronic or mechanical means, including information storage and retrieval systems, without permission in writing from the publisher, except by a reviewer who my quote brief passages in a review. For information contact Cristian YoungMiller at RateABull@gmail.com.

RateABull Books
Visit our Web site at www.RateABull.com

Book Design by Cristian YoungMiller
Cover Illustration by ohsobeit.com

ISBN-13: 978-0-9827132-0-4
ISBN-10: 0-98-271320-7

To all of the guys that are made to feel that they aren't good enough as they are.

Other books by Cristian YoungMiller:

Everybody Masturbates

'Everybody Masturbates' is the perfect gift idea for anyone from ages 8 to 42 yrs old. In the style of the classic book 'Everyone Poops,' 'Everybody Masturbates' is designed to make boys and girls of all ages feel comfortable about masturbation. (It also makes a great party gift for adults.)

Everybody Masturbates *for Girls*

'Everybody Masturbates *for Girls*' is the perfect gift idea for girls between the ages of 7 to 38 yrs old. Also, in the style of the classic book 'Everyone Poops,' 'Everybody Masturbates *for Girls*' addresses the specific issues that girls have accepting their emerging sexuality. (It also makes a great party gift for adults.)

Buy Fall 2010:

Happiness thru the Art of…
Having Sex like a Porn Star:

A 'Novel Guide' to Sexual Positions, Multiple Orgasms, Increasing Your Sex Drive & Other Sexual Secrets*

'Happiness thru the Art of… Having Sex like a Porn Star' is the sequel to 'Happiness thru the Art of… Penis Enlargement'. Follow the further adventures of Ben and his talking penis 'the Brotha,' as the Brotha tries to stop drinking, and Ben attempts to make his new relationship work.

The First Day After Life:

A Spiritual Adventure about Why Bad Things Happen & How to Shape your Future*

'The First Day After Life is a story about a psychic who dies, tours the afterlife like he's backstage at a theme park, and as a result, discovers the real explanation for why God lets bad things happen to good people.

Contents

Chapter 1
Meet Ben and the Brotha..1

Chapter 2
How Ben and the Brotha Met.. 20

Chapter 3
How Do You Make a Penis Happy?.. 32

Chapter 4
How to Enlarge Your Penis 49

Chapter 5
The Journey of Two Inches Begins with a Single Jelq 63

Chapter 6
Taking the Brotha Out for a Test Drive 100

Chapter 7
How to Last Longer in Bed... 118

Chapter 8
The G-Spot & How to Help a Woman have an Orgasm 135

Chapter 9
Ben, the Brotha and a Rose Bush.. 150

Chapter 10
Escorts Need Love Too.. 162

Chapter 11
How Big is Too Big? 177

Chapter 12
Why You Shouldn't Screw a Rose Bush 195

Chapter 13
How to Be Happy 210

Acknowledgements

I would like to first thank Michael Presky for all of the hard work he put into proofing this book for me. It was a pleasure working with you. Katy Bea, your devotion to this project was invaluable so I thank you for it. Paul McMahon, your encouragement and honest assessment of how people would respond to my writing was, in part, why I wrote the book. Maria, thank you for all of the dinners that we shared while I wrote this book. They helped more than I can express.

And when you're writing a book, being able to talk endless about the process is always essential; so Paul Rubenstein and Keith Hammons, thank you for at least pretending that you were interested in my ramblings. And last, but most of all, I would like to thank the guys on RateABull.com who encouraged me to write a book years before I considered it myself. Your interest and questions were the basis of my story. I hope that this story helps you as much as your thanks have helped me.

Happiness
Thru the Art of…
Penis Enlargement:
A 'Novel Guide' to Jelqing, The G-Spot,
How to Last Longer in Bed
& Other Sexual Secrets

CHAPTER 1
Meet Ben and the Brotha

What does the word 'adage' mean? If you look it up in the dictionary you might find the definition as follows: a traditional saying that expresses something considered to be a general truth. But I don't think that's it. The word takes on a whole new meaning when you consider its Latin root 'bondage,' which in Latin means: ye twisted game where thou betrothed dost dawn the highly shined skin of land beast and attaches said betrothed to thou'st bed posts and precedes to lash thou betrothed body until both are writhing with pleasure. See when you consider the Latin root of a word the word always takes on a whole new meaning. That's why Latin used to be taught in school and resulted in smarter students.

No, the word adage has a much more insidious origin. It's rooted in twisted games of power that may or may not include the use of patent leather. It is a word meant to subjugate and humiliate. It is a word meant to create two classes of people where one is enslaved to the other. It was a word that Hitler used many times during his most famous speech to the German people. Only people don't realize it because he said it in German and in German the meaning is different.

No, the word adage is not a friend to us, or to society, or to humans as a species. It is a word that mocks us in its existence. It laughs at us every time we foolishly utter the word again. And every time a folksy person slips the word 'adage' into a sentence to make himself seem a little smarter, he chips away at the chains that hold back the doors of hell. Aren't the fire breathing demons that constantly bang on the doors enough for the chains to handle? Must we add to our eventual demise by chipping away at the chains ourselves? I say we should avoid it at all costs, but hey, 'you can lead a horse to water, but you can't make him drink.'

Since I probably can't get those types to stop using adages, I would like to throw out a few random examples of why adages destroy the foundations of life as we know it. Do you know the adage that says that the size of a man's penis is directly related to his height? How about the adage that says that the size of a man's penis is directly related to the size of his feet? And here's another one: the size of a man's penis is directly related to the size of the man's hands with the thickness of his thumb being related to his penis' thickness. And of course, there is the adage that black men have large penises.

    Now these are just random examples and I could have chosen any of millions. But let's be honest, if these adages were real, as a six foot six black man with size 14 shoes and hands large enough to palm a basketball, my penis would be so large that it would stretch down my pant leg and I would trip over it as I walked around. If adages were true I would need to tuck the head of my penis into my shoes. And when old Mrs. Fey drove her walker by me as I walked to work, I would have to tell her that I keep a dead snake in my pants.

    The head of my penis would probably be all black and blue from it being dragged across the ground. And when women ask me about it I would be all like "no baby no. These are love scars that I got because I was dreaming about you and my penis kept scraping the ceiling." She'd be all like "oh baby, you so sweet. I want you to push it all the way in me." And I'd be like "you know it baby." And then I would pass out as all of the blood rushed out of my body to fill my penis. And then, passed out, I would rock her world. And in a few hours after I came to ("came," get it?), she would beg me for more.

    But that's not how it goes. Instead, I wake up in the morning and go to take a piss and sometimes when I reach down I find something missing. I start to scream the manliest high pitched scream you ever heard because I think my penis is gone. Yeah I find it. Sometimes it takes two hands to pull it out like a calf out of a cow, but it's there.

    After I take my morning piss I turn on the shower, get naked and do my best not to look at myself in the mirror. And if I do catch a glimpse I try to keep it above the waist. If I'm looking into the mirror I usually take the opportunity to check my hairline to make sure it's all still there. And then I check my teeth to see if any of last night's dinner still remains. And if I'm feeling very adventurous I keep looking down at my chest and then my stomach. And then if I'm feeling lucky I look further down, hoping that I won't find him looking back at me. But he always is.

"What, you starin' at me?" he usually says.

I look away but I know how the rest of the morning is gonna go.

"You got a problem with me? You got a fuckin' problem? Bring your ass around here and I'll show you a fuckin' problem."

"I don't have a problem," I sometimes say back.

"Well it seems like you do. It seems like your little shit for brains has a problem with me."

I usually do my best to ignore him by turning on the shower and going about my business. I pull out my toothbrush, paste it up and get to work. But once he gets started there's no stopping him.

"When you think you're man enough to look me in the eye then you look back down. You hear me talking to you? What, you think you could ignore me? You can't ignore me bitch. I own you. You hear me? I own your sorry punk ass. Your sweet punk ass is mine."

That is usually where the seduction begins.

"Why don't you take your sweet ass into the shower. I said get into the shower, bitch."

I know that if I don't do it he's just going to get angrier, so I do.

"Yeah that's right. Why don't you bring your fine self down here and let me feel your fine looking fingers. Oh yeah, that's right. Why don't you tell me whose bitch you is."

"I'm your bitch."

"I want you to scream it bitch. Tell everyone listening whose bitch you is."

"I'm your bitch," I scream, knowing that if I don't all of this will just get worse.

"You damn right you my bitch. Now work those fingers bitch. That's right pull it back. Make me feel it bitch. Make me feel it. Work the soap bitch. Oh yeah! That's right. Make me feel it bitch. Oh yeah, ho! That's right! Oh yeah! Right now. Right now! Ahhhhh! Zzzzzzz."

And then my day can begin.

I try to keep as close to a routine as possible. I get out of the shower, towel off, and then get dressed. If it's during the week I wear underwear. On the weekends I don't. For work days I have all of my work shirts aligned in my closet by order of which one I most like to wear.

After picking out the day's work clothes, I sit down for a bowl of cereal. At the table is when I allow my mind to relax again before my day really begins. I can think about what's going to be on TV that night or which bus driver I'm going to get on my way to work. I consider this 'me' time and I do my best to use it to the fullest.

Dressed and ready to go it's a three block walk to the bus stop. I do have a car but it is a straight shot from my bus stop to the bus stop in front of work. So since I usually bring a TV dinner every day for lunch, I don't really need my car. I also find it easy to let your mind go as all of the buildings and cars blur by your unfocused eyes.

Besides, once I get to work and the action starts it becomes all about everyone else. Retail management is a deceptive phrase, because what you are mostly managing is people. You manage people that pierce the parts of their body that can be seen through their work shirts. You manage people that hook up with other people in the storage room, and people that don't come into work after a hard Wednesday night of drinking.

Managing the product is easy. Incline press benches don't come into your office in tears because their boyfriend gave them VD. No, the employees do that. The most the equipment does is trip an unsuspecting customer as they walk down the aisle. And I would say that 99.99% of the time the equipment doesn't do it intentionally. No, managing a sporting goods store is not for the weak. That is why at least twice a week I do an hour at the gym.

Usually on the days that I go to the gym I take two protein bars to work with me. I eat the first one at 4 and then the second on at 6 when my shift ends. I then head over to Power Palace for a workout.

Managing a sporting goods store also has its perks. Like when I was looking for a gym, Power Palace chased after me. They called me more times than I could count and when it came time to decide on a price they threw in a 15% discount and towel service. The price was so low that the guy had to call in the floor manager to okay it. I don't like to throw around my influence, but I'll be honest, sometimes it feels good.

My routine at the gym is pretty consistent. I alternate between upper and lower body days. On the first visit of the week I do upper body and on the second my lower body. On everything I do three sets of between 5 and 8 reps. If you can do more than 8, you have to increase the weight.

Upper body day starts out with 45 pound dumbbells in a seated shoulder press. I then grab the 95 pound dumbbells for what I call the "start the lawnmower"; I do three sets with either arm. I move on to bench press which I do with dumbbells instead of a bar so that I can work either arm independently. With the bench press I push 55 pounds per arm, but any day now I'm going to 60.

Next are the bicep curls, which I do with my elbow planted on the inside of my knee instead of on the curls bench. Yeah, I sell that crap. Curls benches cause you to shoot your bicep but you don't get a total arm workout. You need to let all of your arm's twitch muscles get into the action. That's what gives you mass in your arms. I work it with 50 pounds.

After that I finish up with a blast on my triceps. I can do about 35 pounds. Ok, maybe more like 30 pounds. Or let's call it 30 pounds on a good day and 25 most days. We all have our problem areas and I'm not ashamed to admit that triceps are mine. I blast it, I shoot it, I get those twitchers working, and I still can't get that weight up. It's my personal shame.

On my lower body day it's simple. I come in and set the stomach crunch machine on 165 pounds and do three sets of twenty. After that I move to the calf master where I max out the machine at 200; I do three sets of eight. Then I do 150 on the reverse crunch machine, three sets of eight. And finally I move downstairs to the incline squat machine. There I put on six 45 pound plates, two 35 pound ones, and two 10 pounders. I do the three sets of eight there and then I'm done.

To be honest, hitting the steam room after my workout is my favorite part of the day. And when I get there and there's no one else there, it makes my week. I take off my sweaty clothes, wrap a towel around me and head for the room that puts my body at ease. When the steam starts warming up my muscles is when the talking starts.

"Hey Ben."

"What, man?" I reply, not trying to sound too annoyed, knowing that I'd pay for it later.

"No one's here. Why don't you open up that towel and allow me to enjoy some of that steamy goodness?"

"Someone could come in," I say back.

"The door has glass in it, dumbass. You see someone coming and you wrap back up."

"I don't know man. I don't feel comfortable with that."

"Oh, I'm sorry. I made that seem like a question, didn't I? No, I meant, open the fuckin' towel and let the brotha get some air."

I've found that just opening the towel shortens the conversation and reduces a lot of the stress that I have in my life.

"Ahhh yeaaah! See that's what the brotha likes, a little room to stretch my weary body and let a man be a man."

The steam room relaxes me. And what's even more enjoyable than just taking a steam is interrupting the steam with time under a freezing cold shower. So what I do is wait until I can't take any more of the heat and then I head over to the showers.

"Hey wait, what are you doin'?"

"I'm gonna head over to the shower," I reply.

"No, I'm talking about with the towel," the brotha replied with a sense of boldness that I'd never seen in him before.

"I'm not gonna walk around the gym naked."

"First off, you're not walking around the gym. You're walking 25 feet down the hallway of an empty bathroom. Secondly, you grow a second pair of balls I don't know about, because the last time I checked I own your balls. Now all I'm suggesting is that you get up, walk 25 feet in an empty room. Is that too much for you? Am I asking too much?"

"No. I mean, I guess I can do it."

"Sure you can. It's only from here to there. It's nothin'."

"Ok. Ok I'll try it."

I take hold of the towel that's separating my bare ass from the tiles on the built-in steam room bench, and with uncertainty and a butt load of hesitation I walk to the steam room door, letting the brotha swing in the breeze. Well, the brotha doesn't exactly ever swing. He more just bobs back and forth. That swing would require more length than the brotha is equipped with, but I don't want to get into that now.

When the cool air of the hallway hits the brotha I can tell he likes it.

"*If you're having girl problems I feel bad for you son. I got 99 problems and a bitch ain't one.*"

When the brotha gets happy he usually sings remixes of Jay Z songs. Most of the time it's from DJ Danger Mouse's 'The Grey Album.' He heard it a few years ago and he's still obsessed.

"The years 94 and my trunk is full, in the rear view mirror is the motha fuckin' law. I got two choices ya'll, I could open the car door, bounce on the devil and put the pedal to the floor."

Preparing to step under the shower is always a test of heart. Even with the cold water on beside me I could see the steam still coming off my body. When I step under the cold water, the great part is when my heart seems to skip a beat. I don't know what it is but it takes my breath away and for a moment I can't feel my heartbeat. Whatever's going on it feels great, and it's almost like I pass out for a second. But it's afterwards that really gets my heart pumping.

After my body gets used to the cold water I then step out of the shower without drying off and head back to the steam room.

"I ain't passed the bar but I know a little bit. Enough that you can't illegally search my shit. We'll see how smart you are and what you think I don't know. I got 99 problems but a bitch ain't one."

"Hey there's someone naked in the steam room," I say, surprised at what I see through the glass. "When did he get in there? I didn't see him pass."

"Just chill my man. See, he looked up. He saw you. He knows you're naked too. Just walk in like nothing's up. It's all good."

I know the brotha's advice is often questionable, but this time he's right. In this case I have a split second to decide whether to pretend that my towel slipped or to just walk in there like I'm cool with what's going on. And since I took the time to think about all of this, pretending is no longer an option. All I can do is walk in and sit down like I do this all the time.

We walk in and neither the brotha nor I say anything. In fact I do my best to ignore the guy. I head over to the empty corner of the room, lay my towel down on the bench, and shift my body away from the naked stranger.

I have to admit when you're naked in a small enclosed space, it's hard to think about anything else other than the naked man there with you. It's kinda like when you see a horse with a hard-on. It ain't sexy, but you can't help but think how lucky he is. And once your mind goes there, disturbing things sometimes happen.

In the steam those disturbing things can be hidden by leaning forward with your elbows on your knees, so that's what I do.

"Hey, what are you doin' man?" the brotha whispers so quietly that only I can hear.

I don't answer him because between the two of us it should be obvious.

"He can't see me in all this smoke. Lean back man, I'm tryin' to get my steam on."

And I know he's right. At this point I could barely see the brotha much less the guy across the room, so I relax my legs and lay my back onto the wall. I close my eyes and think about how good it feels to be free. I allow my mind to float in the silence and once again I steal a little me time.

I'm pulled out of my me time when I feel the brotha shifting around. I open my eyes and find that the steam isn't as thick as I last saw it. In fact, not only can I look down into the brotha's beady little eye, but out of the corner of my eye I can see the other guy's as naked as a jaybird. And I'm not sure how naked a jaybird is, but I know this guy is completely damn naked.

I look away and begin to come up with a plan to get out of there without it looking like I'm on the run. I figure that I could just wrap up, get up and slowly walk out. But all of my plans are blown when I hear the loud, clear voice of the brotha say "Sup?"

I look down and see from the way that he is looking over my leg that he wasn't talking to me. When I hear the odd sound of a new voice reply back "Sup?" my heart starts beating in my throat.

'Oh my god, my penis is exchanging "Sup's" in a steam room with another penis. I got to get the hell out of here,' I think. And the terror that rushes through my body is like gasoline in a rocket, because it makes me take off. I grab my towel, tie it around me like a noose and jet to the lockers.

"Hey, hey, hey where you goin'? I was talking there."

"You were talking there?" I say with shock. "Really? You were just striking up a conversation in the steam room?"

"Yeah, what's wrong with that?"

"What, did we just meet? Is this the first time you're meeting me? Do you really need help figuring out what may be wrong with you chewin' the fat with some dude's dick in the steam room?"

"It was quiet so I was makin' conversation."

I hear someone walking down the hall from the steam room so I "shh" the brotha and return to getting dressed. The naked man moves slowly to his locker, which happens to be the one four over from mine. His movements are unhurried and casual. And when I get a good glimpse of him I understand why; he's hung like a horse.

It turns out that this guy is one of those locker room guys that I hate. They treat the room as their own personal freak show and everyone in it as their audience. In fact, my being forced to dress so close to him pissed me off and I would have told him so if I didn't again hear the word "Sup?" yelled from my pants. It was followed by a reply of "Sup?" from the crotch of the naked man beside me.

At this point I am too horrified to speak. I grab my gym bag and bolt for the door. The brotha has done a lot of things to me over the years, but this has crossed some type of limit. And no matter what might happen I know that shit is goin' down over this.

I get to the car and immediately the brotha starts to speak.

"Were you tryin' to be a cock blocker?"

"Cock blocker? A cock blocker for what? What were you planning on doin'?" I ask, horrified.

"Nothin' man. He just seemed like a cool dude."

"Why, because he was hung? Is that it?"

"No that ain't it. I was being social that's all. You know what that is? Do you remember what it is to be social? It's when you talk to other people. It is when you bring home someone for the brotha to play with. Remember that?"

"Ok, stop talking, people are beginning to stare at me," I say.

"You don't tell the brotha what to do. The brotha tells you what to do, got it?

"Stop talking. Ok? Just shut up for a little while."

"You don't tell me to shut up. I tell you to shut up. No one tells the brotha to shut up. Goddamn, wait a minute, you just told me to shut up. Who the fuck do you think you are?"

The brotha continued to talk and eventually I was able to tune him out. The tone of his voice used to grate on my nerves constantly but then I learned how to grab some me time in the middle of his rants and things got better. For someone that uses his mouth to look through and pee out of, he sure can say a lot.

I knew that this rant like most of his others were all caused by something I said. And in this case it was the fact that I told him to shut up. Certain things set him off. Calling him "little" anything will set him off. Getting him caught in a zipper will set him off. Any sort of blow to the crotch will actually quiet him down. But five days later when the post-traumatic stress disorder wears off, and he stops thinking that every bend in my jeans is a bat to the crotch, he will go off like you can't even believe.

No, this was just caused by my telling him to shut up, so I imagine by the time I get home he will be done with it. But that doesn't solve the problem. And now I can see that this is a problem. I can't have him yelling things from my pants to naked men's penises in the locker room. Because even if they don't ban me from the gym, I won't be able to show my face in there again. The gym is my sanctuary. I can't have that.

I drive in silence, trying to ignore the brotha's ramblings, which eventually quiet to a few curse words followed by inappropriate terms for sheep. And when I get home we are both quiet. I use the time to warm up some leftover baked chicken and rice and flip on the TV to watch whatever's on.

By the time I get into bed I am seriously reconsidering having the conversation. I'm not big with confrontation and the brotha seems to thrive on it. 'How am I supposed to express anything that I want to say once the brotha starts talking?' I ask myself. But then I get an idea. I get out of bed and head to the kitchen for a glass of water. I pick out one of the Coca-Cola glasses I got from McDonald's and fill it to the brim from the sink.

I pretend to take a few sips out of the glass as I walk it back to the bedroom. When I get there I place it on the nightstand. I then slip off the gym shorts I sleep in and whip off my underwear. The brotha, who was almost asleep, looks up at me.

"Hey man, what's up? Were you in the mood for some makeup sex?" the brotha asks.

I then grab the glass, place it on the bathroom floor, get onto my knees and dunk the brotha in right down to the balls.

"Ahhhh! What are doing? I can't breathe. I can't breathe!" the brotha screams back.

"Shut up! Shut up! Do you hear me? Shut up!" I say in a relatively calm voice.

"Ok, ok!" the brotha screams back.

"Are you going to let me talk?" I ask calmly.

"Yes, yes, I'll let you talk!" the brotha screams from inside the water of the glass. "I can't breathe."

"Ok, I'm going to take you out. And when I take you out you're going to listen to what I have to say, right?"

"Yes, I'll listen!"

"You'll listen right?" I ask again, calmly.

"Yes, yes, I'll listen."

With that I pulled the brotha out of the glass and watched as he gasped for air.

"You stupid bitch!" he spit out as he coughed. "Who the fuck do you think you are? I will fuck your ass up. You hear me? I will fuck your ass…"

And that's where I dunked him again.

"Ahhhh! Alright, alright I'll listen," he promised again.

"And you're really going to listen this time, right?"

"Yes!" he screamed back.

"Because you know what's going to happen again if you don't, right?"

"Yes, yes. Take me out, I can't breathe," he screamed up through the glass.

I pulled the brotha out of the glass and even so he couldn't help but slip in one more insult.

"You stupid bitch!" he said.

I considered dunking him again, but after that comment he remained quiet. I grabbed a towel and dried him off. I took him in my hands and laid down on the bed. I let a few moments go by so that we could both catch our breath, and then I tried to start the conversation as respectfully as possible.

"Now, can you explain to me what was going through your head today at the gym?" I ask softly.

The brotha takes a moment to answer, but when he does he's civil. "I don't know, man."

"What do you mean you don't know?" I ask.

"I don't know. You never let me out. And I just wanted to feel the cool breeze too, ya know."

"No, I'm talking about in the steam room."

"What, you mean with that other dude?" he asks, genuinely confused.

"Yes, I mean with the other dude. Why would you start talking to some strange dick in the steam room? What were you possibly thinking when you did that?"

"I wasn't thinking anything man. I just looked over and saw him hanging over that dude's leg starin' at me and he seemed cool so I gave him a 'Sup'."

"He seemed cool?" Now I'm confused.

"Yeah, you know, he looked cool. He was just hanging all the way across the dude's leg and I thought he looked really cool like that. And since he was staring at me anyway, I thought I would say hey."

"You thought he looked cool?"

"Yeah. What you didn't notice?"

"No, I didn't notice. I don't go around staring at other dudes' dicks."

"So you're trying to tell me with all that porn you watch you don't notice any of those guys' dicks?" the brotha asks.

"No," I reply.

"Come on, you don't notice how huge those guy's dicks are?"

"No."

"So it's just luck that every video you watch has the word hung in the title?" the brotha insists.

"That's not true. I just click on it based on the thumbnail."

"And you never notice that there is a dude fuckin' the woman that you are supposedly staring at?"

"Yeah I do, but I'm not staring at him."

"So you don't notice how huge and thick those guys' dicks are?"

"Well, they might be big. I don't know."

"And you don't wonder what it would be like to hold a dick that big. You don't imagine what it would feel like to rub your hands across all those big veins?" the brotha says in a softer tone.

"Oh my god!" I say as a thought flashes though my mind.

"What?"

"My penis is gay!"

"What?" the brotha screams back.

"Oh my god, my penis is gay," I say as I feel a cold sweat build on my forehead.

"Ok, that's it. Shut the fuck up!"

"I have a gay penis."

"Ok, stop talkin'. Shut the fuck up and roll your ass over and go to sleep," the brotha says, as much embarrassed as he is angry.

"My penis is gay," I repeat, trying to wrap my head around the idea.

"I'm not fuckin' gay! Just forget about it ok? Just fuckin' forget about it."

"I don't think I can. I have a gay penis. I have a gay penis."

"Yeah, you want to know who's gay? Bring your ass around here and I'll show you who's gay. You want me to do that bitch? Bitch, is that what you want?" the brotha asks, returning to his normal level of anger.

"No man. Just chill out."

"Then shut the fuck up, roll over and go to bed. You hear me?"

"Yeah, yeah."

I roll over but I can't sleep. I'm too busy thinking about what this means about me. I can't be gay. I love women. I love the way they talk. I love the way they think and the way they look. I love women, yet somehow my penis is gay.

I continue to think about my situation and every so often I can hear the brotha say something under his breath. I'm sure it's some new form of denial, but whenever he did I quieted down and listened, hoping that it would give me some new understanding about what's going on.

Eventually I fall asleep. My dreams aren't good. I dream that I'm in a field of those Vienna sausages. You know, the little sausages that come in those little cans. But in this case the sausages are grown on stalks like corn. I'm walking through the field and at one point I pick one of the sausages and eat it. That is what I call a disturbing dream. I am not proud of that dream, but I guess you can expect dreams like that when you find out that you have a gay, homosexual American penis. Yes, since I now have to deal with this, I figure I should start using the politically correct terms.

I open my eyes to find that it's still dark. I roll over to take a look at the clock and it says 2:02 am. It's still way too early to get up so I roll back over and stick my hands between my legs for a little warmth and comfort. But when my hand settles, something feels different. It's a familiar feeling but there's something that definitely different. I then reach around a little bit to get a better grip on the brotha and that's when I realize what's different. The brotha is gone, balls and all.

"Ahhhhhhh!" I shoot up in bed, screaming like a ten-year-old girl. Panic sets in. It is my worst nightmare and there is nothing in world that can console me. 'Oh my god, I'm now a woman,' I think. But then after feeling around for a snatch I don't find anything.

Still screaming uncontrollably I pull apart the sheets on the bed, hoping he just fell off and caught up in the covers. But after ripping everything apart I don't find anything. I then lean over the bed and check the floor around the bed, thinking that even if he left intentionally he couldn't have gotten far. But after making the full rounds on the bed, I don't find him there either.

After I begin to see stars I realize that I have to figure out a way to take a breath. But in the brief time that I thought it, the stars black out my vision and I feel myself land backwards on the bed. I lay there not thinking for a second and it feels good to be calm. But even in that hazy state I realize there is something that I should be doing, and when I realize that it's finding my penis I start screaming again and the process starts over.

The second time I come to, my throat has locked so I can no longer make that high-pitched scream. It's good though because now I can let air in and can spend more time pulling apart the house looking for my penis.

I dive into the closet thinking that he may be hiding in one of my shoes. I then open up all of my drawers and pull all of the clothes out, shaking them as I go. After I have looked everywhere in the bedroom, I run through the house to the office. The lack of balls while I run is a disturbingly free experience. It is only natural to have a few things bouncing around when I run, and now I'm afraid that I may never feel that feeling again.

In the office I look under the desk in the jungle of wires and there's no penis there. I look on the bookshelf and in the corner of the room where all the dust balls end up, but there's no penis in those places either. I then run into the bathroom and whip open the shower curtain. Nothing. I look in the cabinets and the medicine cabinet. Still nothing. And then it hits me, the toilet.

I throw myself onto the ground in front of the toilet and wrap my arms around it while staring in. I was beginning to understand that I had pushed the brotha too far. I should have seen how sensitive he was underneath. He always put on a tough front but he was just a sensitive gay homosexual American penis underneath, and he had taken his own life because of me.

I began to cry over the loss of someone that was more than just a friend, he was more like family. In fact, I don't know if someone could be closer than family, but if they could, he would have been that. But as my tears dripped into the toilet water I realized something even worse. I had drunk half of that Coke glass full of water and now there was no way for it to come out. I was going to have to hold it forever.

I leaned over the toilet crying and feeling more nostalgic because of the smell of pee that encircled the bowl. I used to think that I should clean the bathroom more often, but now I realized that, if I had, I would now have nothing to remember the brotha by. The sharp smell of urine gave me comfort in this dark time and I rested my head on the edge of the bowl to remember how lucky I once was.

Just as the tears dried up, I heard what sounded like the jingling of keys outside my front door. I got up off the floor and dragged my half-naked, dickless body into the front room. Whoever it was was having a problem with the key. The person tried many times and only on the fourth or fifth attempt did they get it in. The lock snapped back on my end and the doorknob twisted. As the door opened and the streetlights shined in through the crack, I saw my penis step inside. The brotha was drunk off his balls.

"Where the hell have you been? Do you have any idea how worried I was?" I yell at him, with manly tears forming in my eyes.

"I'm not fuckin' gay, alright?" he spits back with lips weakened from alcohol.

"You're drunk? I'm here scared as hell that something happened to you and you're out getting drunk? Do you know what you put me through?" I say, managing to hold back the tears.

The brotha closes the door behind him and stumbles over to the kitchen. I go over and lock the door before following him. The brotha opens the fridge door and gets lost staring into it.

"I'm so fuckin' drunk," he says for my benefit.

"So that's it? I'm on the bathroom floor thinking that you flushed yourself down the toilet, and you walk in mumbling about how you're not gay and everything's supposed to be cool?"

"Don't be such a little bitch," he says, still staring at the endless rows of condiments.

"You feel like you're gonna throw up?" I ask, recognizing the room anchoring pause.

"Nope."

"Because if you get in bed and throw up… I swear to god." I wait for him to reply, but he doesn't. "Are you going to throw up?"

"Nope."

He spits out the one word answers like he is trying to shoot it into the sink of a spinning kitchen. So I ask again. "Do you need a glass or something? You want to go to the bathroom?"

"Nope."

"If you throw up on the floor I'm gonna be pissed. You feel like you need to throw up?"

"Nope."

"You sure?"

"Nope."

"So you think you're going to throw up?" I ask.

"Yep," he replies with his thin lips tightly perched.

"You want a glass?" I asked, concerned.

"Nope."

"You want to be taken to the bathroom?"

"Yep."

The brotha doesn't look very good when I reach down to pick him up. He is so retracted that he looks like he is talking from a snatch between his balls. When I pick him up it must have jiggled something loose because he makes that sick puppy sound and puke comes shooting from his mouth.

"Oh no, not on the carpet."

And just as I said it, just to be a dick he threw up again.

"Oh no, no, no."

I make it to the bathroom and hold him by the balls as he leans over and pukes into the toilet.

"Oh my god, I'm gonna to die," he mumbles, with puke dangling from his lips.

"You're not gonna. I won't let you."

"I'm gonna die," he mumbles again before puking up.

"I'm not gonna let you die. You hear me?" And just as I jiggle him to get his attention, all of the puke on my hands makes him slip and he falls into the toilet. He immediately hits the water with a splash and screams back up.

"Ahhh, I can't swim."

"Hold still, I'm gonna get you."

"Don't flush the toilet," I hear, as his head dips in and out of the toilet.

"What?" I scream, shocked as I wade back and forth in the puke-filled water. "I'm not gonna flush the toilet."

"Don't flush the toilet," I hear again.

"I'm not. I'm not."

The scene is getting frantic as I start cupping the toilet water out of the toilet, hoping that the pressure from my hands doesn't cause the toilet to automatically flush.

"I wanna live. I wanna live," I hear coming from somewhere. "I've never even felt another man's penis."

"What?" I say, horrified, but not sure what I heard through all of the noise. Just then I find him and pull him out by the balls.

"Is this how Jimi Hendrix died?" he says in a soft voice that I've never heard him use before.

"You're alright. I've got you. You're alright," I say, holding the brotha gently in my hands. "You're gonna be alright."

The brotha, still shaky, still scared, turned to look me in the eye. He then began to say something. It looked like he was going to thank me. It looked like he was going to tell me how much I meant to him. This was going to be a moment between us. I, for the first time, was going to know what was in his heart. But all he had in his heart was puke, and once he opened his mouth it all came rushing out. The moment was all I expected it to be.

After washing him off in the sink, I put him in the bed next to me and got in. I left my pants off to make it as easy as possible for him to find his way home.

"I'm gonna leave my pants off, so that when I wake up in the morning you'll be back where you belong, ok?" I say, feeling a little more powerful after saving his life. "Did you hear me?"

I look down at the brotha and he looks all tired out.

"Did you hear me? I said that I'm expecting that in the morning you're going to be back where you belong."

He doesn't respond so I lean into him a little closer. He opens his eye and looks back at me.

"Hey," the brotha says, "you wanna have makeup sex?"

"No, I don't wanna have makeup sex," I say, a little pissed. I lay on my back above the covers making it as easy as possible for him to get where he needs to go.

"Hey Ben?" he says.

I don't answer.

"Hey Ben, you wanna make out?"

"You're still drunk."

"Hey Ben?"

I don't answer.

"Hey Ben?"

"What!"

"You wanna kiss?"

"Common brotha, don't be gross."

"Don't be actin' all proud like you never tried to kiss me before."

"That's not true and you know it."

"You were breakin' your back tryin' to kiss me. Stickin' your tongue out like I was a lollipop."

"Roll over and go to sleep, man."

I roll over with my back to the brotha, knowing that if he found his way out he could probably find his way back. But now I know that there's no controlling him tonight.

"So you say you don't want to make out, but then you roll over and show me your ass. I'm gettin' mixed signals Ben."

I quickly roll back over so my face is head to head with his. I try to lie there as still as I can. I'm hoping that my stillness will give him nothing to respond to and he will in turn go to sleep. After a few minutes of silence I open my eyes to see how he's doing.

"You got pretty eyes, Ben," he says staring back into my face.

Learning my lesson I shut my eyes tightly and do my best to fall asleep.

The next morning when the alarm went off, I was still very tired. It took me a second to remember the night before and to reach down to find out if the brotha was back to where he was supposed to be. I can't explain how happy I was when I found out that he was.

With the relief of a normal life setting in, I rolled over and fell back asleep. When the alarm went off for the second time I was sure to turn it off and not just hit snooze. If the brotha was still asleep I really wanted to get through my morning routine without his color commentary about how good I am at being a bitch. It just wears on you after a while, and then it makes you do things that you later regret.

I get up and take the time to enjoy the feeling of taking a piss. It feels like a good belch that completely relieves all of the pressure build-up. It feels like magic.

But even when taking the piss I refuse to look down. I instead use my honed sense of piss hearing to find the bowl. The first sound is more of a splat and that's the floor. I move to the right and the next sound is more of a hiss and that's the sound of the rim of the bowl. I shift up a little hearing the hollow sound of the toilet cover, before bringing it back a bit and hearing the splashing sound of the bowl. Bull's eye! Again, another perfect piss.

I next brush my teeth and keep my eyes above my shoulder in the mirror. I'm very tempted to take a quick look down to see if the brotha is absolutely like he should be, but I don't. I even hit the shower with my head slung back. I try to not make it obvious that I'm avoiding him, because that would cause a response as well. Instead, I just pretend that I'm inspecting the mold on ceiling of the shower.

When it comes time to soap up the brotha, I do it quick. I run my fingers along the seam of where we connect and everything feels as it should. I then quickly move to all of my other touchable parts and I'm done without a peep.

By the time that I towel off and get dressed I feel like I've raided the lost ark. I feel I've dodged the spears and escaped the big rolling ball. Cereal seems that much sweeter after that and I eat it with a smile.

As the last of the cereal is eaten and I'm about to lift the bowl to my mouth, I hear a familiar yet softer voice.

"Ben?"

"Yeah my brotha?" I reply back hoping he doesn't launch into one of his usual tirades just as I have to leave for work.

"I'm not happy."

The tone and gentleness that he used told me that he wasn't accusing me. He wasn't trying to drag me down or build himself up. What I heard from him was an expression of how he really felt. And after thinking about the many things I could do to cheer him up, what came out of my mouth surprised me.

"Me too, my brotha. Me too."

Chapter 2
How Ben and the Brotha Met

I grew up in a small town in Wisconsin that was on the border of Wisconsin and Illinois. Beloit was a 75 minute drive west of Milwaukee, 105 minutes north of Chicago, 45 minutes south of Madison, and 15 minutes south of Janesville. Unlike the other cities surrounding Beloit, Janesville had to earn its fame. Janesville had one of the first General Motors factories in the United States but that's not how it earned its fame. No, Janesville was considered the northern headquarters of the modern day Ku Klux Klan. In fact, Janesville later rose to its peak fame when Geraldo Rivera did a special on his daytime talk show from Janesville and had his nose broken by a flying chair. We called Janesville 'The Jewel of Wisconsin.'

Beloit was very different. While Janesville was an industry town that was 95% white, Beloit was a college town that was 15% black. So by Wisconsin standards Beloit was the Africa of the midwest. My mother was a piano teacher who taught most of her lessons at home and my father worked in the GM plant in Janesville.

I had one sister that was younger than me by two years and two guy friends that I spent most of my time with. I met them when we were all in the first grade. We were friends ever since.

Josh and Tommy were both good students though not great, and both had a parent that worked in the factory. Out of the three of us, it was I who struggled the most with things like school, girls and break dancing. Because, let's be real, break dancing was hard.

And it was Josh and Tommy that I grew up with both physically and sexually. When we were kids our mothers would make us take baths together. So when we hit nine it was only right that we started playing the games that boys do together like 'let's see' and 'bouncy pants.' Bouncy pants was a game where we would bounce as hard as we could on Tommy's parents' bed and try to pull down our pants and pull them back up during the bounce. Really. 'Let's see' was an extension of 'bouncy pants.' It was the obvious compromise that happened when Tommy's mother threatened to spank us for constantly messing up her bed. Oh, by the way, both games, Tommy's idea.

'Let's see' was a much more direct game. It is kind of like the classic game 'face it,' but in 'let's see' you were sitting next to each other as opposed to facing each other from the other side of the bathroom. 'Let's see' really answered a lot of questions about what another guy looks like, where as 'face it' just answered the question in generalities.

There was a night when Josh and I both slept over at Tommy's house and they told me that they had a new game to play. This one started like all of the other games, we got naked and… well, really that's it. But this one, after getting naked you went to the bathroom to get lotion and you did something that was novel to say the least. It involved taking the lotion and applying it to your hard wiener and then rubbing it back and forth.

This didn't seem fun to me. Why would someone take lotion and then rub it back and forth on your wiener? Seriously, where's the fun in that? And why the wiener? Why not a finger or a foot? I just didn't get this game. And what was worse, when Josh and Tommy did it, it made this horrifying sloshing noise that I couldn't stand.

That noise became the limit on our games. Seconds into them starting without me I told them how disgusting it sounded and told them to go do it in the bathroom. Josh made a comment on my wiener's size that Tommy causally agreed with and then they headed for the bathroom. But I can tell you that a partially closed door does not block out the sound of sloshing. I struggled through it.

A funny thing happened about a year later though. One day I was at home and the girl that I had a crush on was taking piano lessons from my mom. I don't know why but when listening to Lori play the piano I thought about Josh and Tommy's game. I remembered how much they swore to me that the game felt good. At the time I assumed that they were just trying to get me into their little club, but listening to Lori play the piano I became less repulsed by the idea.

I left my room momentarily to get the vaseline petroleum jelly. This is what Josh and Tommy used and I wanted to stay true to the sport. With jelly in hand I got a handle on things and it wasn't a bad feeling. In fact, if you could ignore the sound it made, it was actually kind of pleasant. And it seemed that the more you pulled back and forth the more pleasant it got.

And not only did it get more pleasant, but if you kept at it the feeling got down right good. The feeling was like your naked body was covered with G.I. Joe dolls, the six inch not the twelve inch, and they were all being moved around at once. But it seemed that just when it was getting good, really good in fact, I was forced to stop because I had to pee.

The trick at this point was to get my pants on, clean my hands off, rush to the bathroom without anyone seeing me and without me peeing in my pants. Luckily Lori's playing covered the sound of doors opening and closing. And luckily I got to the bathroom with a few moments to spare. But here's the funny thing. When I got safely to the bathroom I wanted to keep playing the game even though I had to pee. And finally when I did pee, nothing came out. Weird, right? That's what I thought.

Afterwards, when I was sitting in the bathroom, I thought about Josh and Tommy and how wrong I was about them. They weren't perverts at all. They were really onto something and should have been commended for their originality. Who else would have thought of such a game? Lord knows I wouldn't have.

But all of my praise for my friends was short-lived when I next looked down at my wiener. It seemed that as good as the game felt it came with a very steep price. In the midst of all of the pushing and pulling I must have broken something because my wiener was now deformed. What it looked like was that my wiener was all red and it was wearing a wiener jacket with a really furry collar. The area right below my wiener head was incredibly swollen and wasn't going down.

It's hard to describe the panic that sets in when you think that you've broken your wiener. I guess I would say, imagine having a wiener, and then imagine it being broken. That's pretty much is how it felt. And imagine that you broke it because you had stupidly decided to play one of your friends' dumb games. And because you had played the game, your wiener would forever look like a lion in a sausage suit.

After about ten minutes of panic I knew that I had to leave the bathroom. Lori's lesson was only so long and the last thing I wanted was for her to go to use the bathroom and see me coming out. How would I explain myself? No, I had to get out.

Mournfully I pulled up my pants and headed back to my bedroom. There I lay until dinner time and there I returned when dinner was over. It was a sad night in the Thompson household that day. Regret hung in the air like a thick petroleum jelly. And more than just my normal looking wiener died that day. My adventurous nature died along with it.

Three days later when my wiener returned to normal it was a gift from God. All of the prayer that I had done really seemed to pay off. And all I had to promise in return was that I would never play that game again. Did I feel bad when I broke that promise to God the next day? Yes. But what I learned from the experience was that sacrilege got easier the more you practiced it. And it seemed that after God realized I wasn't going to stop, he stopped making the effort to swell my wiener. See, we both learned something from the experience.

Although I had really gotten into playing Josh and Tommy's game, I wasn't about to tell them. Instead this was something that I would keep to myself. So the first time that my wiener spoke to me was also a surprise.

I was in the shower one day doing the things that you do in a shower when I noticed that things were up down there. Or more to the point my wiener was up. But, knowing that each time I played the game I was spitting in God's face, I wanted to avoid extracurricular shower activities.

But as a kid who could still sneak by on taking a shower every few days, when I took the shower I had to be thorough. That was the deal I made with my mom. I only had to shower every few days, but when I did I had to make sure I was really clean afterwards.

It was in that spirit that I kept going back to my wiener just to make sure it was clean. The truth was also that it felt really good. It was pretty much a loophole to the game. It was a way of getting the pleasure from playing the game without actually spitting at God. I wondered if anyone else had ever discovered this, or if I was the first one.

Unfortunately my loophole didn't hold. Josh's father kept a gun in their house and part of his safety training for his family and all of Josh's friends was that 'you never play with a loaded gun.' I understood what he was saying, but I never really got it.

It was that night in the shower when my gun went off. And when it did, something white shot everywhere. It startled me at first, but man did it feel good. But just as the last shots were coming out I heard a cough, a spitting, and then a clearing of someone's throat. And with that I heard a voice say "Happy New Year."

As I stared down at my wiener I couldn't help but wonder what else it could do. It was already filled with surprises. And I wondered if anytime soon it would perhaps grow wings so it could fly me places. But I guess there's no reason to have to say that it didn't. Skipping ahead a little, I will tell you that all it ever did was bring me pleasure when I touched it, and talk of course.

"Did you just say 'Happy New Year?'" I asked hesitantly.

"Happy New Year," it said again.

"You can talk," I said, with as much surprise as anyone would.

"Happy New Year," it said again.

"Can you say anything else other than 'Happy New Year?'"

"Do that thing you did again," it said.

I knew what it was talking about. It was all the rubbing it got with the soap.

"No, I don't think so. I promised God that I wouldn't do that anymore."

"Please," it said to me, looking up and ready to go again.

I figured that God was smart enough to realize that he had been screwed on our deal. And with all of the times that I had done it before, one more time wouldn't make much of a difference. I cleaned myself just the way I did before and realized that the only difference with this and what I was doing before was the lubricant. Apparently the game worked with more than just petroleum jelly. Apparently soap was just as good.

With the gentle wipes back and forth my wiener purred. It liked what I was doing and after it again coughed up the white stuff, it twitched uncontrollably and then seemed to fall asleep. I felt very relaxed myself. But more than just being relaxed, I was energized.

I toweled off, got dressed and headed into the living room. There my father sat on the couch watching TV. At that moment I felt very drawn to my father so I sat down next to him and placed my head on his shoulder.

"Hey dad, what are you watching?" I asked, not able to cool the juices that were revving me up.

"Jake and the Fat Man," my dad replied.

"What's it about?"

"It's about Jake and this fat man that solves crimes."

"Dad, did you know that fat was caused because of calories?"

"I did know that," my father answered, amused.

"Did you know that calories are a unit of energy?"

"Yes I did."

"Did you know that…" I really didn't have anything else to say but I wanted to keep talking to my dad so I had to make up something quickly. "…that umm." I really didn't have anything to say. "Dad?"

"Yes Ben?"

"Can I go to Disney World with you?" I asked.

"Maybe next time Ben."

"But I could be real quiet the whole time."

"Boy, you sure are talkative after taking your shower. Maybe you should take showers more often. Maybe you wouldn't be so quiet all the time," my father said, changing the topic.

On the shower point he was right. From then on I would take a lot more showers. But the topic that he was trying to avoid was what I really wanted to talk about. My dad was very fond of Disney World. At least three times a year he would drive to Florida, spend two days at Disney World by himself, and then drive back. The trips usually took five days all together. He called it daddy time.

My mother never talked about these trips. When she knew that one of his trips would correspond with something that I wanted dad to attend, she would simply say that "he wouldn't be here." As far as I could tell, the only ones that had a problem with his trips were me and my sister Lil. We liked Disney World. And it was our never-ending mission to convince our dad that we did. He obviously wasn't taking us because he thought that we had grown out of it. But we hoped an endless campaign of begging would convince him otherwise. It never did.

The year that I most wanted to go with him was the week that he scheduled a trip on my fourteenth birthday. I thought that it would have been a great opportunity to mix one of his favorite things, going to Disney World, with one of my other favorite things, getting stuff. He disagreed.

I instead made him promise that he would call me on my birthday. Usually when he went on one of his trips, we wouldn't hear from him again until he drove up onto the driveway. But with my birthday days away, I wanted him to make an exception. I even made him repeat which day my birthday was on.

"What day is it Dad?" I asked.

"It's Saturday."

"And how many days away is it?" I followed up with.

"It's two days away."

"And you're going to call me, right?"

"Yes, I'm going to call you."

And with that I knew that he would call.

On Saturday Josh and Tommy told me that they had arranged something for me. It was all kind of exciting, because they never really did things like that. I thought that it was really cool of them to put something together for my birthday and I just hope I liked it.

On Saturday when Tommy's mother picked me up, Josh was already in the car with Steve, Billy and Tony, three other guys from school. It seemed like this was going to be a full-on party. Tommy's mom dropped us off at the quarry and I immediately knew that this was going to be a beach party.

The Stateline Quarry was simply known to us as 'the pit.' This is where we went when we needed a little r&r. And the rest and whatever the other 'r' stood for never felt as good as when we were there. It was a large pit the size of a football field that filled up with water when it rained. Next to it sat a digger crane, and when there were road projects going on, the pit was where they would get the limestone. But during the years when there were no road projects, we considered it our beach.

The party started at five pm. And because it was my birthday, Tommy's mother agreed to wait until eight before picking us up. Tommy's mother knew that we could all swim, and as far as she knew, none of us drank. So to her it seemed like a little harmless fun.

When we got to the beach, the first thing we did was dive into the water. Like usual the water was ice cold. It was tradition to run in and then dive forward. Once you resurfaced the first thing you had to say was that it was 'brisk.' We felt it always added a little class to our good time.

We swam around for a little bit, and then got out to have some fried chicken that Josh's mom had bought for us. The swim was good, the chicken was good, and the company was great. When it started to get dark we did something that we knew that we weren't supposed to do. We started a little campfire. Technically it was illegal to swim at the pit, so a campfire was doubly illegal, but in for a dozen, in for a pound we always used to say.

It was Tony's idea to go skinny dipping, but I was surprised just how quickly everyone went along with it. It's not like we hadn't all seen each other naked, but still; this was a public beach and who knew who could be around.

I was also a little surprised when I turned out to be the only one voting no on the idea. I had thought that at least Josh would have hesitated, but he didn't. Not wanting to be a party pooper I decided to go along. It was now a little colder out, but it being the middle of summer it was still pretty warm. We dropped our trunks at the water line and then we all ran and dove in.

"Brisk," each of us said.

We all started floating close to each other and I soon realized that all of them were staring directly at me.

"What?" I asked.

And then, without a word, everyone went running for the shore, and grabbed their trunks with someone else grabbing mine.

"What's goin' on?" I asked, a little scared of where this was going.

"You'll see," Tommy answered back.

And after the guys pulled up their trunks they disappeared into the woods.

"Guys?" I yelled. "This isn't funny, guys."

I heard someone coming from the other direction and my first thought was that it was a beach ranger. That is what we called the cops that patrolled the pit. I walked out a little deeper and crouched down until the still water was just below my nose. The campfire lit the person up as they approached.

"Hello?" the person said from the woods.

It was a girl's voice. And what's more it was a familiar voice. It was Cristine, the cool Filipino girl from school that I was kind of crushing on. This was what the guys were talking about. 'Not bad,' I thought. 'Well played.'

"Hi," I replied.

"Ben?" she called out to me.

"Hey."

"Where are you?"

"I'm in the water."

"Oh," she replied as she located my bobbing head. "Where's everybody else? Tommy told me that there was going to be a party."

"There is. They just stole my shorts and took off into the woods."

"Oh. So you're naked?"

"Either that or my nads just shot into my body for nothing."

"What?" Cristine said with a chuckle.

"Nothing. Do you happen to have a towel?"

"No, I didn't bring one."

"Wanna join me?" I asked, trying to judge the vibe.

"No," she said with an embarrassed laugh.

"Just checking." I look around trying to think of what else to say. "Yep. So have you seen Michelle or Diane?"

"Yeah, they're both working at the Beloit mall," she replied with a laugh. "Are you just going to keep talking to me naked?"

"Yeah, you're right. I'm just gonna come out and we can go find the guys with my pants. Ok?" I say with a sense of resolve.

Cristine begins to blush, but she tries to play it cool. "I guess."

I first reach down to make sure that I'm not hard. I then do a little pull on it to get as much length as possible. And when all of the maintenance is done, I walk out of the water like nothing's different. I watched Cristine as I walked up. She looked nervous and not sure of what to do. But what I also noticed was that she never stopped looking me in the eyes. I walk up to her and not only does she look great but she smells great too.

"So, I saw them take off in that direction," I say as I'm staring and pointing at the woods. When I look back at Cristine she's still looking me in the eyes but her face is different. I can't quite tell what the difference is. She's more confused looking than anything and she seemed less playful.

"Do you want me to walk in front of you?" she asked very soberly.

"Yeah, ok."

She walked in front of me in silence. Even her movements were less playful. I wondered what the difference could be. I rubbed my face to make sure that there was nothing on it. And when that came up clean I looked down at my body. Without realizing it I had gotten a stiffy. For a moment I thought that that could have been the cause of her mood change, but then I realized that she never looked down. I thought for a moment and remembered that I turned away to look at the woods. Could she have sneaked a look in those two seconds when I looked away? Nah, she was one of those good girl types so she wouldn't have done that. And besides, girls in general never seem to notice anything. It's no wonder they always get along with each other.

But whatever caused it she was different now. She was still talkative, but something had changed.

"Are you working anywhere this summer?" I asked.
"No."
"Going anywhere cool?"
"Yeah."
"Where?"
"Colorado."
"Visiting family?"
"Yeah."

Yeah, something had changed but I couldn't tell what. But I have to say that there were times when I was younger when I would worry that a girl would call me and I wouldn't have anything to say to her. That used to be a big fear of mine. But now I saw I had nothing to worry about. Because I'm sure that if it wasn't for our conversation, things might not have been going as well as they clearly were.

We eventually found the guys and Cristine did all of the work of getting them to give me back my pants. Afterwards she moved to the other side of the group. I tried a couple of times to get close to her but she moved away. I figured that the whole situation embarrassed her so I would have to give her a little time.

Cristine's reaction kind of made the rest of the night a downer. Later that night, after jacking off several times to the idea that I was standing naked with a girl, I asked my wiener if he had noticed anything. He told me that she did check him out when I turned away. Apparently she was quicker than I thought. But when I asked my wiener's thoughts on the situation, he just looked away.

That turned out to be a pivotal night for me. For whatever reason, my wiener's attitude changed after that. He would get quiet for long periods of time and then when he did speak he always seemed a little angry. He started drinking way before I did. He would start off by suggesting that we both drink, and then when I would refuse he would start calling me things that weren't nice. Eventually I would pour some liquor from my father's cabinet into a short glass and slowly lower my wiener into it.

After a while I began to wonder if my wiener had a drinking problem. But in those days they didn't make after school specials about how to tell if your wiener was an alcoholic, so I was never sure. Instead I started drinking with him. After that his drinking didn't seem like an issue anymore.

I guess there were times when I wished my fourteenth birthday had gone a little differently. Maybe it would have been better if the guys hadn't invited Cristine and stolen my pants. But hey, you could analyze a situation to death. Anything that happened that night could have caused anything. Someone could even say that if my father had called me that night my life would have been different. But seriously, you can never tell these things.

When my sister turned eighteen I was living on the Beloit College campus. There was a rule that all students had to live on campus for their first three years. I only went home about once a week so it was by phone that my sister told me that Dad was moving out. She didn't have many details, but what Mom had told her was that Dad was moving to Florida.

It didn't really surprise me that he was going because as the years went on, he wasn't even there when he was sitting there. His trips to Disney World got up to five times a year, and they were all by himself. I wasn't looking forward to going home and talking to Dad about his move, so it just made it easier when I arrived home and he was already gone. I asked my sister what he had said to her and she said that she was in her room when he left so he didn't get a chance to say anything.

I graduated from college with a degree in theater arts and communications. And then Tommy and I decided that we were going to get the hell out of Dodge. We were considering a couple of places. We thought about Los Angeles, but were too afraid of the earthquakes. We considered New York, but didn't want to get mugged. We thought about Dallas, but decided that the odds of us striking it rich digging for oil was so slim that we shouldn't go. We also thought about Chicago, which was an obvious choice.

But in the end we decided on Orlando. It was either him or me that pointed out the possibility of beach babes running around everywhere. And I know it was him that eventually pointed out that there were no beaches in Orlando. But we both decided that it was still Florida and the beach was never that far away.

I wanted Orlando because I thought that I could find a job in broadcasting. Disney made a lot of movies and TV shows and I figured that I could get a job as a host or something. We moved down a week after graduation and within the next week Tommy had a job working on the landscaping crew at MGM. I found a job working as a waiter at a dinner theatre. These were both temporary jobs though. These were just the jobs that we had as we waited for our real lives to begin.

For Tommy his real life began when he decided to move back to Beloit. His dad had gotten him a job at the Janesville GM plant that paid twice as much as he was making at MGM. My real life began when I started working in retail. I like to think that my communications degree was a good preparation for retail. After all, your main job is to communicate with the customers. And after a few years at the high end clothing store I worked at, I was able to buy a house.

It was a few years after that that I decided to move on. I didn't like having to dress up every day for work, so when I found out that there was a manager job open at a sporting goods store I jumped at it. Now I had a house, a good job, and my entire future ahead of me. The brotha and I were rolling high and wanted for nothing. That's why it surprised me so much when I heard myself say that I was unhappy. What did I have to be unhappy about?

Chapter 3
How Do You Make a Penis Happy?

On the day that the brotha told me that he was unhappy I knew that something had changed. The brotha and I had stopped being close a long time ago. Sure, we still had a lot of sex, but we had lost our connection. The sex had become kind of cold.

For us it made no difference if we were watching TV or doing taxes. There were just times when he would say "let's have sex," so we did. I guess this is kind of corny but I missed the way it used to be.

I remember when we first started having sex; it was special. I would feel the brotha in my pants so I would slip away to the bathroom. And sometimes I would just sit there looking into his eye, and other times we jacked off like rabbits. There were even times when we would lay naked and I would just hold him all night. I missed those times.

Those were the times when the brotha would say such nice things to me. Back then the brotha would start early, like in third period. I would be sitting in class bored and the brotha would pop up and say "hey." That's it, just "hey." And knowing he was there just made me happy. And once I learned the trick of putting my hands in my pockets, I didn't mind the times when he would stick around as I walked between classes.

Back then the brotha would start what he did at 11:15 am, come back later at 2:00 pm, and then slip around a bit at 3:15. So by the time I got home at four I could barely wait to be alone with him. It was an all day thing with him. Now I'm lucky if he gets all the way up before he starts yelling, "come on bitch, make me feel good." Things have just changed.

But when he told me that he was unhappy, it felt different. It felt like I was seeing a side of the brotha that he had been hiding from me. Now I felt bad about threatening to drown him in the Coca-Cola glass. And I understand why he wanted to get away from me. If I were unhappy with someone for as long as the brotha must have been, I would probably have tried to leave too. But after those few words though, things would have to be different.

The brotha and I didn't have much to say to each other as I walked to the bus. We were also quiet as I arrived at the Sport Castle. I had arrived a little late so Chip and Rose were already there.

"We were gonna call you," Rose said in her dry, monotone way. "Weren't we Chip?" Rose turned to Chip, who heard her but couldn't be bothered to answer.

Chip was not a morning person. And to the disappointment of all of the morning staff, Rose was. I often wondered if the pink stripes in her hair and heavy mascara were all just for show, because she was way more upbeat than any gothic twenty-year-old that I had ever met.

I take Chip's lead and ignore Rose. If I started the day responding to her backhanded accusations, then who knew where the day would go. I unlocked the door and walked into the quiet building. It always felt nice the first thing in the morning because it felt like I had the opportunity to do something good with my day.

As usual I let Chip and Rose in, and then locked the door behind us leaving my keys in the lock. Rose was our cashier so she headed back to the office to wait for me. Chip headed to the stockroom where, if today was like every other, he would put away his lunch and then head to the fort he made out of boxes and sleep for another fifteen minutes. He is supposed to come in early to restock. But every good manager knows to not focus on the process.

His process was that he intimidated the late shift staff into stocking before they left at night. That way he only needed to bring out a few items in the morning. Chip did that in the fifteen minutes he had between his nap and the store's opening. I wouldn't call it a fair process, but you can't argue with what works.

After everyone was in and the doors were relocked I usually turned on the lights and air conditioning. I then took the long way to the office so that I could see what needed refilling. It was a detour that I began when I realized that Chip went in back to nap. Now it was habit.

As usual when I got into the office Rose was waiting for me. She was a short, pale girl with a round face. But I have to admit I didn't hire her for her experience. From the moment she applied, I thought she was really cute. And from the times when she chose to wear clothes that were almost too revealing for the workplace, I could tell that she had one of those effortless twenty-year-old bodies.

Hers was the type of tight body that came from being young and not from spending time in the gym. It was the type of body where if you touched it, you would feel no muscle tone at all. She would feel like a big Pillsbury dough girl and she would giggle if you did. But despite all of the jiggle and pudge, when she stood naked in front of you there would not be a bulge that wasn't designed by God to make her body go 'boom.' Yeah, it's too bad that her boyfriend gave her VD.

"So, how's that penicillin working for you?" I ask.

"Good," she says with a big smile, happy that I had taken an interest in her.

"Are you staying away from him?"

"He called me again last night and I told him 'you gave me VD you freak.' And he was like 'I didn't give you VD,'" Rose says in a mocking tone. "I was like, who else would I get it from? And he said 'I don't know.' He's such a dumbass."

"Did you tell him that you didn't want to see him anymore?" I ask while I unlocked the safe to get the cash register float.

"I don't have to tell him. He knows."

"If you don't straight out tell a guy something, trust me, he doesn't know."

"Really?"

"Yeah, guys aren't that bright," I say while counting out the cash in the float.

Rose lets the moment go by while she watched me count.

"What about you? Did you do anything fun last night?" she asked with an indecipherable smile on her face.

I stopped counting and looked up at her to make sure that she didn't know more than she should. Looking at her caused a sudden flash of heat to shoot across my face. That feeling was quickly followed by a pain in my chest that made me think that I could be having a heart attack.

'What if Rose ran into the brotha at whatever bar he went to to get drunk?' I think. The thought was too embarrassing for words. I desperately started scanning her face for any indication that she knew more than she should, but as usual her face was an unknowable combination of smiles and piercing.

I look back down at the cash on my desk and my face feels like it's on fire.

"Oh my god, are you blushing?" Rose asked with delight.

"Black people don't blush," I reply back, changing the topic.

"You are so blushing. I can't wait to hear what you did last night," she said as I handed her the cash, hoping that it was correct since I'd now forgotten how to count.

"I went to the gym then went home and went to bed. It was a boring night."

"I don't believe you," Rose said in a way that told me that she didn't see the brotha. Or if he did see him, then she didn't realize who he was.

"Nope, sorry to disappoint, but that is all I did," I say with a little more confidence.

"Well, I don't believe you but that's fine," Rose said as she got up with the cash and register tray. "I guess it's up to me to find out then."

Rose left with a blushing smile which could only mean bad things for me. I leaned back in my chair and thought about what happened the night before. I tried to remember how the brotha acted when he got drunk. What came to mind was the fact that he became a know-it-all. When the brotha got drunk suddenly he became an expert on everything. He once spent two hours screaming at me about how salt miners used to run the world. So I think it's safe to say that not only did he become a know-it-all, but he also became an idiot.

The question was though, would he be the type to talk to other people about his problems when he got drunk, and would he mention me by name. Well, since he didn't talk to me about anything, why would he suddenly start sharing with perfect strangers?

I look down at the brotha who is up and about. He was obviously listening to my conversation with Rose. It's funny, I always thought that he had a thing for Rose. But of course, that was before I found out the brotha was a gay homosexual.

For a moment I got lost in the memories of all of the times that we shared together as two straight individuals. I'm not gonna lie, thinking about it put a sad feeling in my heart. And what's more, I couldn't shake how much those times felt like yesterday. I guess time moved slower with a heavy heart; yet another mystery of life.

Once the memories were gone I noticed that the brotha's attentiveness was too. I looked up at the clock and it was five minutes before opening. Rose usually let in the other employees, but I was the one that usually unlocked the door for our official opening.

I got up and took my last walk through the store. Besides a few misaligned weight benches the store was ready to go. I unlocked the door and placed the keys in my pocket. I looked across the counter at Rose, who smiled back enthusiastically. I stared at her for a moment because the look in her eye reminded me of a gremlin that was holding a chicken wing at the stroke of midnight. Somehow you knew that there's gonna be trouble.

I then looked around the store for the other employees. Tammy was a black chick that worked in the clothing department. My challenge with her every week was to get her to moderate her nail length and her attitude. She was from one of the islands off Florida, Barbados or Bermuda or something, and every time something happened that she didn't like, she made a sucking sound with her lips. Apparently it's some type of island mating ritual because when she talked with her boyfriend on the phone she did that sucking thing so much that parts of her weave got caught in her teeth.

I walked toward the clothing section and found Tammy re-sorting the polos.

"Good morning Tammy."

"Good morning Ben. How are you doing this morning?" She says with a playful smile.

"I'm good Tammy. How are you?"

"I'm good. See, I remembered to say it this morning," she says with a big smile.

"Yes you did. Isn't that more pleasant than 'hey, hey what ya say lova boy'?"

"It's a term of endearment. I was just having some fun with you."

"And I appreciate that, but when we're at work, we have to act like it, right?"

"I know. I got it," she says with a more serious look on her face.

I smile back at Tammy, genuinely happy that she was making an effort, and afterward I look around for Justin. Justin worked in the shoe department and was usually the most reliable of the bunch. He was also very clearly a homo… I mean a gay, homosexual American. But for whatever reason he would never admit to it, so everyone else in the store had been forced to place wagers on how much of a gay homosexual he was.

My bet was on him being so gay that he would jerk off to Madonna music. But not the 'Sex' book/'Justify My Love' Madonna. I meant the 'I'm looking way too muscly because I'm 50 years old and I do way too much yoga'/Beautiful Stranger Madonna. There's a big difference between the two. During the 'Sex' book time she was bold enough to get naked and say, look, no balls. Now, she kind of looked like a tranny that left one ball attached to supply a little extra juice.

And Madonna was a strange cat too, so she could have left the one ball. And I'm sure that if she wanted one of Guy Ritchie's balls she would have just taken it. But anyway, that is how gay I thought Justin was, gay enough to jerk off to Tranny Madonna.

Rose had bet that he was "I fight myself every day not to get highlights in my hair" gay. Chip bet that he was "I'm not gay but I'm having sex with a guy that I'm working with" gay. I have to say that it was a little weird when he said that because there was only one other guy working in the store besides the two of us and Brian had a girlfriend.

Brian thought that Justin was "my knees are permanently scarred" gay. But everyone else agreed that that wasn't very nice. And Tammy wasn't asked to join in because she had to learn professionalism first.

I spotted Justin coming out of the storage room walking toward the shoe section.

"Good morning Justin."

"Hey Ben."

"Ya know, I was coming into work this morning and I heard 'Ray of Hope' by Madonna…"

"You mean 'Ray of Light'?" Justin corrected.

"Yeah! And I wouldn't admit this to anyone usually, but it got me kind of excited. You know what I mean?"

"I guess," Justin said, unenthused.

"I mean when you hear her, I mean with her newer stuff, not her older stuff, doesn't it just get you excited?"

"I guess."

"And here's a great thing about this store. There's a spot back in the storeroom where you can really be alone with your thoughts. You know what I mean?"

"Isn't there a security camera back there? Isn't that how Colin and Jenny got fired?"

"Well, yeah, but you know, the camera doesn't cover the entire area. And sometimes, you know, how can you control yourself when you're listening to Madonna. Am I right? I'm right, aren't I?"

"Ummm, sure."

I keep smiling at Justin and he keeps staring back. But what I'm really doing is waiting for him to look away so I can look down and see if all this talk about Madonna has brought about a little action on his downstairs. What can I say, the pool was now at 50 bucks.

Justin looked away for a second and I looked down. From all of the other times I looked at his junk I could tell that there wasn't much movement at all. But before I abandon my search I notice some movement.

"Ben, are you..." Justin began.

"What?" I say cutting him off and quickly looking up.

"Were you just..."

"No! What?"

"Ok, that was strange."

"I'm not sure what you're talking about. I need to go check on Brian."

"Ok."

I turn to walk off when I again hear Justin's voice.

"Oh, Ben, I met someone you know last night."

I immediately get a flash of the brotha chatting it up with Justin using all of the information that he would have overheard to impress the pants off of him.

"No, you didn't," I reply back as I whip around.

"Yeah, sure I did," Justin says with a pleasant smile.

"Where'd you meet 'em?" I say quickly.

"It was in a bar?"

"Which bar?" I shoot back.

With that Justin shut up. In fact, he looked like a guy that was hiding a gerbil in his mouth. This told me two things: first, he met the brotha last night and the brotha mentioned me by name; and second, it was in a gay, homosexual American bar.

"Ummm," Justin muttered.

The other interesting thing about Justin was that he wasn't very quick for a gay, homosexual American. You might even consider Justin to be a slow talker, but somehow his talk still managed to outpace his brain.

"I don't remember which bar," he said taking his declaration back. "In fact, you know what, it was another Ben that he knew. Old Ben."

"You mean Old Ben Kenobi? That wizard is just a crazy old man."

"What?" Justin replied, confused.

"Star Wars?" I said in a way that should have made Justin feel stupid for not getting it.

"I never saw it."

And with that there was no need to ever question whether or not Justin was gay.

Brian was late every morning so there was no need to check on him. It was sad to say, but Brian had a legitimate reason. Unfortunately Brian's girlfriend was crazy. I had sympathy for him because sometimes these things happen to the best of us.

The way Brian described it was, one day everything was normal, sex was good, and she's doing things to him in the bedroom that others would only dream about. And the next thing you know she's setting his clothes on fire and threatening to spit in his food when he wasn't looking. I think this is an epidemic that is far too often overlooked. I'm surprised it isn't mentioned more on the news. And for this reason I cut Brian a little slack on his lateness.

Chip has less sympathy for Brian. However, Chip was always ready to step up if necessary. Once his arrival nap was over Chip was usually within his section straightening the equipment and making his last rounds or restocking. Chip was a good guy. Chip was that guy who everyone knew that took a nap in the morning at work and then took another one at lunch. You know, he was that guy.

Sometimes I wondered what he did all night that made him so tired all day. But then I remembered his wager in our gay Justin pool and I decide it'd be better not to ask. Because until I had proof that someone else had won, I still considered that 50 bucks mine.

"Morning Chip," I said as the official beginning to his day.

"Morning," he said back in a voice that sounded like he'd been up for hours.

"Hey listen, we're gonna receive that late shipment this afternoon. Can you arrange with Brian when he gets here to get it built and on the floor today?"

"Sure, when he gets in," Chip replied.

"Are you and Brian ok?" I asked.

"No, I'm just saying 'when he gets in'."

"Ok good," I reply casually. But when you have been a manager as long as I have you start to pick up on the subtle hints that a person gives off that indicate what they're feeling deep inside. And although Chip was acting like all was well, clearly it was time to have a chat with Brian. That's cool though, because I liked chatting with Brian. We had had great, deep conversations together.

I walked back to the counter and leaned over to whisper to Rose.

"Can you tell Brian to see me when he gets in?"

"Sure, are you going to fire him?" she asked, a little too excited.

"No, I'm not going to fire him. That's crazy! No, just send him my way when he gets in." I finished the statement with a few taps on the counter with my college class ring. For whatever reason it always made the situation seem more serious when I did that. And I'm not going to lie, I liked the feeling of power.

"Ok," Rose replied with a smile.

I headed back to my office thinking about what I decided would be one of the more interesting days this week. Usually I didn't get to discipline anyone. And to be honest, I've always kind of liked it.

When I got back to my office, I closed the door and considered what I was going to say. Certainly Brian knew that he was often late. And certainly he knew that it wasn't a good thing. Convincing him that something had to change certainly shouldn't be that hard.

With that thought I shifted my attention to other things. The brotha's announcement that he wasn't happy lingered in my mind. And my own announcement that I wasn't happy seemed just as foreign to me. When did I stop being happy? Was it on a particular day or after a particular event?

I can guess when it was when the brotha stopped being happy. It was my fourteenth birthday at the pit. That was the last day that the brotha was a guy you could chat with. But I didn't see what the brotha saw. My experience of that event was very different.

At that moment I heard a knock on the office door. I remembered Brian and decided that it was him.

"Come in," I said, returning my thoughts to work.

Brian stuck his head in through the crack. "Hey, you wanted to see me?"

"Yeah, come in and shut the door."

I would describe Brian as a high school and college jock type. He was about 6'2", solidly built, blonde, and always clean shaven. Brian looked like what you would imagine Thor would look like if he had a professionally short haircut and was in his mid-twenties. Brian was also a little soft spoken and very chill. He didn't get rattled very often, and he knew how to let loose and have fun once in a while. He was just a chill-laxin' guy; that would be a word that was a combination of being chill and relaxed.

Brian came in, closed the door behind him and took one of the seats in front of my desk.

"So, what's going on Brian?" I asked to get the conversation going.

"Yeah, you know, the same. My girlfriend is driving me crazy. She doesn't like having to leave earlier to drop me off at work, because she says that she then arrives too early at her work and she just sits there for a half hour."

"That's rough man," I threw in for a little moral support.

"Yeah, I'm thinking about getting my own car, but you know, the money. And I'm trying to save up money so that we can move out of my apartment because it's kind of cramped."

"Right. How's that going? Do you have first and last saved yet?"

"No, I had to help my girl with a medical bill this month because things were really getting tough on her."

"Oh, has she been sick?" I ask with genuine concern.

"Yeah, she's been feeling a little sick lately."

"Contagious?" I ask, wondering if I had to cut the meeting short.

"No, no. Nothing like that. She's just been feeling a little queasy all the time."

"Is she pregnant?" I ask to lighten the mood.

Brian looked up at me and a pink glow suddenly shot across his slightly tanned face. I looked into his grey eyes and saw nothing but emptiness. It was like he had been transported somewhere else and all that was left was his body. After staring for a second longer I began to think that he hadn't considered that option before and that it was a good guess.

"Brian, are you ok?" I ask, getting concerned about his blank stare.

In response, Brian turned to me, opened his mouth, and instead of words, let out a stream of projectile vomit. "Ahhh," I yell while propelling my rolling chair back.

His spew missed me. However, it did get my desk, my paperwork, my pen holder and maybe there was a little bit on the ceiling. But like I said, it missed me. I looked up at Brian who was now redder than I had ever seen a white man. He was too disoriented to feel embarrassed and when he opened his mouth again I was greeted by another stream that got my company checkbook, my stapler and the floor on the side of my desk. Luckily though, he completely missed my trash bin which sat right next to him.

I reached for the trash bin and handed it to him. Brian took it and immediately started to shake his head with sorrow. He went to speak again, and I lifted my hand to stop him, fearing that with enough words my office would look like the bedroom from 'The Exorcist.'

"Yeah, you need to take a moment before you speak," I say, not as a request.

Brian sat with his head hanging over the bin. I look around my puke covered desk and started to wonder what the managerial rules were with cleaning up puke. Do you ask the person that copped it to mop it? Can you ask one of your other employees to do it? Or since it's my office, do I have to do it? Looking over at the red-faced Brian, I remember that Brian's a cool dude, but we really weren't that close.

I pushed my chair out as far as I could and then stood up.

"Um, I want you to take a moment and catch yourself. After that you know where the cleaning supplies are kept. And be sure to get to it before the smell gets into the carpet."

Brian shook his head but never stopped staring into the bin. I worked my way around the desk and the chunks splattered on the floor. I then cracked the door open and slipped out. And while I slipped through the aisles of clothes it became clear to me why Brian didn't make it to the professional ranks in sports. He was not good under pressure.

I headed over to Chip who was manning the sporting equipment section.

"Brian's here, but there were things that came up while we were talking, so he's gonna join you on the floor later."

"Ok. When are we expecting the new equipment?"

"Sometime soon, but don't worry, if he isn't back by then, I'll help out on the floor until he is."

"You're the boss," Chip says as a statement of fact.

I figured that I would help out Chip until Brian cleaned himself up, but the truth was that Chip wasn't much for conversation and the store didn't get busy until after ten. This was the time I usually spent covering all of the important things on my to-do list. But I was sure that Brian had covered my to-do list as well. So now I was forced to kill the time on the floor.

A few people entered the store while I was standing there and all of them headed toward Tammy and Justin. The majority of the store's profits were made in women's clothes, shoes and apparel. And, surprisingly, the most popular size in women's clothes was large.

Big women seemed to love shopping at sporting apparel stores. Although our biggest bump in sales came one day from men after Oprah did a show about men's health. Dr. Oz said that you can gain a half an inch of penis for every 40 pounds you lose. That week, every fat man in Orlando came into the store. It was like a county fair, you know, without all the inappropriate erections. Though once the guys walked past the female fitness mannequin, I guess it was the same.

But without Oprah getting the hopes of fat men up, the majority of the people coming into the store were women getting ready for their first yoga class. Having two people working the equipment section is only possible because the profit margin on the equipment is so high. It seems we could put any price on those things and they would still sell. Those benches must be the most expensive bookshelves ever made.

But my feeling was that the intentions behind buying the exercise benches were always good. When people shopped here it was because they were trying to make themselves better in some way, so I could get behind that. It would probably be cheaper to just put down the cookie, but hey, who am I to say what works.

As I let my mind wander I saw a man in his mid-forties walk into the store. He was a white guy that I would say was pretty average looking, but it was always hard for me to tell with white people. He looked like he was forty pounds away from being fit and he was recently shaven. There was no doubt that he would work his way through the store and then stop at the exercise equipment.

As I watched him scan the equipment behind the counter without scanning Rose, his motives were clear. This is a guy that has probably worked at the same place for a while. There was probably someone there that he has been interested in for a while.

In frustration with not being able to get anywhere with her, he probably shaved the beard he had had since they met. She probably complimented his face without it and he enjoyed the attention. Now he figured that if he could lose a couple of pounds the attention would continue. So the next day before work he stopped off at a sporting goods store.

To not scare him off, Chip and I move to the far end of the room. This is an instinct that you develop the longer you sell fitness equipment. By moving away the intimidated customer doesn't feel confronted with what they are considering doing. It's sort of like a fat man at the world's heaviest woman tent at the county fair. Does he enter? What happens if the world's heaviest woman is actually fifteen pounds lighter than him? What would he do then? If a person is standing at the entrance trying to get people to come in, the fat man can't have this mental debate.

The guy enters the equipment section, looks down at the first bench press bench and then stops. I look over at Chip letting him know that I would talk to him and then I wait. You have to wait a little bit before you approach a customer in sporting goods. Customers don't really see anything for the first few seconds of staring at a bench. What they're really doing is asking themselves if they're really going to do this. After a few seconds of that, they are then staring at the price and wondering whether that amount was worth spending for the opportunity of more sex.

And only after they have decided that it clearly was, was it ok to approach. It's kind of like a fat man at the county fair staring at the Ferris wheel. Wait, did I mention that I went to the Orange County fair last weekend? It was like the store the day after Oprah said that you can gain penis size by losing weight. There were a lot of fat people. It left an impression on me.

"What's great about this bench is that it's inexpensive," I said to the man to break the ice.

"Well, it's cheaper than that one, if that's what you mean," the man said pointing at the bench next to it.

"The reason why that one is more expensive is because it can hold more weight."

This guy isn't heavy enough for that statement to be a trigger. But for people slightly heavier than he was, that phase made them walk away from the cheaper bench and never look at it again.

"Yeah, but how much weight am I going to be lifting?" the guy said, turning to me. I think that that question was meant to be one of those questions that don't require an answer, but the upsell has to begin sometime so why not now.

"Probably about 60 pounds to start off with, but if you do it consistently, you could probably get up to 120 pretty soon."

"Double the weight? I think you have more faith in me than you should," the guy said with a smile.

The truth is that if he used the equipment longer than a month then it would be a miracle. But sporting good stores in Orange County don't sell reality, they sell dreams. "I don't think so. If you stay with it, 120 pounds is realistic."

"Well, that's very nice of you," he said before scanning the rest of the equipment.

"What are you looking for?" I ask, knowing that our relationship has been established.

"I'm trying to find something to help me get rid of this." The man put both of his hands on his gut and shook it a little.

"The only way to lose weight is to burn calories. The fastest way to burn calories is to build muscle because large muscles are less efficient than small muscles and need more calories just to sustain themselves. So you can either focus on building muscles or burning fat."

"Can't I do both?"

"No. The reason why muscles get larger is because they develop very small tears in them when you work out. And when the muscle repairs itself, it does it in a way that can better handle the stress the next time. The most important part about muscle growth is rest.

Muscle growth doesn't happen when you're lifting the weight. It happens during the time you are allowing your body to rest.

On the other hand, muscle growth from cardio workouts don't create as many tears. So the way that you lose weight doing cardio is from creating a calorie deficit. 3500 calories equal a pound. So you have to burn an extra 3500 calories to lose one pound. So when you're doing cardio, the goal is to burn those extra calories as often as you can, preferably five days a week."

The man stared at me. Clearly he was impressed. "You know I'm a doctor and I didn't know any of that. You really are an expert on this stuff."

"That's my job." I find that by being humble the customer was more likely to accept me as a god. "So what do you think you are more likely to stick with, weights or cardio?"

"Umm, I don't know. Is there something that does both?"

And that is always the next question. It's amazing how consistently that worked.

What's important in the next step is not to scare the customer off. You have to make a quick decision on how much the customer was willing to spend and then find something that was only slightly outside his price range. If you can sell the customer on the benefits of the product, they would gladly increase their range by 50 bucks. But the odds were really low that a customer would increase his price range by $200. The trick was to upsell the customer without being greedy. It was an art.

Judging by the fact that he stared at the cheapest piece of equipment in the section for as long as he did, his upper limit was probably about $150. So to answer his question I was going to show him a piece of equipment that was $225.

"This is a rowing machine. It's great for cardio, and it builds muscle at the same time."

"I thought you said you couldn't do both?"

"You're not going to get huge using a rowing machine."

"I don't want that," he said happily.

"Some people do, and this is not gonna do it for you. But whereas running or the stairmaster only build up your legs, this will also work your other muscles. It won't make any of your muscles big, but it will make a few of them denser and hence less efficient."

"Because less efficient muscles burn calories?"

"Exactly."

"I got that," he said with a smile. He looked down at the price tag. "$225. That's a little more than I wanted to spend, but I think it's worth it."

Sold and sold. "That's good. I think you'll like it. It comes with a pamphlet that has recommended exercises so that should be helpful."

"Nice."

"So tell me something," I said, trying to change the topic. "You said that you were a doctor?"

"Yeah."

"So I got this situation." I stop when I realize that Chip is still in earshot so I turn to him. "I have this customer, Chip." Chip took my lead and headed over into the shoe section. "I know this guy who I've known for a while and out of nowhere he tells you that he isn't happy. What would you tell him?"

"I'm a doctor of chemistry," he said, with an uncomfortable look on his face.

"But that's kind of the same thing right? Everything's about chemistry right?"

"This is not my area of expertise," he said, with a funny look on his face.

"But you're a smart guy, right? Smart guys have smart ideas. What do you think I should do?"

The guy looked away in thought. "You know what," he began. "I would say that you should tell your friend that he should try to figure out what makes him happy and then do it. I'm sorry, I don't know what else I would say to him other than that."

"No, that's good. You're right. If he's not happy, he should figure out what makes him happy and then do it. You're right. So simple," I said feeling a little lighter than I had before.

"So can I pay for this now or…?"

"No, no. You can tell Rose what you're purchasing and I'll have Chip bring one out for you. It comes in a box, but it doesn't really require much assembly."

"Good, because I can't do much assembly," he says with a chuckle.

"Naw, it's easy. I promise."

"Thanks for your help," he says.

"You too. I'm sorry, what's your name?"

47

"Toady."

"Toady?" I asked while trying to suppress my natural instinct to take his lunch money.

"Well it's Tod, but friends call me Toady."

"That's cool," I said, while wondering if people who give someone a nickname like that could truly be considered a friend. "I'm Ben."

"Nice to meet you Ben. Do I pay over there?"

"Yep, right over there."

I walk over to Chip and let him know which machine Toady needed and then I briefly considered taking Justin's lunch money just to get it out of my system. I don't though because Justin had enough things to worry about, like the unfortunate things that gay homosexual Americans are forced to do with other guys. His was a tough life, and I didn't need to make it any tougher.

Instead, I paced around the store looking at everything but not really seeing anything. What Toady said was right. I needed to sit down with the brotha and we needed to figure out what it was that would make the both of us happy. And once we did, we had to do it. It was simple but very true. Oh, and you know what, as a chemist, I bet he also would have known how to get the smell of vomit out of carpet.

I look at the counter and Chip was already helping Toady out the door. It would be unprofessional to chase after him as he was getting into his car so I let him go. Instead I considered what he said. He was right. When you're unhappy, you just find something that makes you happy and do that. I guess happiness and sex are similar in that way. Who knew? But now the real question was, 'what would make the both of us happy?'

Chapter 4
How to Enlarge Your Penis

Although my relationship with the brotha had taken a turn after that incident at the pit, it really changed the first time we banged a woman. She was this really tall, very blonde chick at Beloit College. My buddy and I were hanging out in his room when Barb, the blonde, came in with her friend Cindy. Maybe Barb wasn't her name, but she really reminded me of Pig Farm Barbie. It was one of Barbie's less popular versions.

So Barb and Cindy come in drunk, but Cindy is 'I'm going to pass out soon but right now I'm not stumbling or slurring so you don't have to worry about feeling bad about having sex with me' drunk. I barely knew Barb, but I knew Cindy pretty well. And when Cindy and I spoke, she made very clear how much she wanted to have sex with my buddy. So when my buddy gave me the look that told me to get the fuck out, Barb and I went upstairs to Cindy's room.

Since this was the first time I had really spoken to Barb I had no way of knowing just how much she liked black guys. Later when we spoke more, she told me how she had dated some white guy all through high school, but how much she was looking forward to going to college so that she could have sex with a black guy. And since we were both freshman, and it had only been three weeks since the beginning of college, I was the first one that she had gotten to know.

I wasn't aware of the college rules on being a wingman when women come to a friend's room to have sex with them. Were you supposed to sleep with the girl's best friend or not. I wasn't sure. But when Barb started playing the slow songs of George Michael on the cd player, how could I resist. And remember, this was the 'every woman wants me' George Michael and not 'I have sex with men in public bathrooms' George Michael. So, back then that was a pretty bold move on her part.

I can't remember for sure, but I think she was the one who made the move on me. I think she was the one that jumped on me like a big blonde cat and stuck her tongue down my throat like she was snaking the drain for her lost jewelry. Again, I'm not sure whether it was her or me, but I think that it was her that yanked off my t-shirt and kept whipping my chest with her long blonde hair. And if memory serves me right, she then started rubbing her jean covered snatch against the jean covered brotha until she couldn't take it anymore. She then took off her pants before taking off mine and then jumped on me like a cowboy jumping off a roof onto his horse.

But really, who initiated it and who did what first is unimportant. What is important was that the brotha got his first bit of pussy. Was it what either of us had expected? Not really. You hear these stories about "fucking tight pussies," but that's not how I would describe it. I guess I would describe it more like throwing stones into a cave. Sure the stones hit the sides of the cave every so often, but for the most part, it's a whole lotta nothin'.

Now don't get me wrong, I was still having sex for the first time. So after a very appropriate minute or two I pulled the brotha out and allow him to spit up on her. And hey, I'm not going to complain about anything that allows me to touch boob. But overall, the whole experience wasn't what I expected. And again, this was a long time ago, so I can't remember whether it was her or me, but I remember that one of us had a disappointed look on our face that said 'wow, as a black man I thought he'd be bigger.'

It was after that that the brotha got kind of weird with me. He became very demanding about stuff. Like for example, he would make me walk to the bathroom wearing pants while everyone else wore a towel. And on the rare occasions when I saw some other dude's junk, he would make me describe it to him in really uncomfortable details.

But that wasn't the worst of it. The worst was that the brotha wanted approval over who I had sex with. I couldn't just meet some girl at a party and then go back and bang her. I had to first find somewhere I could be alone with the brotha and describe her to him. If he liked her then I could invite her back to my dorm. But if what he saw when he met her didn't live up to her description, then he would go limp in protest.

Going limp was something he saw on TV one night when we were watching a show about protestors. The protestors pointed out that dead weight was heavier to carry than a stiff body. So ever since then, whenever I wanted to do something that he didn't, he would go limp in protest. That's why I now always wear underwear while watching TV.

The first time he pulled that shit on me was with this girl that always used to come to my room uninvited. The first time she came over I discussed her with the brotha. His answer to my request was no, or to be more exact, he said 'there ain't no thang like a chicken wing,' which I have to think meant no.

But she kept coming over and she kept acting like I was the man, so eventually she got to me. One night she was in my room when I was falling asleep. She didn't like the fact that I was falling asleep on her so she kept asking me questions. One of the questions was 'what was I thinking?'

And because I was tired my filter was down, so I said 'I'm thinking about how I could get you to give me a blow job.' And her reply was "all you have to do was ask." It's amazing how hearing something like that will wake you up.

Of course, I then asked and she said "well, we'd have to kiss first."

I think it was a legit request. I would have preferred that she just unzip me and go at it, but she was a sheltered virgin from a small town. I knew I had to take that into account.

We kissed for a bit and then I touched naked boob so that was good enough for me. But why stop there, right? So we continued kissing and I brought up the whole blow job thing again and she said no. I felt so cheap. She had lured my tongue into her mouth with the pretense of a blow job and then pulled a bait and switch.

But being the type of guy that always gives a person the benefit of the doubt, I say, "can we have sex?" And when she said "maybe," I just knew it was going to happen.

As we continue to make out, I reach down to my jean buttons. And very quietly, below the sound of smacking lips I hear the brotha repeating the word 'no.' I start kissing louder to drain out the sound. When I unbutton and unzip my pants I grab her hand and place it on the brotha.

She then starts squeezing it like it was a lump of clay. I'm wondering what she was doing, but I figure that this was the first time that she had ever touched a dick so I'd give her a pass. But after a few minutes of it, she stopped and sat up next to me.

"What's wrong?" she asked.

"What do you mean?" I replied.

"Don't you want to do this?" she said, looking back at me, disappointed.

"Yeah, why?"

Without a word she looked down at the brotha so I follow her gaze. When I see the brotha he is spread out across my midsection, limp. He hadn't retreated into my body or anything; in fact he seemed like he was almost his full size, but he was limp. His head was in one direction, his balls were just hanging there, and his one beady eye was staring right back at me. The look in his eye screamed "hell no, we won't go," but I guess he didn't say it because we both knew that with him protesting, we weren't going anywhere.

I then made up some excuse with the girl about how I had to get up early for a lab class and was too tired to get up for it. She was ok with it. The truth is that she managed to get what she wanted from me. It took her two years but she got it and she was happy. I was the one that had reason to complain. I got screwed by two people that night. And threesomes are never fun when you're the one that ends up getting screwed by the dick.

That incident was when I realized how much of a hold that the brotha had over me and my life. The brotha literally had me by the balls. My heart could want as much as it wants but unless the brotha was ok with it, the heart wasn't going anywhere.

So, how is a guy supposed to respond to a person that has you by the balls? I don't know what an expert would say, but I have found that giving them whatever they want seems to pretty much keep the peace. When the brotha says jump, I usually ask 'was that high enough for you?' The answer is usually "no. What are you a fuckin' bitch? Jump higher." You learn to live with it.

But now I have something on the brotha. After our night of enhanced sharing, I knew that he was unhappy… and maybe gay. But the unhappiness was what I would focus on. And what I'm hoping is that if we both focus on it, we could make his life better. And if we made his life better, maybe my life wouldn't be so crappy.

You know what, I don't wanna give the wrong impression. My life wasn't crappy. I owned a house. I had a great job. It was just that…

Well, I don't know. The brotha wasn't always the best company. And sometimes I wished that I had... Man, I don't know what I wish. I just wished things were different.

And I knew that if the brotha were a little happier he might let me date. Maybe if the brotha were happier I could do more than just touch naked boob. Naked boobs are great, right. But knowing that if I take off my pants I'm going to find a passive protestor makes me want to not take off my pants.

When I arrived home I took off my jeans and pulled the brotha out of the flap in my boxers.

"What's up bitch?" the brotha immediately said.

"Hey. I've been thinking about what you said about being unhappy."

"Yeah, I heard you talking to some guy about my business. That's my business, you hear me. That is not for you to go spreading around to strangers."

When the brotha said that I thought about how he got drunk and rattled off his big mouth to someone I worked with. But I knew that if I brought that up he would get defensive, and then someone would just end up crying again.

"I was talkin' to an expert. I was tryin' to figure out how to help."

"He was a chemist ya dumb fuck. And on top of that, he was stupid enough to buy one of your crappy rowing machines. What does this guy know about anything?"

"First, the name calling doesn't help."

"Speak for yourself, ya taint."

"Second of all, it did help because he gave me some good advice."

I was waiting for a comeback but nothing came.

"I have decided that if you're unhappy, then we should do something to make you happier."

"If you want to make me happy, why don't we move over to the bedroom and make a little love," the brotha added in that low voice he uses when he is trying to seduce me.

"Ya know, we have sex whenever you want, and yet you are still unhappy. Doesn't that tell you something about what makes you happy?"

"What that tells me is that you ain't worth shit when it comes to having sex. Maybe what I need is to be in someone else's hands. You know someone that knows what they're doing."

"Oh no, no no. No no no no, no. That ain't gonna happen."

"Then you betta step things up. You betta learn how to do it left handed or something because this brotha needs to feel himself some strong hands."

I don't think that I can express how much that statement disturbed me. I know that I usually give into every one of his whims, but, how do I say this, hells no!

"My brotha, have you ever considered the fact that there is something else out there that could make you happy other than sex?" I asked, hoping to get him to open up like he had for that brief moment this morning.

The brotha was silent for a while before he said "get me a drink."

This was a little early for him to start drinking. Usually he didn't start until around ten. But I decided to cut him some slack today because I knew how hard it was for him to open up. And usually when he drank he turned into an angry drunk. But I'm going to hope that instead of being angry, this time he'd start to share.

I went to the kitchen and looked through my extensive liquor cabinet. I knew that when the brotha started drinking in the afternoon, he drank beer. When he started drinking right after work he drank hard liquor with a soda or juice mix. When he started drinking at ten it was usually hard liquor straight. But since it was after work, I made him a vodka cranberry and poured it into a shot glass.

The brotha polished off that one pretty quickly and then asked for another. I made him another and he knocked that one back just as fast. The brotha was quiet as he waited for the buzz to kick in. While he did I warmed up some leftover white rice and a few pieces of chicken from the 20-piece bucket I'd bought at the beginning of the week.

When it was warm I took my plate to the couch and flipped on the TV. There was nothing on so I stopped on an old episode of Happy Days and relaxed. After about twenty minutes I was done with dinner and the brotha was starting to mumble to himself. I turned off the TV and sat up on the couch.

"So what's up?" I asked, a little afraid of what he was going to say.

"You think you could just do whatever you want and I can't do shit about it," he said, a little more drunk than I expected.

I did mix his drinks a little strong but it usually took a more potent mix to get him talking.

"You think that you could just snap your fingers and I will just do whatever you want? Well, no. You can't."

As I listened I tried to figure out where the hell this was coming from. Because as far as I knew, I'd been the brotha's bitch for as long as I could remember.

"You think you could just bring in your floozy whores and they could just look at me how ever they feel and I just have to lay there and take it. Fuck no. You hear me? Fuck no!"

This is where I started to question whether or not I should speak. He was clearly thinking of something in particular. But the question was whether or not he was willing to say it.

"How are the girls looking at you?" I asked in as calm a voice as I could.

"Like you don't fuckin' know. Like you don't see it too," he added.

"I don't know what you're talking about."

"Then either you're blind, or you're too fuckin' stupid to see it. Which one is it? Are you blind or just too fuckin' stupid?"

"I guess I'm blind. What am I missing?"

"You should have said that you are too fuckin' stupid."

The brotha was quiet for a minute.

"I need another fuckin' drink."

"No, no more. If you want to tell me something just say it. How are they looking at you? Just tell me. Just say it!" I yell, starting to get angry that there has been something that I may have missed. "Just say it goddamn it!"

"That I'm fuckin' small all right!" the brotha yelled back. "They all look at me like I'm some sort of disappointment to them."

"You're a disappointment because of your whole passive resistance thing. That's why they're disappointed."

"No. They all look at me like they can't believe that I'm the one that's attached to you."

"I don't understand what you mean," I ask a lot more calmly.

"You're just so fuckin' tall and you're black, and you're so fuckin' cool. And then they see me and they're all so disappointed looking."

I lean back for a second to absorb what I'd just heard. Never before in my life had the brotha ever said anything nice about me. I always thought that I was the problem. I thought that I was the 'stupid fuck' as he would often say. I didn't know how to respond to these revelations.

"I know you're just fuckin' embarrassed by me. I know you wish that I was someone else, someone bigger, thicker, someone that matched you more."

I wasn't going to tell the brotha, but what he was saying was true. I did think about what it would be like to have a brotha that was longer and thicker. It's true that I wondered what it would be like to have a brotha that matched me a little more. I didn't really like the fact that in the morning he would retract so far into my body that I felt like a eunuch. I didn't like the fact that I was 6'6" and one of my hands almost covered my entire dick. I didn't like the fact that women didn't squeal when I stuck the brotha in them. But this was all stuff that I thought. I would never say any of this aloud, even if the brotha already knew.

"I need another fuckin' drink," the brotha said soberly.

I got up and fixed him another drink knowing that he would be fucked up for the rest of the night. When I sat back down I sat on the edge of the couch leaning forward so that the brotha could reach the shot glass I was holding. He finished off that glass as well and then fell over lifeless.

I was used to him passing out. After drinking three shots right after the other he usually only has about ten minutes of consciousness and then he was dead to the world. I learned that the hard way one night when I thought that I would get him drunk so that he wouldn't screw things up with a chick I was with.

I got myself a bottle of Jack, offered him a few half shots and he was out. I then tried to hook up with the chick and the brotha may as well have been an oversized clit because that's what he looked like. I'm not gonna say that it was embarrassing when she reached up and felt for my Adam's apple, but it certainly wasn't pleasant. After that I learned that there were no ways around the brotha. I had to either work with him or keep him in my pants.

Over the last few years I have mostly chosen to keep him in my pants. In fact, I don't even bother to start things up with women because I know what I will have to go through with the brotha. But having heard what he just told me, everything made a lot more sense.

If I think back to that night at the pit, the brotha did say that she checked him out. I didn't see it when she did it, but she was definitely different towards me afterwards. And if she did see the brotha it would have been after swimming in that freezing water for about twenty minutes. Not only was she looking at the younger, smaller brotha but she was looking at him with shrinkage because of the cold water. I've seen him like that. It's not an attractive sight.

Now I have to assume that the brotha did see her look down. And that how he acted toward me afterwards was because he was embarrassed by her reaction. He started drinking and started acting like a total dick because he felt bad about himself.

And I'm sure it didn't help when I had sex with Barb and one of us, probably Barb, looked down at me with that look that said that she thought it would be bigger. I imagine that if the brotha saw that, it would have just made him feel worse. Wow, all this time and I thought that he was just being a dick. I didn't realize that this bothered him. I didn't realize how sensitive he was.

The unfortunate thing about all of this was that there was nothing that we could do about it. He was the way he was and women would always react the way they did. The unfortunate thing was that we were stuck with each other and there was nothing either of us could do about it. I would have to learn how to live with the names and the "bitches" and the drinking and all the rest. Unfortunately, this was my life and this was all it would ever be.

On that pleasant thought I decided to go to sleep. The brotha would be out for hours and not getting enough sleep the night before, I felt tired. It was a warm night so I felt comfortable sleeping naked. Also, if the brotha woke up and had to puke I wouldn't have to fiddle with my pants as I ran to the bathroom.

My dreams that night were not very interesting. In fact, the dreams were a lot like the dreams I usually have. There was a chair in my dad's office back in Wisconsin that I always liked. And my main dream for the night was about there being some sort of nail or staple in the chair. I would sit down on the chair and I would feel something stick me so I would get up to look for it. But no matter how much I looked I couldn't ever find it.

After what seemed like five minutes of talking to people about the chair I had to pee. So at that point, the chair became a toilet and I took a piss in it. And after a really long pee I still felt like I had to go so I realized that I was dreaming and I woke up.

My first thought when I got up was about whether or not I had peed the bed. I moved my thigh around looking for wet spots and when I didn't find any I rolled over and relaxed for a second longer. Once enough strength returned to my body I dragged myself up and sat on the edge of the bed.

With my eyes still closed and my body feeling heavy, I rocked myself forward onto my feet. Back when I was buying my bed I made sure to buy a high bed because I liked the feeling that came with having my feet dangle while sitting on the edge of the bed. At 6'6" you don't get many opportunities to feel small and dangling my feet off the side of the bed reminded me of the good parts of my childhood.

I reached for the wall and doorways as I made my way to the bathroom. And once there I rested my left hand on the wall to keep me up. With my right I reached down for the brotha. Instead of the brotha I felt a burning sensation in my chest when I only grabbed air.

In a second I was fully awake reaching and grabbing between my legs hoping that he was just caught between my thighs. When I didn't find him there something primal came from inside me. It was a scream that could've been made just before hunting lions on the plains of Africa. It was a scream that could have been made during the pre-war tribal ritual of my people who had long since been packed up and shipped to America.

It could have sounded like that. But what it actually sounded like was a six-year-old girl who screamed at the top of her lungs because her brother took her black Barbie from her and kept sticking it in his pants. I'm not really proud of that scream, but it is what came out, so what am I supposed to do.

Like the night before, I rushed back to my bed and started shaking out the sheets. When I didn't see anything fly up, I searched the floor next to the bed. When I didn't find anything there I ran into the living room to see if my house keys were still in the bowl. When I found them there I reached for the knob and found that the door was still locked.

With these clues I figured out that he was still in the house. I ran to the kitchen and looked around. The bottles were where I had left them and he wasn't in the fridge.

The panic that I first felt changed a little bit when I realize that he's somewhere close by. Instead of my heart beating at a mile a minute, the beating slowed down and became very hard. It felt like my heart was straining to beat and each beat was causing my heart to stretch to twice its size. I wondered if I was having a heart attack. That only caused my heart to hurt more when I thought about someone finding my naked dead body on the floor missing a penis. I didn't want to be forever known as the naked eunuch found dead on arrival. That was not how I wanted Rose to remember me.

As I stood in the pitch black kitchen I noticed a light coming from under the door to my office. I rushed over to the door and opened it slowly. The light was coming from my laptop and as I entered the room I saw the brotha sitting on the laptop keyboard staring at the screen.

"Didn't you hear me scream?" I yelled at him. "Why the hell didn't you answer? Do you know you almost gave me a heart attack? Why the hell do you keep running away?"

But as passionately and loudly as I said it, the brotha didn't respond. In fact the brotha didn't even move. His little body and head remained motionless staring at the screen. I got a little closer to him and yelled a little louder.

"Hey! You can't keep doing this. You hear me. I can't keep waking up in the middle of the night to find you gone. Do you have any idea how that feels?"

Still the brotha didn't respond.

"Hey!" I yelled louder. "Hey!"

As if the last one was loud enough to wake him up he turned and looked at me. As he turned a tear rolls down his head… or maybe it was a drip of dribble that came out of his mouth. Either way it was heartbreaking to look at. In that quiet moment the macho, son-of-a-bitch attitude that he carried around was gone. All that was left was a small, very vulnerable penis with tears or dribble rolling down its body.

I stopped yelling at the brotha and turned toward the screen. The brotha was on YouTube and he was looking at a video called 'Jelqing or How to Enlarge Your Penis.' Yeah, the brotha wasn't dribbling, he was crying. I saw what he saw in that video. And what we both saw was the chance to be happy.

I pulled out my desk chair and sat down in front of the computer. I reached around the brotha and started the video up from the beginning. It started with a black guy saying "How to increase the size of your penis?" and then holding up a pink balloon saying "this will be our penis."

There was something very calming about this guy. It felt like I was him and he was me. And in spite of his strangely feminine name that he kept repeating over and over again, I knew that this was a guy that I could relate to. I knew that this was a guy that could possibly help me to be happy.

Here is what he said:

Jelqing or How to Enlarge your Penis

"How to increase the size of your penis? Ummm... (Lifting up a pink, penis shaped balloon) This will be our penis.

There are three basic exercises. One is milking. Think of it as if you were squeezing something out of a hose. While you are half or three quarters erect, you take your thumb and pointing finger, and you make a little OK out of it. And you grab from the base of the penis and you do a little squeeze and then you pull it out. (Cristian pulls his OK shaped fingers along the length of the water balloon past the tip.) That's one. This is after you've lubricated because if you don't you'll just tear the outside of your penis and that would not be fun. So you lubricate it with lotion or soap, whatever you want. So you've made the milking motion, with the OK sign and that's one.

Then when you've reached the end of your penis with the other hand, you start again. (Cristian switches hands so that his other hand is now gripping the base of the balloon.) And you do the same OK and you pull. And that's two. And you continue three, four, and so on.

So for the first five days you do 40 times. (Cristian simulates the milking motion as he counts) So one, two, three and so on. And from day 6 to day 10, so that's the next five days, you increase it by 40. So you start off at 40, and day 6 to day 10, you go up to 80.

From day 11 to day 15 you go by another 40 so you go up to 120. And from day 16 to day 20 you go up to 160. And from day 21 and onwards you do a minimum of 200 milks a day.

Still being half erect or three quarters erect, you hold the base of the penis and you shake it. (Cristian shakes the balloon with single thrusts like he is trying to get a water droplet off of the balloon.) One, two, three... And you do that 40 times.

The third one, the last one was never my favorite. What you do is you take your thumb and your pointing finger, you hold the end of your penis and... you know when you're peeing, you're urinating, and you want to stop the stream, you clench? You kind of clench that muscle. Well what you do with this third exercise is you hold your penis with your thumb and forefinger. You pull outwards with your fingers and you clench back. And you do this for ten seconds.

You then do it again and you rest. And you do it a total of twenty times. After the twentieth time you're done for the day. You do these three exercises six days a week and you take the seventh day off before you do it again.

Now, what progress would you expect to see? I can tell you what my experience was. I started out..."

Here the video stopped and was replace by graphics that said "See the full vlog for free at RateABull.com; the place for advice and relationships."

The brotha and I both stared silently as the screen once the video had ended. I didn't say anything because I was amazed at what I had seen. The guy in the video seemed just like me. He didn't seem crazy or shifty. In fact, he seemed the opposite.

There was something about the way he spoke and the way he smiled that made me trust him. He seemed friendly and comforting. He had clearly been where I am now. And here he was on the internet talking about it like it wasn't humiliating. I could trust this guy.

"I want to do it," the brotha said.

"That seems like a lot of work and it could take months," I added, considering the commitment that was required.

"I don't care how long it takes, or how hard it is, I want to do this. And I want you to want to do it too," the brotha added.

I stared at the screen again thinking about the reason that the guy in the video would put this on YouTube. At the end of the video it said "see the full vlog for free at RateABull.com." This video was clearly trying to get me to go to this other site. When I got there I would probably have to sign up for it and do something else that I wouldn't want to do. No thank you.

This video told me everything that I needed to know thank you very much. Guy on the video, I trust you and I think you have made me happy, so thank you very much.

"Yeah, let's do it," I said to the brotha. "Starting tomorrow, you are going to be bigger."

The brotha turned to me and another tear rolled down his body. I think the brotha was happy.

Chapter 5
The Journey of Two Inches Begins with a Single Jelq

After watching the video three or four more times, I took the brotha to bed and we fell asleep without any further discussion. The next morning the brotha was again where he should be. His silence continued as I reached for the retracted brotha and took my morning piss. It continued while I stared in the mirror at him and brushed my teeth. And it continued as I took a shower. Even a handful of soap suds didn't start his usual suggestions of sex.

I'm sure that a lot of the silence had to do with how much he had drunk the night before. But I'm also sure that somehow his silence was a sign that he was looking forward to what would happen once we got back home. I didn't have the time to start Cristian's Jelqing technique before I left for work. And that night was a gym night so it would have to wait a little longer. But I was sure that most of his silence was because he was trying to contain himself so that tonight would be special.

After getting dressed I poured my usual bowl of cereal and sat down for breakfast. As I stared out the window at the big fichus tree in my front yard and the houses across the empty street, I began to feel how special the day was. This was going to be the last day of my inadequate life. It was going to be the last time I had to be self-conscious about changing in the gym locker room. And it would the first day of a new relationship between me and the brotha.

Maybe that new relationship would be one of actual friends. Maybe I would begin to enjoy sexing him up again. Maybe he would allow me to enjoy having sex with chicks again. Maybe we would have the type of relationship that I imagined that other guys have with their dicks. Maybe it would be fun and maybe I would even grow to love him.

And as if on cue the brotha broke the silence. "Ben," he said.

"Yeah brotha?" I said with a small smile on my face, almost glad to hear the voice of my new friend.

"I think I'm gonna be sick."

'The silence...,' I thought, just before the brotha puked in my pants.

I spent the next couple of minutes kneeling in front of the toilet with the brotha hanging in the bowl. There wasn't a lot that had to come up. And once it did, the brotha became silent again and then fell asleep.

I took the brotha to the sink and washed him off. I took my time because I knew that I would miss my bus and would have to drive to work. That gave me an extra few minutes to look for another pair of pants and to remember the nice things that I was thinking about the brotha.

When I arrived at work I found Rose and Chip waiting like usual, but with them was Brian. As I unlocked the door I noticed a slight smile on Chip's face. I would like to believe that it had to do with Brian being on time to work. I wondered if his newfound joy would interfere with his morning nap, but as usual once I opened the door he headed immediately to the storage room where his improvised bed await him.

"Good morning Ben," Rose said with a smile and then headed back to my office.

"Morning Brian," I said when Rose and Chip were out of earshot.

"Morning," he said back.

"Feeling better today?"

"Yeah, yeah, I'm fine."

"Did you talk to your girlfriend about what you were nervous about yesterday?" I asked in a fatherly sort of way.

Brian looked up at me and without a word shook his head 'no.' Silent he walked toward his section.

"These aren't the droids you're looking for," I said, loud enough for him to hear.

"He can go about his business," Brian replied.

"You can go about your business," I replied.

"Move along," Brian said loud enough to be heard clearly across the store.

64

"Move along. Move along now," I said, before switching on the lights and heading back to my office.

As I opened my office door I heard "does it smell strange in here?"

I got in and closed the door behind me. I played it casual for a second and then denied everything.

"No, no it smells the same."

"It definitely smells strange in here," Rose continued.

"Maybe the night crew cleaned the carpets."

"No, it smells more like someone got sick in here and then tried to cover it up with Windex or something."

'Boy does that girl know her puke smells,' I thought. 'I guess experience is the best teacher.' "Naw, I don't smell it. So how are you this morning? Everything good?" I knew that that would distract her. And as automatically as being called to the board as soon as you get a hard-on, a huge smile appeared on Rose's face.

"My boyfriend is such an idiot. He doesn't get that I don't want to speak to him anymore."

"Did you tell him that you didn't want to speak to him anymore yet?" I asked.

"No."

"Like I said, men aren't that bright. We need to be told things if you want us to know them. You can't expect us to figure it out on our own," I said as I handed Rose the till.

A typical day followed from there. As usual I had to go over to Tammy and remind her to smile, and as usual I talked to Justin about the unmistakable sexual appeal of the new Madonna. Justin didn't seem to give an inch.

At about lunch time the brotha woke up and became restless. More than once I had to stick my hand in my pocket and make a quick adjustment. And I was more than happy when six o'clock came and my shift was done. When Jennifer, the cashier from the night shift, arrived I counted out Rose's till and waved good-bye as she headed out. I then handed the new float to Jennifer and the night shift began.

I balanced Rose's till with the receipts and when everything checked out I put all of it into the night depository pouch and waited for Jerome, the night manager, to arrive. I always considered Jerome to be an interesting guy. He was the only white Jerome that I had ever met. He claimed that Jerome was a Greek name and listed a bunch of saints and stuff. But as far as I'm concerned Jerome is the guy you pick up in your skyblue Buick Skylark on the way to meet Tyrone at the Hooch Hut for malt liquors.

I had never worked with Jerome because we were both hired as managers, but he seemed like an uptight guy. And he didn't seem like he was uptight in the way that kept the store clean. He seemed uptight in the way that he needed to control what everyone did. I'm going to guess and say that it came from constantly being mistaken for a black guy. I imagine that could make a white guy uptight, especially if you grew up in Orlando. Yeah, Disney is right around the corner, but Central Florida isn't exactly the most liberal place. And I'm saying that as a guy that grew up in Wisconsin.

When I was finally able to leave, the brotha was wide awake. When I changed at the gym I saw that he was more excited about the night's activities then I thought. I didn't remember him getting all the way up, but the spit marks on my boxers showed something else.

I quickly slipped on my long pants and considered whether or not the wet marks would soak through to my shorts. I had brought the thinnest of my shorts, not thinking that it would make a difference. Deciding to gamble, I changed my shirt and shoes, stuck everything into a locker and headed down to the free weights.

It was amazing how much energy I had while going through my routine. After only one rep I decided to increase almost all of my weights by five pounds. I had been stuck at my previous weights for weeks and this was the first bit of progress.

I burned through my routine in twenty minutes and was back in the locker room in no time. I considered taking a steam but by the last rep the brotha was up and hadn't gone back down. I figured that if I tried to get comfortable for a steam he would spend the whole time either asking to come out or asking to head home so that we could get started. Instead I stuffed my work clothes into my gym bag, hopped in my car and headed home.

When I got home I dropped my shorts, helped the brotha to poke through the flap and heated up some leftovers.

"So are we doin' this or not?" the brotha piped up.

"Let me grab some food, rest for a second, and then we'll begin."

I could tell the brotha was happy when he broke into a little Jay-Z from the Grey Album.

"There's never been a nigga this good for this long, this hood, for this pop it's hot, or this strong. With so many different flows, this one's for this song. The next one I'll switch up, this one will get bit up.

These fucks too lazy to make up shit. They crazy. They don't paint pictures, they just trace me. You know what, soon they forget who they plucked they whole style from and try to reverse the outcome. I'm like TUCK."

Meanwhile I popped a few pieces of chicken into the microwave and munched down. When I was done I moved into my office where I went to YouTube and found Cristian's jelqing video. The brotha and I watched it, memorizing the amount of time for each exercise, and then moved to the bedroom, where I had a bottle of lotion under my bed.

I grabbed the lotion, pulled off my boxers and then stopped.

"Are we supposed to be standing or sitting?" I asked the brotha.

"Why the fuck would it matter? Come on, let's start," the brotha barked back.

"You're right." I sat on the floor and looked down at the brotha.

"What?" the brotha said, looking up at me.

I got back up, walked back to the desk in the office, pulled out the ruler and returned to my place at the foot of the bed.

"What are you doing?" the brotha asked with hesitation in his voice.

"I'm gonna measure you so that I have a record of how much you've grown."

"No, you're not," the brotha replied with a little fear in his voice.

"Yeah man, how else are we supposed to know if it worked?"

"No, you're not gonna measure me. You're not going to write that down where someone else could see it."

"Ok, I won't write it down, I'll just remember it."

"No, you're not."

"Come on man."

I ignored the brotha and reached down for him when he yelled, "Passive protest!" And then went limp.

"Damn passive protest. Come on, firm up."

"No."

"Firm up."

"No."

"Ok, I'll just measure you limp. If the number's really small I guess that's what will have to be written down."

"Passive protest!" As he yelled it again he shrunk down to a smaller size.

"Get big."

"No."

"Get up, goddamn it!"

"Hell no. I won't go!"

"Goddamn it! That's it, we're not doing it."

"Are you threatening me?" the brotha retorted.

"Maybe I am," I replied, full of confidence that I had finally found something that the brotha really wanted.

"Oh, then you must not want to have sex ever again. You must not want to have sex ever again. Because I'll leave, and this time I will never come back."

"Ok, look, I was just kidding," I said, while trying to muster up a smile through all of the flop sweat that had immediately appeared on my face. "You know you're the man, right?"

"I'm the man?" the brotha asked with attitude in his voice. "Am I the man, bitch?"

"You're the man."

"So are you going to put that goddamn ruler away?"

"Sure man, whatever you want."

"Alright, then now we can begin."

I put down the ruler realizing that he would always have the upper hand. But even with that I was still sure that I had something I could bargain with and that today would be the day to exploit it.

"One thing though," I said as I reached for the lotion.

"What's that?" the brotha said with a little anger.

I considered backing off, but figured that it was now or never, so I asked.

"Do you think you could lay off the 'bitches'?"

"If I lay off the bitches the only thing left is dicks and I know how you feel about that. You may like that all up in you but that ain't my thing."

I sat for a moment and considered what my gay, homosexual American penis was saying. Then I realized that he was making a joke. "No, I mean I am requesting that you stop call me a bitch."

"I know what you're saying, dumbass. You can't tell when a brotha's makin' a joke. You better laugh, goddamn it."

I let out my laugh that kind of sounds like I am clearing my throat, hoping that satisfied the brotha.

"Wow, you laughed. Now how can I stop calling you bitch if you don't stop acting like one? That would be like me calling you by someone else's name and expecting to you reply. Come here Billie Jean. Come here Dirty Diana. Come here Ben."

"I know that you were just listing Michael Jackson songs, but my name actually is Ben. So if you called me Ben I would reply."

"And when I call you bitch you reply."

"Look man, I'm just saying we are about to start this thing that is probably going to take months. I have to be prepared to do it consistently six nights a week. It would simply be a nice gesture on your part if you stopped calling me bitch."

"So that's what you're going to spend your token on?"

"Yeah. Wait, why? What else could I have gotten?" I asked, knowing that I hadn't considered my position long enough.

"No, no. That's fine. No more bitches. You got it. So let's do this ho."

"Ah no, come on man!"

"You said no more bitches!"

"I meant just call me Ben."

"That's not what you said."

"Come on man!"

"Alright, alright... Ben. I feel like a bitch just saying it. Ben. That name sounds like the little white kid on the news dying from leukemia. Wait, are you trying to tell me that you have leukemia, Ben?"

"I don't have leukemia! It's just my name. Come on, leave me alone."

"Wow man, I'm just playing with ya. You don't have to act like such a little Ben."

I quiet down for a second and wonder whether he would spend the next few years redefining my name for me so that whenever I heard someone say it, I would think that they are using it to refer to me as a female dog. Certainly I wouldn't put it past him. He was right.

I did spend my token poorly, but what else could I have spent it on? Well, now that I thought about it, I guess I could have spent it on trying to get him to stop turning me into a nighttime penis tucker. So I guess there's that. Damn!

"Are we doing this... Ben?"

It's amazing that he's not saying it, but I can still hear the 'bitch'. "Yeah let's do it," I say, a little defeated. "You need to get one-half to one-third hard."

"How much is that?" the brotha asked.

"I don't know. Half as hard as you usually get."

"How hard do I usually get?" the brotha asked.

"I don't know, go till three o'clock."

"What?"

"You know, get hard until you're pointing forward, like you're a hand on a clock pointing to three o'clock."

"So you just want me to get hard?" the brotha asked.

"Brotha, you get hard when the wind blows. So yeah, I just want you to get hard."

"First, yeah I do. Thanks for noticing. Second, if you can make the wind blow, I'll get hard."

I think for a second and then lean over and blow on the brotha.

"Don't be an ass. That's not gonna work. Oh wait, it worked a little. Keep doing that."

I keep blowing and he got a little fuller but not to where he needed to be.

"You know what it was? It was all that, 'don't call me a bitch' bullshit. It pissed me off and now I can't get up."

"I'm not going to take that back... unless I can exchange it for something else."

"Nope you're stuck with it, get used to it."

"Damn," I say, really wanting to exchange it for him not taking off in the middle of the night. "So what do you want me to do?"

"I don't know, think of something... Ben."

'How is he doing that? Now all I can hear is 'bitch'.' "You want me to fantasize about something?"

"Yeah try that," the brotha said.

I closed my eyes and leaned back against the bed. I thought about the day. I thought about Rose. She really was very cute in spite of the unfortunate VD thing. And at twenty her body was so tight that she probably didn't even bounce when she jumped. Ahhh Rose.

Then I thought about my workout at the gym and how great it felt to lay on a bench doing bench presses with no one around and the brotha up and about. That thought then reminded me of the brotha in the steam room giving that hung guy a 'sup,'

"Ok, I'm up," the brotha said.

'Wait, wait! Is he up because of my thoughts about Rose or because of the guy in the steam room? Oh, this is not good!' I thought.

"What are you waiting for? I'm up," the brotha repeated.

I look down at the brotha and start to feel hot by what I see. And I'm not hot in the good way. 'This is not good!' I thought again.

"My brotha, you are too hard."

"Why thank you," the brotha replied.

"No, I mean you are supposed to be at three o'clock. You're at one. Why are you so hard? I don't get why you are so hard."

"Why question, why don't you just bring your hands down here and make use of it."

I pause for a second because I wasn't sure if I was going to be sick. Once that passed I reached both hands down to the brotha and grabbed him.

"Oh yeah, that feels good," the brotha moaned.

I looked for where the crease mark was between my pinky and my hand and I lightly rested it on top of my balls. I then lined my other hand on top of it. When I did that I noticed that the brotha's head reached to the top of the middle finger of my right hand. I decided to use that as a mark to judge his growth. If I wanted I could even get a measurement from it later.

Having outsmarted the brotha I felt a little better.

"Come on, hold me. Make me feel good… Ben."

'Amazing,' I thought. "Ok, but let's do the jelqing first."

"Well, if you can think of another way to get me down, you can go ahead and try," the brotha said, getting comfortable in my hands.

"I think that we should jelq first," I said again.

"Ok, go ahead."

"And I think you should stop leaving me in the middle of the night."

"Oh damn, here we go," the brotha said.

The brotha drooped a little bit, and when he did I squirted some lotion on my hands, grabbed him and got ready to go. I made an 'OK' symbol with each of my hands while putting the 'O' around the base of the brotha. With my left hand closest to the base I squeezed it tight enough to trap the blood in the brotha. Then with my right hand I squeezed and pulled my right hand forward until the brotha's head expanded with blood. I then kept pulling past the head and off of the brotha.

"What the hell was that?" the brotha said.

"That was a jelq."

"That was it? At least you could warn a brotha before you start. That kind of hurt. It felt like you were trying to make my head explode."

"Well, I'm about to do thirty-nine more, so you're warned."

I then put my right hand at the base of the brotha and retained the trapped blood. Loosening the grip of my left hand, I then pulled my left hand down the brotha taking about three seconds to get from the base to the tip. And like before the brotha's head expanded to its largest possible size and then popped through the 'O' of my fingers.

"Two," I said.

I then put my left hand at the base of the brotha and pulled my right hand down the length of the brotha. I kept alternating back and forth for a few until I noticed that the brotha's head was no longer expanding. I took both hands off of the brotha and the brotha stood fully erect.

"Why did you stop?" the brotha asked.

"You're hard."

"Was I not supposed to be?"

"You know you're not supposed to be. You're supposed to be one-half to one-third erect."

"Well, stop making it feel so good," the brotha replied, with a little self consciousness in his voice.

"Look, we can't continue if you stay hard."

"You think I'm doing this on purpose?" the brotha asked.

I thought for a second, trying to come up with something that would bring the brotha down.

"You know Brian from work?" I asked the brotha.

"Why are you bringing him up?"

"He told me about a story that he read online about this guy who was sticking his junk in a fan. He ended up cutting the tip of his junk off. Can you imagine that?"

The brotha remained quiet and then like a falling redwood clasped down between my legs.

"Wait, wait, too much. You should be a little harder than that."

"Then don't tell me a story like that. How do you expect me to respond to a threat like that?"

"I wasn't threatening you…" I thought about it for a second. Could this be the ultimate bargaining chip? "Or was I? I guess you'll have to wait to find out. Now I need you to get harder."

"You expect me to get hard after that?"

"Come on." I begin to jelq again with barely enough blood in the brotha to make his head expand. "Doesn't this feel good?"

"See! Now all I can think about is that fan."

"Come on now, relax. Think about how much bigger you're going to be in a few months. Think about how you are gonna rock some girl's world. You will be King Kong, man."

"Actually apes have very small dicks in relation to their body size," the brotha said matter-of-factly.

"Whatever man, you'll be big. Can you see how big you'll be?"

"Yeah, I can see it."

With that the brotha got up to half erect and I continued the count from where I left off. I was able to continue to forty without a problem and when the last one was done, he spoke up again.

"My head hurts a little," the brotha said.

"Did I do it too hard?"

"How the fuck am I supposed to know what's too hard?" the brotha said, annoyed.

"Does it feel like you popped a blood vessel in your head?"

"Am I supposed to have popped a blood vessel?" he asked, a little scared.

"No, if you did feel that way, then it wouldn't be good."

"Oh, then no. It just feels like the skin around my head has been stretched more than it should be."

"Hmmm. I don't know. That sounds about right, don't you think?" I added.

"I swear to god, if you break me, I will kick your ass," the brotha said in as threatening a tone as he could.

"I'm sure you'll be fine. The rest, I think, are easier."

I grab the base of the brotha again, doing my best to trap all of the blood in the brotha. And then with all of the force that I can muster I flicked the brotha.

"One," I said afterwards waiting for a comment from the brotha. When he said nothing I did it again. "Two. Is this ok for you?"

"No, it's cool. What is this supposed to be doing?"

I continued flicking while I spoke. "I'm gonna guess and say that it is supposed to be getting the blood to circulate around you after doing the jelqing."

"Ok," the brotha concluded without much argument.

I go through all forty and then I get ready for the third part.

"One more right?" the brotha asked.

"Yeah, why? How are you feelin'?"

"Chill out man, I'm feeling good. That first one was a little questionable, but the second one was cool."

"Ok. So for this one we are going to have to work together. You know when we're peeing and we want to stop the pee from flowing?" I asked.

"Yeah, yeah, I know the drill. We have to clench back like we are trying to stop ourselves from peeing our pants and at the same time you are going to grab my head and stretch it as far as you can."

"Yep, are you ready?"

"Yeah."

"Ok, let's go."

I grabbed the brotha's head and got as tight a grip as I could but my fingers slip off. So then I pinch the brotha's head between my thumb and pointing finger and I latched on like a vice grip.

"Ow, ow, ow, ow," the brotha repeated.

"What?"

"Goddamn it man, that hurt!" the brotha exclaimed.

"Brotha, you're kind of slippery. That's the only way that I'm gonna hold on."

"Then wipe me the goddamn off then! Don't just squeeze me like some whore's tit. Damn!"

I got up and went to the kitchen for a hand towel while the brotha continued to talk.

"What do you think I am, a please take a number tab? You think I'm a pimple? You think I'm a tick you're trying to pop? Have some respect man."

"Ok, ok. You're clean. Let's just do this. You ready?"

"Yeah man, just have some respect next time," the brotha said in an almost whiny voice.

I grabbed onto the brotha's head again and again the brotha complained.

"Ow, ow, ow, ow."

I let go. "Look, what else am I supposed to do? I need to get a good grip on you, and the only way I can do it is by pinching down."

"It just hurts, alright?" the brotha said in anger.

"You want me to stop? You want to stay this size forever?"

"No, I want you to continue."

"Ok, then stop complaining."

I grabbed again and stretched the brotha out as far as he can go. I then clench back on the muscles that stopped me from peeing and I tried to count to ten. I made it to six before I let the brotha go.

"Why'd you stop? You were supposed to hold until ten," the brotha said tiredly.

"This one is frickin' hard. I don't think that that muscle is strong enough."

"Hey, if I could suffer through the pain of this, you could hold it for ten. You hear me? Let's do this."

I stretched the brotha again and as soon as I do, I clenched back again. I made it to six again before I let go.

"Are you pussin' out on me? Are you pussin' out on me solider?" the brotha said.

"No, it's just tiring," I replied out of breath.

"I don't want any excuses. Now you grab my head solider and you squeeze it like your life depended on it. Do you hear me?"

"Yeah, yeah," I said, still trying to catch my breath.

"What did you say?"

I know what the brotha wanted to hear so instead of arguing with him, I just said it. "Sir, yes sir."

"That's right. Now grab my head like your sex life depends on it."

The brotha's motivation was effective mostly because I figured out that it was true. I hadn't had a lot of sex in my life and most of the reasons were because of the brotha. Between his vetoes and his passive protests, the little bugger had gotten into my head. I barely tried to have sex anymore because I never knew what would happen once I whipped the brotha out.

All of the women that I tried to have sex with were all pretty attractive so it wasn't that. But for whatever reason, in my head, I would hear "Oh hell no" coming from the brotha, followed by "passive protest." That was always what told me that I was done for the night.

I did get pretty good at going down on women as it turned out. But, as good as I could be, most women still liked to feel the guy in them, and the brotha was too much in my head to let that happen. And instead of disappointing people I just decided to give up on getting laid all together. So when the brotha said that I should do this last exercise like my sex life depended on it, I knew he was speaking the truth.

I grabbed onto the brotha as tight as I could and I pulled him out until my arm lost strength. I then used every bit of strength I had to clench back. This time I made it to ten but the last few were quick counts. After a five-second break I did it again. And then after another five seconds I did it again.

I kept going until I had done it twenty times. And when I finally let go there was a deep imprint in the brotha's head. The brotha looked up at me a little wobbly and in a soft, vulnerable voice said "hold me."

I wrapped my warm hands around the brotha and as he grew in my hands I knew what he was thinking. Without him asking I reached over and squirted a little lotion in my hand. I slowly wiped it all around him and then rubbed him down until he spit.

The brotha was quiet for the rest of the night and so was I. As we watched TV together I sat with him in my hands. I have to admit that the closeness that we both felt was nice. We didn't have to speak. It was just about us being together. I guess there's a bond that develops between two people after they've experienced the horrors of war. And what we had just gone through was our Vietnam.

It was tough, but we survived it. And we enjoyed the quiet of this night, the soft murmur from the TV, knowing that we would have to survive that horror again. And after we have survived it enough times, we would return home, to the real world, stronger, tougher and more like men.

That was what we thought about that night. And for the rest of that night we just let the comforting theme from The Tonight Show remind us of the world we left behind; a world that had nothing for men like me and the brotha. No, we were outcasts in that world, and after what we had gone through this night we both knew that there was no going back… except for work… and shopping. But other than that, there was no going back.

The next night was just as tough. The sound of screams echoed throughout the room only to reach me sounding like a series of 'ouches.' And the fatigue that I felt afterwards could only be soothed by the closeness that is shared by two men who have survived the horrors of battle. That soothing came from what happens in a foxhole at night in the jungle when it is just a man and his brotha. Just two people trying to escape the experiences of war. It was what I needed and it was what the brotha needed.

The third night really wasn't that bad. It would be described more like a short hike than a long war. And by the fourth night it was all good. We started off with the jelqing as usual. There was still a bit of a challenge to keep the brotha from becoming fully erect, but we were able to dance the line. I made sure that even when the brotha got a little harder I was still able to make his head expand when I jelqued the blood toward it.

The second exercise was as easy as the first time I had done it and the brotha felt the same. The third exercise got a little easier when I realized that putting a piece of paper towel between my fingers and the brotha's head meant that I didn't have to squeeze as hard to get a tight grip. The brotha was grateful.

"Goddamn killer gram!" he said afterwards. And considering that none of the words were 'bitch', 'ho' or 'I gonna fuck you up you motha fucka,' I practically considered his response praise.

On the fifth day I woke up at the usual time. It was a work day and I went through all of the usual motions. I hit the snooze alarm once and then tiredly dragged myself into the bathroom to take a piss.

However, this morning, was unlike every other morning that had come before. On this morning, when I reached my hand into my boxers to find the brotha I found him on the first pass. That struck me as a little unusual but not enough to get me to say anything.

But along with his easy access, the brotha felt different. I wasn't sure if it was my imagination or not, but the brotha felt heavier. I was very familiar with how the brotha felt in my hands. I knew how he felt when he was hard, semi-hard, halfway hard, a little hard, soft after just being hard, not hard at all, and retracted into my body. But this time the brotha felt unfamiliar in my hands. It almost felt like I was holding someone else's dick. I paused a moment to see whether that thought caused a change in shape for the brotha. And when it didn't I had another reason to feel good.

I had to assume that this change in weight was being caused by the jelqing. But it had only been five days so the thought was a little hard to believe. Although I wanted it to be true, it was hard to believe that the cause of the brotha and my problem could be solved in five days.

And honestly, how could it be solved at all? Jelqing wasn't much more than jacking off. And if jacking off was enough to do it, I would have to walk around with the brotha tucked in my shirt collar.

But I guess I had to admit that jelqing was a lot different from jacking off. Jacking off was more like slipping the tongue to a flower than it was jelqing. Jacking off was soft and enjoyable. Jelqing was more like treating your junk like a stress ball that you were trying to pop.

Yeah, jelqing made the brotha excited, but it was more like the way he got excited after a great day at the gym, than it was like when he was in the changing room afterwards… I mean, it was more like the way that he got excited after a great day at the gym than when we were watching girl on girl porn on the internet. Jelqing is 'I'm jacking off outside in my neighbor's back yard exciting.' It is 'I'm going to walk around my house all day with a clothes pin on my nipple exciting.'

But even though I could understand why the brotha might be feeling a little heavier in my hand, I wasn't confident enough to say for sure that it wasn't just in my head. And since I wasn't completely sure, I decided to not mention it to the brotha.

When I got home from work on my seventh day, I decided to watch the video on YouTube again. I typed 'Jelqing or How to Enlarge Your Penis' into the search box and Cristian came right up. I watched it again, but this time I did it looking for any hint that he could be making things up.

I was never great at reading faces, but as far as I could tell he knew his way around a dick. And he spoke with such confidence that he had to be packing something powerful in his pants. I don't know if it was because of the jelqing, but he said that it was.

After the video ended I stared at the web address for Cristian's website. I considered whether or not I should visit it. I continued to stare instead of visiting because I didn't want to feel like a chump. I didn't want to go there and then realize that he was making all of it up just so that he could get people to buy an Austin Powers penis pump or something.

But after I had stared at the web address long enough I typed www.RateABull.com into the browser and the page popped up. It wasn't a porn site. In fact it was very tame. It was what I would describe as an advice website. There was a section on the home page where people could post questions and send it to other members. And there was a section that included featured videos.

I scrolled down to the featured videos and found the one called 'How to Enlarge Your Penis.' But when I clicked on it a box popped up saying that I had to sign up for the site. That is when I left the site and went to my favorite girl on girl porn page.

"Seriously, again?" the brotha asked.

"What, you don't like girl on girl porn?" I asked the brotha.

"Sure man, it's great. I'm just saying it wouldn't hurt to have a dick or two thrown in the mix. I mean, what am I supposed to be watching?"

"You're supposed to be watching the girl on girl porn! Why, what are you usually watching?"

"I'm watching the shaved snatches. Chill out motha fucka. What's wrong with you? What do you think I'm watchin'?" the brotha asked defensively.

Without a word I switched to the section on the site that had the girl/guy sex.

"Hey wait, what are you doing? I was watching the twin peaks, put it back," the brotha said firmly.

"No, I was tired of that anyway," I said to make the brotha feel better.

"Oh I see. You need to let your gay boy fantasies out," the brotha said with some bite.

"Just relax ok," I said, trying to calm him down.

"How can I relax when I'm attached to a gay dude and at any moment I could wake up and find myself balls deep in ass?"

I looked down at the brotha and paused for a second. "Are you getting hard?" I asked with a hell of a lot of confusion."

"No!" the brotha screamed back defensively.

"What the fuck? You saying that just got you hard."

"NO!" the brotha repeated.

"Goddamn killer gram," I said while resting my face in my hands. 'Oh wait, I get it now.' I think. 'A killer gram is something that is small but still deadly. So when the brotha used it to refer to me, I didn't understand what it meant. But when I use it to refer to him, it works.'

"NOOO!" the brotha yelled back.

I switched off the computer and headed into my bedroom. Without a word I sat in my usual place and got the lotion from under my bed. The brotha was still kind of hard from 'the incident which cannot be spoken of' so I started in on the jelqing. At the end of the night I jacked the brotha off as usual, but I felt a little dirty when I was doing it. It definitely wasn't the first time the brotha made me feel dirty so I waited for him to spit up, hopped in the shower and then frantically tried to scrub the memory away. Man, if I had a quarter for every time I had to reach for the abrasive cleanser I would have a roll big enough to keep in my pocket and never have to jelq again.

After two weeks of jelqing I decided to take a measurement again. I knew that it was still very early and I shouldn't have expected to see any change, but I was really curious. So after our jelqing session I lightly rubbed the brotha until he got completely hard.

"That's right, rub it nice... Ben," he said in his inappropriately aggressive manner.

When the brotha was completely hard I wrapped both of my hands around him again. I placed the heal of my left hand lightly on the brotha's balls and placed my right hand lightly on top of my left. It was amazing but the hard brotha felt thicker in my hands. It wasn't hugely thicker, but it was enough to feel different in my hands. It actually felt pretty good.

That wasn't the goal though. The brotha wasn't thick to begin with but I didn't think that he had a problem with thickness. What he was was short. The brotha needed some length. So when I wrapped my hands around the brotha, extra length was what I was looking for.

I let the brotha settle in my hands.

"Yeah, that's it. Hold me," the brotha said in his Barry White voice.

I gave him a little squeeze to try and get a little bit of extra stretching before I looked. And when I finally opened my hand I saw something that was a little hard to believe. Whereas before the brotha only reached the crack between my middle and pointing finger, now he reached more than halfway through my pointing finger.

The change was a little hard to believe so I took my hands off of the brotha and put them back on. Trying to remember how hard I had rested my left hand on the brotha's balls the last time, I placed them there again. I placed my right hand lightly on top of my left and looked again. And once again the brotha reached more than halfway through the thickness of my pointing finger. I was amazed.

"Wait, what are you doing?" the brotha asked, looking up at me.

I looked down at the brotha and he was looking directly into my eyes. I thought about whether or not I should tell him considering he reacted so badly when I tried to measure him.

"Before the first day we started jelqing I measured you using my hands," I said hesitantly. I was waiting for a yell of "passive protest" and for him to go limp in my hands, but it never came.

"And what's the result?" he said instead.

"I think you're bigger," I said, with an obvious look of confusion on my face.

"You think I'm bigger, or I am bigger?"

"Well, the first thing I noticed was a week ago when I held you during our morning pee. It felt like you were heavier in my hand. But just now when I held you with both hands you felt thicker. And not only that, you are longer than you were before."

"Now stop Ben. Don't fuck with me. I'm not in the mood to get fucked with. You think I'm bigger or I *am* bigger?"

"I don't know," I said still confused. "Could I have just not noticed that half-inch before? Maybe your balls are hanging lower now."

"That's possible, maybe all of the jelqing stretched them out. Do my balls look like they're hanging at all now?"

I look down at the brotha's balls and they look as tightly pocketed as they could be. "No, you look tight."

"Look again, because this is important," the brotha said.

I grabbed hold of the brotha's balls and tried to slide them back, but they didn't move. "No, they're tight."

"So what then? What could it be?"

"I don't think that I could have misplaced that extra length all of the times that I held you before. No, that's…" I thought a little harder about what the difference could be.

"What?" he asked, in a slightly higher voice than normal.

"It's working" slipped out of my mouth before I could get a chance to reconsider saying it.

"It's working?" the brotha asked with restrained joy.

"Yeah, it is," I said, still confused about how it could be true.

"And I know it's true. You know why because *fifty-two cards went out, I'm through dealin now; Fifty-two bars come out; Now you feel 'em now; Fifty-two cars roll out; Remove ceiling in case fifty-two broads come out; Now you chillin' with a boss bitch of course S.C. on the sleeve, at the 40/40 club, ESPN on the screen; I paid a grip for the jeans, plus the slippers is clean; No chrome on the wheels, I'm a grown-up for real; Geee.*

"Now you gonna make love to me bitch, or do I have to smack you around a bit."

"You promised to lay off the 'bitches'," I remind the brotha.

"Now how are you gonna ask a pimp to lay off the bitches? *I'm a hustler homey, you a customer crony; Got some, dirt on my shoulder, could you brush it off for me? If you feelin' like a pimp nigga, go and brush your shoulders off; Ladies is pimps too, go and brush your shoulders off; Niggaz is crazy baby, don't forget that boy told you; Get, get, that, that, dirt off your shoulder; You gotta get, get, that, that, dirt off your shoulder; You gotta get, get, that, that, dirt off your shoulders. Yeahhhh. Best rapper alive!*"

"Look man, I know you're happy, but we made a deal. I would make you bigger and you would stop calling me a bitch."

"What, you want to ruin the good time now? Ok, yeah I promised. My bad. I said it was my bad, you feelin' better now? Damn man!"

"Hey, we had a deal that's all."

"I said you were right. I'm just feelin' good that's all. Now, you gonna be like this all night or are you gonna hold me, huh?"

"Be like what?" I ask, to see if he's going to say it.

"Ahh no. I see what you're trying to do. Bein' like how you bein,' a little pussy."

"That's not any better," I told the brotha.

"Well if you don't want to be called a little pussy, then stop actin' like a little pussy."

"Yeah ok, I'll stop doin' that. I'll stop a few other things while I'm at it." I got up and headed into the kitchen to get something to drink.

"Wait, where are we goin'. We're not done here. You forgot a little somethin'."

"No, we're done. You just don't know it yet."

"Aww, what the fuck does that mean?"

I didn't answer the brotha. Instead I poured myself a glass of juice.

"What, you gonna be a little Ben about this? You gonna be a little Ben about this?"

"I don't appreciate that either."

"Appreciate what?"

"Using my name instead of 'bitch'."

"You said that you wanted me to use your name?"

"Don't act stupid, you know what I mean."

"You're such a little Ben."

"See that's exactly what I'm talking about. Don't use my name in place of the word bitch. Because I know what you're thinkin'. You think I don't, but I do."

"You are one paranoid motha fucka ain't you?"

"Hey, don't think you're in control cause you ain't. I'm in control here," I said, even though I knew that I wasn't.

"Don't be a little bitch," the brotha said.

"What did I say about calling me a bitch?" I asked the brotha.

"I didn't call you a bitch. If I would have said don't be a little bitch, bitch, then I would have called you a bitch."

"That's it. I hope you like the size you got because that's all you're gonna get."

"Now you are being a little bitch, bitch. You think I don't know that you like my growth spurt as much as me. You think I don't know about how you fantasize about fuckin' a pussy from ten feet away. Who you think you're talking to, bitch? This is my house. I rule this joint. You got me? I rule this joint."

I didn't have much to say to that. He's right that I did fantasize about being able to fuck some chick from ten feet away. How he knew that I don't know. And I did like his growth spurt as much as he did. So he was right, I wasn't going to stop now that I saw some gains.

But he was wrong about something. He wasn't in control anymore. I was in control. With just this little gain that couldn't be more than a half-inch I felt I wasn't helpless to the brotha anymore. There were things that I could do to change my life. I just needed to figure out what they were.

The brotha was quiet for the rest of the night. I watched some TV and even pulled the brotha out of the flap in my boxers so that he could watch. When I saw that Letterman didn't have any good guests I went to bed. It was a warm night so I tucked the brotha back into my boxers, kicked the sheets back, and allowed myself to drift off.

At about two o'clock I'm awoken by loud yelling.

"What the fuck in god's fuckin' name?" the brotha yelled as loud as he could.

I didn't open my eyes right away. I took a moment to enjoy what I heard because to me it sounded like music.

"You motha fuckin' bitch-ass son of a bitch," he yelled again.

I opened my eyes and slowly got up to close the window that was directly behind my bed. I have neighbors and although their bedroom window was two hundred feet away, I knew this conversation was going to get loud enough for them to hear.

I rolled to the edge of the bed and looked over. What I saw was the brotha hanging from the bed by a noose made out of string. He swung back and forth and the string had him by his circumcised neck.

Looking the brotha in his one squinty eye, I calmly asked him the obvious question. "How did you get down there, brotha?"

"Ah, you son of a bitch; you son of a motha-fuckin' bitch."

"Come on now, no need to bring our motha into this."

"Oh you think you funny motha fucka? You think you funny? Bring your bitch ass down her and I'll show you how funny you is."

"Tell you what, I'll just roll over here and wait for you to get back up." I then rolled back over, closed my eyes and smiled to myself.

"You bitch. You bitch!" he yelled even louder. "You cut me down, you bitch."

I didn't answer, because once again his voice was sounding like music to my ears.

"Ben. Ben! Don't you leave me hang, Ben."

I rolled back over and looked down at the brotha. "Oh, so you remember my name now? That's interesting. Before I was 'bitch', now I'm Ben. You know what? I figured this might happen. I figured that some time tonight you would call me by my proper name. Because you know what you're missing?"

The brotha didn't respond, but I wanted to hear him reply so I asked again. "I said, with all your so called power and attitude, do you know what you're missing?"

"What?" the brotha said, angry and resigned.

"Opposable thumbs motha fucka!" I said yelling back as mockingly as possible. "And you know what comes next? You know what comes tomorrow? Spandex motha fucka! Span with the motha fuckin' dex!" I yelled back and it felt good.

What happened was that after I fell asleep I had a dream about my dad. I dreamt that he was back in the house that I grew up in. And that he and my mother were still together and they were happy. The only thing was that when I saw him he wasn't wearing anything but a pair of bicycle shorts.

When I saw him with his belly hanging over his way too tight shorts, I asked him to put some clothes on because my friends were coming over. But instead he told me that if I loved my mom I wouldn't have a bunch of people coming over to visit. I thought that his response was strange so I told him that I used to have friends come over all the time when I was a kid and mom never minded. His response was that I shouldn't backtalk him because he was my father.

That last thing he said was strange because that's not something that I ever remembered him saying when I was a kid. I then stared at him wondering why he had said that when I looked down at his bicycle shorts. What I noticed was that there was a string tied around his ankle that went up his leg and under his shorts. I stared for a second trying to figure out why there was a string going underneath his shorts. Then I realized that it was there to keep his dick from running around on him. That was why he was still with mom, because he had figured out how to keep his dick from running around.

That was when I woke up and I knew everything. I couldn't immediately figure out what it was that I knew, but I knew that I knew it now. I looked down at my shorts and as far as I could tell the brotha was still there and he was sleeping. So I gently got out of bed and searched the house for some string.

The only string that I found was thread so I made the thread a couple of layers thick and got back into bed. Without waking the brotha I then tied one end of the thread to my ankle and the other I ran up my boxers. Creating a little loop on the end of the thread I tightened it below the brotha's head and went back to sleep.

Something told me that this was one of the nights that the brotha would take a walk. So I knew that the brotha would wake up and find the thread, I just didn't know when it would be. He would either feel it as soon as he woke up, or it would be after he jumped off the bed. Apparently he didn't notice it when he woke up. Apparently he only noticed it when he jumped out of bed and got an incredible surprise.

I would like to believe that it was my father who sent me the dream. Maybe he was dead now and he sent it to me from the other side. Or maybe he just somehow sensed that I was having problems and wanted to help.

Either way, I knew what the solution to my problem was. It was a pair of lycra boxer briefs that I had once seen at Target. No more boxers. They were a little too loose. From then on, it was only boxer briefs for me.

"You think you won? This ain't over," the brotha said next. "You might think this is over, but this ain't over. You wait."

I know the brotha meant what he was saying, but it sure felt over to me. What else could there be. The jelqing was working, and I knew how to keep the brotha close at night. I wouldn't have to worry about waking up and finding him doing god knows what with god knows who. It sure felt over to me.

The next day after work I skipped the gym so that I could go to Target. I spent $100 and got twenty pairs of lycra boxer briefs. And when I got back home and tried them on I actually found them pretty comfortable as well. This was a good decision and there were now multiple reasons that I was glad that I had made it.

Over the next week, the brotha didn't say much. I tried to keep him happy by offering to make him drinks which he accepted and by taking my towel off in the steam room so that he could look around. It became clear that the brotha was getting bigger.

In the first three weeks what I noticed was that his soft size increased. That made it easier for me to walk around in the changing room naked. The brotha liked that. He would often crane his neck around checking out what he one night referred to as "the competition." And when the brotha got a little too excited I would reach for a towel, get dressed and leave. The brotha didn't complain when that happened. For the most part he just lived with it and I was a little happier for it.

At the end of three weeks I did the hand measurement again. Now when the brotha was hard he reached almost to the top of my pointing finger. The jelqing was definitely working, and if felt good.

The gains slowed down after that. I wasn't sure if it was something I was doing wrong so I decided to watch Cristian's full video at RateABull.com. It surprised me how much detail he went into. And the more I heard the more I could relate to him. This is what Cristian said in the video:

Hello. My name is Cristian, Cris-tee-in, Cristian. And this is my vlog. How to increase the size of your penis.

I did mention in an earlier vlog that when I was 18 years old, I had exceptional amounts of insecurity. And one of the topics that I was insecure about was the size of my penis. I am 6'4" and I am black. And if you didn't know, there are a couple of stereotypes about black men. And there are a couple of stereotypes about tall men. I was both. And at the time I thought that I was very small.

A couple of statistics. First, back then, there was no internet so I couldn't find this stuff out. But the average penis for a man, as opposed to the average female penis, (he smiles at his mistake) is between 5 inches and 6 inches long. Some say the average drops to as low as 4 ¾ and as high as 6 ½. But essentially it's between 5 and 6.

And keep in mind that like men's penises, women's vaginas come in different sizes. Some are very small and some are larger. And also keep in mind that if you are a, let's say, shorter, smaller guy, statistics say that you are going to end up with a girl that is smaller than you are, shorter than you are. And shorter, smaller women tend to have shorter, smaller vaginas. So it might be that, the size that you have right now, might be the perfect size that you will ever need. You will never need anything larger. And if you got something larger, you might end up hurting the person you're with. And if you do… ok, she'll put up with it for a little while, but eventually it will become very unpleasant and not pleasurable for her.

And she will have sex with you less, until she will have sex with you not at all. So keep all this in mind.

Now I am a taller guy and I will end up with a taller woman. I felt that my penis was disproportionate for my height. And when I had to take off my pants and I had to take a shower, I never felt extremely comfortable. That's when I was younger, and when I got older it didn't really make that big a difference, but it still kind of played on my mind.

So, sometime around the year 2001, I started to see all these ads, these internet ads that say 'increase the size of your penis.' You know, there are all these pills and various things and I did some serious research on it. It turns out that there was one technique that didn't require pills. It was as someone described it to me recently, it's sort of like yoga for your penis.

I checked it out. I checked out a couple of these sites, and decided to buy one of these programs. I paid $30 for it. It was in a Word document. And I read it, I tried it and it worked. So now I'm going to describe the process to you.

(Lifting up a pink, penis shaped balloon.) This will be our penis. But trust me, if this is the size of your penis and you aren't fully erect, you don't need to do a thing. Believe me you don't have to do a thing. But this is for demonstration.

A little bit of biology first. The reason why these exercises work is because there's no cartilage or bone or anything like that in your penis. All it is is fat, a little bit of muscle and a lot of blood tissue. And the way that you get erect is this: the blood vessels that feed your penis, when they're flaccid, when they're soft, they're constricted, they're not letting a lot of blood in. Which means that there's only a little blood flowing into your penis and it becomes soft.

When you become excited, what happens is your blood vessels open up, letting more blood in, allowing it to flow into your penis and causing it to become hard. Now because there's no bone, or anything hard, theoretically it's like a muscle. And the way that your muscles become hard is that you go and lift a heavy weight that causes your muscles to slightly tear inside. That's one of the reasons that you are sore afterwards, because they are torn.

You give your muscles time to relax and heal itself, and to repair those tears. And when it repairs itself it goes, "you know what? We should repair ourself stronger than we were before in order to compensate for that strain." So it heals back, and heals bigger. Same thing with your penis. Essentially what you will be doing is tearing the insides of your penis.

And at this point I should say this: You should consult a doctor before trying any of this stuff because you can cause long-term damage. And you really could. If you do it too hard you really could injure yourself and there it is for the rest of your life, no more Mr. Fun Man. You know what I'm saying?

That last part was even painful to think about. The brotha would not have been pleased if that happened. But the rest of what Cristian said made sense. I was very familiar with how muscles increased in size. And I knew that muscle and tissue responded the same when it came to stress. When a muscle gets micro tears from working out with increasing amounts of weight, it grows back larger and stronger. It would only make sense that the penis would respond in the same way. I understood now.

What he also said about the average penis size was also interesting. I always assumed that the average penis was about seven inches. I had no idea that the average penis was only between five and six inches. I know that in all of the porn that I've watched the guys were always bigger than seven so I figured that the average guy was just a little smaller and that I was way below average. I do remember taking a measurement of the brotha when I was still in college and I was around five or five and a half. That would mean that I wasn't small. I was average.

But like Cristian, I'm a tall guy. Cristian may be 6'4" but I'm 6'6" and a 5.25 inch dick looks like an 'A' cup on a woman with a big ass. Yeah, 'A' cups are fine, but with an ass that big, you just expect to find a 'C'. I am a male 'A' cup and I got a big ass.

And I thought it was interesting what Cristian said about women having different sized vaginas as well. I guess I always assumed that all women had the same size. But now that I think about it, of course women had different sizes. Women have different sized breasts, hands, feet, brains, hearts, lungs, mouths and everything else. Why wouldn't they also have different sized vaginas? And men have different sized penises so there's got to be a different key for every lock.

But here's the thing that Cristian didn't talk about. I'm a tall guy, so what happens if some woman with a huge lock came to me looking for a big key. I'm going to end up disappointing her, and I don't know if I would like that. And big locked, tall women would probably look to me first because I'm black and tall. Man, I would hate to disappoint.

Turning back to the video I realized that Cristian had taken chunks of this video and edited it together for YouTube. I realized this because the section that described the exercises was the same on both. After that there was more new material though. It continued:

Now, what progress would you expect to see? I don't know. Some people say that if you do it enough, you can increase by 2 ¾ inches. Some people increase less. I've seen some say that they have increased by only ½ an inch and they have done it for months.

I can tell you what my experience was. I started out the middle of average, which is 5 ½ inches. In the first nine days, which is incredible, I increased by half an inch. Nine days, that's pretty quick. That's considered on the very quick, very large side, very soon.

After eighteen days I was up by three-quarters of an inch. After seventy-two days I was up by an inch and a quarter. And then it took about four months for me to get up to an inch and a half. So I ended up at 7.

Now, a little bit of warning. You probably want to be happy or stop around 6 ½ or 7. Because the truth be told, me being 7, I have had women say "ok well, that hurt... just enough." And if you're into anal with women or with men 7 is almost too much. In fact I've been told, "no, too big", "stop that hurts too much" or "too big, and that's not going to happen." So if you're into that, you might want to consider smaller.

And yeah there's that whole thing about "yeah, I'm big, I'm huge, I'm horse hung." But if you talk to those guys that are 8, 9 and stuff like that, they might get those girls or guys that say "Oh, it's a fascinating thing," "It's huge and I like it a lot" and stuff, but their partner may get sore. And their partner may not like it after a while.

The truth is that for long-term happiness you want to be just average. Because in actuality, the female's g-spot is only an inch to an inch and a half inside her vagina. So as long as you are an inch and a half long you have all you need. And anything else you need would just be a technique and a little bit of extra lovin' and you will be just fine with an inch and a half. Is that enough information?

I would like to add that penis size is not everything and most of the time it is not the most important thing. The vast majority of women care more about intimacy, closeness, and foreplay then they care about the size of your penis. So even if you were extremely small, but you made her feel loved, and you made her feel like you cared about her, and that you guys have a very close relationship, the size of your penis wouldn't matter at all.

So before you do this, keep all of this in mind. Also keep in mind that these exercises can make your penis less sensitive. Is that a good thing? Will you enjoy sex as much? I don't know.

I can tell you that the effect that it did have on me was that I was able to last longer. So I can last a very long time now. Did I lose a little sensation? Yes. Did it come back? I don't know. I can't remember. It's been a long time.

Do I still enjoy sex now? Yes I do. Because not only do women enjoy feeling a connection, but men do too. So it's not just about the sex, it's also about the intimacy and the connection that you have with the person you're with.

So that's what it is. Anytime you see an email that says increase the size of your penis, that's all they're going to show you. They might give you a little more information about the prostrate, but essentially that's it. Or they may give you pills, but the pills don't work. No pills work.

The pills are basically nitric oxide, which is what bodybuilders have used when you see them with those huge veins. What nitric oxide does, it's called NO, and what it does is dilate your blood vessels like when you get an erection. So what it does is cause the blood vessels in your penis to dilate (get wider). And because more blood is then let into your penis, it becomes temporarily larger. It becomes as full as it can possibly be.

But it is just a temporary thing. And as soon as you stop taking the pills, it goes back to normal. But the stretching actually does work. It may do a little damage and it may cause a loss of sensitivity, but if you want to be permanently larger that is what you can do.

So I hope this has been helpful. I hope that you have learned something. And I guess that I will talk to you next time. See you later.

After the video was done, I stared at the screen with my mouth hanging open. I knew the stuff about NO. Back when I was much more serious about body building, I took a lot of NO and I couldn't keep the brotha down. That's when I found out that Nitric Oxide is what makes Viagra work. The active ingredient in Viagra causes the body to release nitric oxide which causes the big stiffies.

But the truth is that I had never even considered that a penis could be too big. I dreamt about being so big that the woman moaned in pain. Man, that would be nice. At the same time though, maybe Cristian was right. Nine inches might be a little too big. I'll try to stop before I get there.

And what was with the insensitivity thing? Why the hell didn't he mention that in the video on YouTube? How much sensitivity would I lose? Cristian said that the g-spot does exist, which was a surprise to me. But also that it was only an inch and a half inside her vagina. Maybe I didn't need to be any bigger. This was something that I needed to talk over with the brotha.

"Hell no, we ain't gonna stop!" the brotha replied. "I don't care if the only way I know I'm being touched is from the blood draining down my body from one of your scanks doin' a blow job wrong, we ain't stopping!"

I didn't like the way that he made that decision for the both of us, because the decision would kinda affect me too. I thought that we would have a discussion about it and then come up with a decision together. But I guess looking back on it, I must have been drunk when I thought that because the next twenty minute conversation we had was about who could take a bigger dick, Minnie Mouse or Daisy Duck.

That's not the strange part because that was an ongoing discussion in my house. The part that made me think I was drunk was when I jacked the brotha off to the thought of the theme park Minnie and Daisy doing it while theme park Mickey watched and played with himself. For whatever reason, the sound of Mickey's laugh while he wacked off, "ah ha, ah ha, ah ha" got me to the finish line. And when the brotha spit up, I couldn't help but imagine Mickey showering the girls with his oversized, felt mouse juice. "Ah ha, ah ha, ahhh!" Yeah, thinking back on it, I was drunk.

But sitting in my office the next day, I reconsidered what Cristian had said in his video. He had described his own decline in gains. That was also very common when you're body building. There was always a point when you reached a plateau and the muscle gains stop. That was usually when most body builders reached for a little added help from the pharmacist. I wondered if there was something here that could help. After all, muscle tissue repair was all the same no matter what part of the body you're working with.

At that point there was a knock on the door.

"Come in," I said.

Rose walked in and I have to admit, no matter what I was doing in the day, Rose's smiling face always made me feel good.

"We have a problem," Rose said.

I never liked hearing that phrase. The last time someone said it to me it was followed by 'I think someone's having sex on the exercise equipment at night.' And the next five days were followed by corporate demanded cleaning of everything we sold.

"I think Chip is trying to win the 'how gay is Justin' bet," she concluded.

I stared at Rose in silence for a moment. It turned out that it was worse than I thought. "What makes you think that he's trying to win the bet?"

"Justin just came up to me and asked me what the deal was with Chip. I asked him what he meant, and Justin said that he thought Chip might be gay because he kept hitting on him."

"Did Justin say whether or not he gave in?" I asked.

"No, but you've seen Chip, it's got to be just a matter of time."

"Yeah. Wait, what?" I said, realizing what Rose said.

"You know, he has that whole 'I'm Puerto Rican, I'm unbelievably sexy' thing going on."

"Yep. Wait, what?"

"You know, he's incredibly hot."

I didn't expect Rose to say that. Sure Chip had that lightly tanned look, with sort of chiseled features and a lean, fit body. But I didn't think Rose had noticed. I never saw Rose talking to Chip. In fact, lately it was almost like she was avoiding him. When he would come into the storage room she would leave. It felt more like she felt uncomfortable being in the same room as him. I would never have guessed that she found him attractive.

"So what are we gonna do?" Rose added, breaking the silence.

I have to say I was at a loss. Not about the bet but about Rose. I always imagined that I was getting the brotha ready for Rose. And now it seemed that she might have a thing for Chip. I wondered when it was that I slipped up.

"Are we just gonna let Chip win the bet?" Rose said, looking for a response from me.

"Hell no!" I said being drawn back into Rose's conversation. Sex with Rose was one thing, but 50 bucks was 50 bucks. I had my priorities in the right place. "Maybe there's something we can do to distract Chip. You think he's 'incredibly hot,' maybe you could put his mind on things other than the bet."

"Ummm, I don't know if that would work," she added.

"What, do you think Tammy's more his type?" I asked.

"I just think he's really focused on this bet. Let's be real, 50 bucks is 50 bucks."

Her logic was flawless. But still we needed something. "Well, what about if instead of focusing on Chip, we focus on Justin. Justin obviously felt like he could trust you. Why don't you tell Justin that you fooled around with Chip and that he was a little soft in the middle, if you know what I mean."

Rose turned a little red. "I can't tell him that."

"Why not?"

"Justin would never believe that."

"Why not?"

"He just wouldn't. I mean if anything I would have to say that Chip was too big and a little too rough for how big he was."

"Yeah that seems more like Chip. And of course, if we tell Justin that, we're going to be short a few bottles of baseball glove leather oil and the bet will be lost by the end of our shift." I pause for a second trying to figure out why the thought of baseball glove leather oil excited the brotha. "I know. Why don't you just tell Justin that you think Chip's straight and that he might be messing with his mind. If that doesn't shrink his dink, I don't know what would."

"Yeah, I like that. I'm gonna do it."

Rose's smiling face returned as she headed out the door. After she left I waited for about ten minutes and then changed the store's music from Dance Hit's volume 27 to Madonna's Immaculate Collection. 'Justify My Love' comes on first and I figured that if anything this would be the song he needed to head to the storage room and soothe himself.

I stared at the storage room camera monitor for a while, but even after 'Justify My Love' turned into 'Poppa Don't Preach' there was no Justin. "My god he's a stone," I muttered under my breath, needing to say it aloud. But even with that I knew that with Chip out of the way, it was just a matter of time before he turned his isla bonita true blue.

With the excitement of the day behind me I turned to the computer and logged onto RateABull.com. Once on I navigated to Cristian's home page and sent him a message. I wrote: *'Hey Cristian, I really love your video about jelqing. I really felt you when you talked about being the wrong size for a tall, black man. I'm right there with you. I have been doing the exercises as you described, but my gains have slowed down. I'm wondering when you were jelqing, did you take any supplements? Thanks again for the video, you're a lifesaver. Ben.'*

I didn't know how long it would take Cristian to write back if he did at all. But I knew that when a guy hits the stage at the gym that I did while jelqing, the next thing to do was to add supplements. When bodybuilding the first thing you add is whey protein. Protein is an essential element when it comes to building muscle and whey adds both calories and protein. Sometimes whey is all you need to get over the hump.

If you've done that and things slow down again, the next thing to add is a multivitamin if your whey doesn't already supply everything you need. It's so simple, so easy. Only after that do you need to start thinking about things like creatine and testosterone boosters. The question was if supplements would help the brotha grow.

That night when I got home I checked my email and found that Cristian had replied to my message. It was kind of thrilling to get a message back from him. After watching his video so many times, he had kind of become a celebrity to me and now here he was writing me back.

I logged onto the site and read what he wrote. *'Hey Ben, I'm glad you liked the video. Yes, actually I did take supplements while I was jelqing. I just happened to be on a glutamine/testosterone boosting supplement. I wasn't taking it for jelqing purposes, but I've been wondering if it actually did lend a helping hand in my gains. I hope this helps. Cristian.'*

The message was short and to the point. I'm just glad that he got back to me at all. I was very familiar with testosterone boosters, but wasn't as clear on glutamine. I typed glutamine into Google and scanned the results. I also clicked on the Wikipedia link and read through it.

What Wikipedia said was that glutamine was the most abundant amino acid in the body. It has been studied for the past ten to fifteen years and had been shown helpful in the treatment of serious illnesses, injury, trauma, burns, and treatment-related side-effects of cancer, as well as in wound healing for postoperative patients. In fact, Wikipedia said that glutamine is known for reducing healing time after operations.

I wondered why Cristian didn't mention his glutamine within his video. It seemed to me to be an important point. If the way that jelqing worked was similar to bodybuilding, then the tissue's ability to heal larger was the most important part.

I did a little research and found out that the tissue within the penis wasn't really a muscle, but was instead a special tissue that was only found in the penis. I could see how squeezing the brotha while he was half hard could stretch out the tissue. And if glutamine could work on reducing the healing time of all of the tissue cut during surgery, I could also see how it could help to reduce the healing time of the penis tissue. And like all tissue, if it was stressed it would heal in a way better able to handle the stress.

From looking at the diagrams of a penis I could also see how the jelqing part of the exercises, the squeezing part, worked on increasing the thickness. But I could also see how the stretching exercise, the third one that both the brotha and I hated, actually did the lengthening. So that meant that if I wanted to see more length gains, I would have to work harder at the third exercise and maybe add glutamine to my diet for faster growth.

I considered the fact that Cristian had said he was also taking a testosterone booster, but after doing a little research I realized that testosterone was only effective where there were testosterone receptors. And as far as I could see there were a lot of testosterone receptors in muscle but none in the penis. So when it came to growing the brotha, testosterone wouldn't help.

The question was 'how much glutamine should I take?' I figured that the best thing I could do was start by asking Cristian how much he took. I wondered if Cristian would respond again. I still wasn't sure when I typed the message, but I sent it anyway. I wrote: *'Hey Cristian, thanks for your response. I really appreciate it. I was wondering how much glutamine did you take while you were jelqing? And why didn't you mention it in your video? Ben.'*

After I sent it I wondered if I was being too rude in my message. I didn't want to sound like I was accusing him and blaming him or anything. I just wanted to know the answer. 'Oh well,' I thought. 'The message is gone now.'

I shut off the computer, grabbed some leftovers, and moved to the bedroom for my nightly jelqing.

Two days went by before I heard from Cristian. And when I did it was on my day off. I arranged my jelqing day off so that it matched up with my day off from work to give me one day when I didn't have to do anything. I found Cristian's message in the morning and here was what he wrote:

'Hey Ben, the reason that I was taking the glutamine and didn't mention it in the video is a long story. As I mentioned in the video I had insecurity about my penis size ever since I was a kid. The insecurity was so bad that it kept me from dating much. When I was 28 I noticed that even though my diet hadn't changed at all and my workout was exactly the same, I was starting to put on weight. It was

only a pound or two every few weeks, but considering that for years nothing had changed I became concerned.

I heard about a product that boosted Human Growth Hormone (HGH) levels and did some research on it. Its main ingredient was glutamine and research showed that at two grams a day it could boost HGH levels. The product claimed that diminished levels of HGH were what was responsible for age-related weight gain, a loss of energy, and diminished libido. I seemed to have all of that so I took it.

By the time I started jelqing I had been on that glutamine product for a few months. I didn't think of it as anything but helping me to lose a few pounds and boost my energy. And although I considered that it could have an enhancing effect on the jelqing, I couldn't be sure if it would.

And you also have to keep in mind that when I made the video I had no idea that over two million people would view it and use it as a guide. When I made it, I was just trying to think of something that would get people to visit my website. So what I decided to do when making the video was communicate the information that was given to me in the manual that I bought and then include that in my results and additional knowledge.

But now that I've followed the results of a number of the guys that posted their results on RateABull, and see how much more I've gained than they do, I have begun to wonder. I'm sure that they have been just as devoted to the regimen as I had been. Yet they are not seeing the same results. I know that results vary for everyone, but no one else has posted that they have had over an inch in results while I had over an inch and a half in four months.

Taking all of that into account, I have to say that the missing ingredient might be the supplements. And the supplement that is most likely the active ingredient for penis enlargement support is glutamine. Studies have shown that it speeds up wound healing so it makes sense that that is the difference here.

To answer your other question, I took two grams a day; one gram in the morning and one at night. And it was in a product called Ultimate HGH. I wouldn't recommend taking that product specifically because it has a few things in it that you don't need and shouldn't have to pay for. But that is what I did and I hope it helps you. Cristian.'

I was amazed at Cristian's response. I really didn't expect anything so detailed. I was expecting a few lines and he sent me a page. I immediately sent him a thank you message back and then considered what he had written.

I completely understood why he hadn't mentioned the glutamine in the video, but still, I wish that he had. With this being my day off I decided to do a little research online for what would be the perfect supplement. I found a cheap glutamine supplement, but instead of ordering it online, I went to the local discount health food store to pick it up.

The more I thought about it, the more excited I got about adding glutamine supplements to my diet. Because not only would it probably help my jelqing, it would probably help my body's recovery after workouts. And if glutamine did increase HGH levels, I'm sure that it could only help me at my age.

After about three weeks on glutamine I did notice a difference in my mood. I felt like I was smiling a little more, and I was able to increase my weight at the gym by a few pounds. Whether it helped with my penis enlargement, I don't know. The next time I grabbed onto the brotha with both hands, the brotha's head was poking above the pointing finger of my right hand. That felt great and the brotha also liked it.

In fact, ever since our spandex fight, the brotha had been very agreeable. We didn't really disagree on anything anymore and he had allowed me to do what I wanted without much complaint from him. And after I started taking the glutamine, he sang a lot more. Usually it was in the shower, but sometimes it was after jelqing and after getting him to spit up.

What I think pleased him most happened one day after our jacking that followed our jelqing. We were still sitting on the ground when he went limp and his head scraped the carpet. This was a milestone for us, because when we first started his head wasn't anywhere near the carpet. Initially it was about an inch or more away from the carpet and now he was scraping it. I was sitting in the same position that I always was and he was touching the carpet.

My non-erect size had increased first and more, and I loved the way it looked. I figured that more people would see me soft than hard so this made me feel like a rock star, or more accurately, a rock star with a big dick. Or, I guess it made me feel like an accountant with a big dick. Well, the point was that it made me feel like I had a big dick and I liked it.

The question now became how long I had to continue jelqing. The brotha and I discussed it and what we both decided on was when his head was completely above the pointing finger on my right hand. After that we both decided that we would take the new size out for a test run and see how it handled the curves.

It took a total of five months to get to that size. And then we did it for an extra two weeks because within his blog under his video, Cristian said that after you stop jelqing, you get a little shrinkage. So what Cristian suggested was that you jelq until you are a little larger than what you want to be and then expect it to shrink by a quarter inch.

The whole process had been amazing though. And every time I held the brotha in my hand and saw how much larger he was than before I started, it made me feel so good. I wanted to show him off now. I wanted other guys to check me out in the changing room. I wanted the opportunity to get naked with a woman, even if it was just to get my pants altered at the tailor. I have to say though that my tailor didn't appreciate it as much as I thought she would.

Throughout it all, what I was most proud of was that I kept at it. When the squeezing exercise got easy, I squeezed hard. When my forearm hurt from squeezing so hard, I pushed through it. When the third stretching exercise hurt less, I stretched the brotha even more. And when the pain from me squeezing the brotha's head became less, I just said "thank god," and lit a candle to St. Faustina Kowalska, the patron saint of mercy. I'm not Catholic, but someone needed praise for that merciful act and I thought a candle wouldn't hurt.

The question now was 'how was I going to test out our new gotten gains?' I had always imagined that Rose would be the main person to benefit from all of my gains, but now I was starting to think that she shouldn't be the first one. I wanted to test out the brotha on someone that I wouldn't have to see every day. That way, in case something went terribly, terribly wrong I could pretend like it never happened.

When the idea finally hit me, I thought 'of course. This is the only way to go.' And after I figured out who, the only question was when.

Chapter 6
Taking the Brotha Out for a Test Drive

When I went into work the next day I had a plan. I arrived by bus as usual and as usual the bus was on time. Just like during the last five months I arrived to find Rose with a smile on her cute round face, Chip practically sleeping by the door, and Brian sitting on the window sill.

Ever since Brian realized that his girlfriend was pregnant he had become much more serious about his work. He was more than just on time, he was early. It wasn't unusual for him to work through lunch, and when someone from the second shift didn't show, he would volunteer to cover for them.

In the beginning I couldn't figure it out. He was a salaried employee. Extra hours didn't earn you more pay. But then I did. He was trying to stay away from the pregnant girlfriend. And honestly, I couldn't blame him. I guess hanging out at work with cool people was a little better than watching the ankles swell at home.

I unlocked the door as usual, turned on the lights as usual, watched Chip head back to his box bed as usual, and then met Rose in my office as usual. Rose had long ago broken up with her boyfriend, and according to her the penicillin had cleared up her VD nicely. So now our early morning conversations were about much more intellectual topics.

"Do you think that Stewie on the Family Guy is gay?" Rose asked.

"Ya know, that's a good question. There is that episode where Stewie travels into the future and meets his thirty-year-old self. The older Stewie is still a virgin and after having sex for the first time Stewie cries for thirty minutes."

"Yeah I saw that one. It was funny," Rose says with a laugh.

"And Stewie is clearly in love with Brian. And there's the episode where Peter sets Chris up on a blind date to help him get over his girlfriend and Stewie shows up in a dress and then immediately turns around when he see Chris and Peter."

"So what do you think, 50/50?"

"Yeah it's about 50/50. He could be, he couldn't be. The show probably hasn't decided yet."

Rose laughs and smiles then takes the till and heads out to the register. Afterwards I pull the ledgers in front of me for two days of book balancing for our upcoming accounts and inventory audit. But just as I flip open the ledger, a knock on the door rescues me.

"Come in."

Brian pokes his head in. "Do you have a minute?" Brian says.

"Yeah man, come in."

I have to admit, Brian had rarely come in to chat since he'd blown chunks all over my office. I missed hanging with him.

"What's up?" I say, allowing the opportunity for personal chat.

"Ummm, can I sit?" Brian asks.

"Sure man, what's goin' on?"

Brian sat in the chair that Rose just left and subtly caught his breath.

"As you know my girlfriend is pregnant."

"Yeah, how's that going? Is everything ok?"

"Yeah, everything's fine."

"Is she showing yet?" I ask.

"Yeah, you can tell now."

"Ok."

"But here's the thing. She now wants to start childbirth classes and all of these other things."

"Do you need some time off?"

"No!" Brian replies, almost with a sound of fear in his voice. "No, in fact I don't know if you've noticed but I have been trying to put in more time here."

"Yeah, I've noticed."

"Cool. I've been trying to put in more time because I was hoping that maybe…"

I look at Brian and he has a familiar look on his face. It's the same look he had before he went exorcist in my office.

"Do you need my garbage can?"

Brian catches himself and shakes his head no.

"Because if you need it, I'll give you my garbage can. The smell in here just went away last week. To explain the smell I had to convince the night manager that the cleaning person tucked one of his leftover dinners in a drawer. I can't do five more months of that smell."

"No, I'm sorry. I should go."

"No, Brian, come on. Talk to me, what's up?"

Brian settles himself and then plants his eyes firmly on my desk.

"I was hoping that there was some type of managerial opening coming up."

"Why, do you know something that I don't?" I ask, wondering what caused this line of questioning.

"No, I haven't heard anything," he says, returning his gaze into my eyes. "You know, with the baby coming, I was hoping that I could maybe earn a little extra money and, you know…"

"Oh, I see." I think for a moment how I should reply. For months now Brian had been putting in the extra effort. And yeah, babies are expensive and he would probably need more money to raise it. "Well, I don't know if they are looking for any new managers, but it's possible that they could be looking for an assistant manager."

"Oh, that would be perfect. Do you think that I could be considered for it?" Brian asked with both excitement and a green tinge to his tanned, white skin.

"Why don't you do this, put together an updated resume and give it to me and I'll see what I can do."

Brian looked down into his lap. "You don't know what this means to me."

"It's all good Brian. I understand where you're coming from and you've been working through lunch, covering people that have been sick. I've noticed."

"Thanks Ben, I really appreciate it."

Brian gets up and shakes my hand before he leaves. As he leaves I realize that getting his girlfriend pregnant had changed him in some way. He wasn't cool Brian anymore. He was responsible Brian. This guy was less fun. I didn't feel like being buddies with this guy. But hey, he had earned a promotion so I'd see what I could do to help him get it.

I gave it a few minutes before I left the office and when I did I looked around the store for Chip. I spotted him in the shoe section talking to Justin. A few months back Rose had spoken to Justin about Chip so now it was kind of sad to see Chip trying to shoot fish in that empty barrel. But the truth was that neither Rose nor I had made any progress with our Justin bet either. So it almost seemed at this point that the bet was scratched.

"Chip!" I yelled across the empty store. Chip got up and came to me. "Hey there's something that I wanted to talk to you about. Did you plan on heading out for lunch?"

"Yeah, I was probably going to grab some KFC or something."

"Can I join you?"

"Sure," Chip replied, with some confusion on his face.

"Cool, what time were you scheduled for?"

"Brian just let's me go whenever I want."

"Does he? Hmm, good to know. Ok, so what time?"

"12:30?"

"Cool. I'll join you."

"Ok," Chip replies.

I head back to the office and turn my focus to the audit. I immediately feel tired.

When 12:30 rolls around I am more than ready to head to lunch. I leave my office and make a sweep of the store. Chip is once again talking to Justin and it is Justin that alerts Chip that I am looking for him.

I head to the door where Rose stood behind the register.

"How's the accounting going?" Rose asks in her sweetly concerned way.

"Like a mule, because if a horse were moving this slow, I would have to kill it."

Rose laughs in the high pitched way that she does and I smile back at her.

"I'm heading to lunch with Chip."

"With Chip?" Rose repeats back with an unusual look on her face.

"Yeah. Be back in an hour."

I don't bother trying to interpret her look because I was never very good at it. Instead I wait for Chip to catch up to me and then we both leave. The walk to the KFC is pretty quiet. I hadn't realized until that moment how little I had to talk with Chip about. I wanted to hold the main topic until we were both sitting. And in the meanwhile I didn't want to talk about work, his personal life, or the news. What was left after that?

"Did you see the last Magic game?" I say, remembering that a few weeks ago we had had a similar conversation.

"I saw a part of it. Dwight Howard's a monster, man," Chip says.

"Yeah he is. Who do you think will win more rings, Dwight or Andrew Bynum?"

"Oh that's tuff, because Bynum has more people around him than Dwight. Dwight has to carry the team. Bynum just has to wait for Kobe to get tired of shooting."

"So Bynum?" I ask.

"Hell no! Dwight all the way," Chip says with the first smile that I have ever seen him show.

When we arrive we both stand in line, silently waiting to order. Once we do I choose a booth as far away from everyone else as possible.

"So here's the thing Chip, I need to get laid," I say, cutting right to the chase.

Chip looks back at me with a look that I could easily interpret, surprise. But the level of surprise isn't nearly as high as I thought that it should be considering what I'd said. "And I'm wondering if you can help me."

Chip's look of surprise continues for another second and then immediately disappears.

"Justin said you would say that," Chip says casually.

"Justin?"

"Yeah, he guessed. He said you had a weird thing for Madonna and when I told him that we were having lunch he guessed it."

"Really? That's odd."

Chip then slouched back in the booth and not too subtly placed his hand on his midsection. The table was tight to the booth so I couldn't tell exactly what he was doing.

"What do you want to do?" Chip asked.

"Well, I figure that you know a lot of people. So I was hoping that you could give me the name of someone that could give me a massage that might end up in a little more."

"You want me to find you a masseuse that will give you a happy ending?"

"Or a little more."

"Someone that may blow you?"

"Maybe a little more than that."

"You want an escort?"

"No, I want a masseuse that might be open if the vibe is right."

"So that's what you wanted to talk to me about?" Chip asked me with another look I couldn't interpret.

"Yeah, do you know of anyone?"

"Yeah man, I know a few people. But you know, a guy like you doesn't have to pay."

"I know, I'm just looking for something very specific."

"Ok. Hey, I got some of that glove oil on my hands when I was stocking. I'm gonna go wash them."

"Ok."

Chip slides out of the booth. And instead of spinning away from the table he swings towards it. I then notice that instead of stepping away he lingers for a second and when I turn to see what's going on, I notice that he looks like he has something in his pocket. I continue to stare and then I realize that he doesn't have anything in his pocket. Rose was right, Chip was huge.

I then looked up at his face and catch his eyes which were staring down into mine. He holds the stare for a second or two and in that time I wonder if he realizes that he had a huge erection. And I also wonder if he realizes how close his giant boner was to my face.

After a second more of him staring into my eyes, I decide that he didn't realize about the stiffy so I pretend like I didn't notice it either. Chip then spun towards the bathroom and I watched him walk away. I then notice a tightness in my own pants and realized that the brotha was up and about. I looked down at the brotha who was trying to find room in my jeans to expand and the question hits me, 'what is it about baseball glove oil that got the brotha so excited?'

I gave the brotha a little help adjusting and then turned my attention out the window. When the woman behind the counter called my number I realized the brotha was still checking things out so I lingered for a bit. I did another adjustment and then slowly made my way to the counter.

As I look down at the leg and thigh sitting on the paper plate on my tray something hits me. 'I wonder if Chip knows that I meant a woman masseuse? Of course he does. Why would he think anything else?'

Although I'm sure it's obvious when he gets back I make a point to describe the breasts of my ideal masseuse. "I like 'B's'," I say as he settles with his food. "And I like Asians. So if you know of anyone that has any combination of that, it would be cool."

With a surprisingly relaxed look on his face he said that he would see what he could do. And then for the rest of the dinner we talked about Justin. I have to say that Chip is overly obsessed with winning that bet. But like Chip said, "fifty bucks is fifty bucks."

Once we got back to work Chip seemed to spend a lot of his time on his cell phone walking in and out of the storage room. And by the end of the day, he had a phone number for me, a woman named Jasmine. At one point I caught Rose staring at me while I was staring at Chip. She was obviously very curious to know what was going on. But I figured that in a way, what I was doing was a gift for her. Rose and I were going to be together once everything was through and I knew that doing this was just going to make what we did more fun for her.

That night I wasted no time in calling Jasmine. I was very nervous about it so I had to first calm myself with two drinks. When we spoke she spoke with what sounded like a Chinese or Korean accent. I didn't know the difference between the two, but either was fine so I was happy.

"Hi Jasmine, Chip gave me your number," I said.

"Who's Chip?" she said in a way that made me think of the term 'dragon lady.'

"Chip? He's about six feet, Puerto Rican, good looking?"

"I don't know any Chip. What you look like?"

Her abruptness was a turn off for me. But not knowing where I could find someone else I kept talking?

"I'm 6'6", I'm in good shape…"

"You sound black," she said cutting me off. "You too big for me."

I didn't know how to respond to this. Do I tell her that 'yes, I'm black and 6'6" but my dick isn't that big'? Or do I say that it started off small and was now only 'big.' Or do I just agree with her.

"You need to find someone else. You too big for me," she said again.

"Do you know of anyone else? I'm looking for a massage and then maybe a little more."

"You looking for a massage? I could give you a massage."

At this point I really didn't want to see this woman. Everything about her screamed 'ball breaker.' I didn't need to expose the brotha to that vice. "But I also want sex," I continued.

"No, no, massage only. I give you a massage."

"But I'm looking for sex also."

"No, you too big."

"Do you know of anyone that might be able to handle me?" I ask, hoping that she would give me a number and go away.

"I give you a number and she give you a massage."

I wanted to make sure that she would offer me sex as well, but at this point, I wanted Jasmine to go away and never be heard from again.

Jasmine gave me the number of Julia. At least I think her name was Julia. Jasmine's accent was very thick. It was either Julia or Ula, and what hooker in her right mind would call herself Ula? Ula was a retarded, Eastern European woman with a unibrow. And where I could see Ula having a very specific and devoted clientele, it wouldn't be very large.

"Man, I hope that her name isn't Ula," I said to myself before I dialed.

"Hi, Jasmine gave me this number. I think I'm looking for Julia."

"Yeah, that's me."

A paused developed on the line as I was expecting her to make it easy on me by telling me what she offered or something.

"She said that you would be able to give me what I'm looking for."

"What are you looking for?" Julia said back in a slightly nervous voice. Her nervousness gave me comfort.

"I was looking for a massage, and if the vibe was right maybe something more."

"I just give massage, sweetie."

"Would you consider more if we had a connection?"

"If we had a connection? Yes. But if I'm not attracted to you or if there's no connection, I will refuse."

"That's fine. That's all I'm looking for. How much is a massage for an hour?" I ask.

"$120," she replies, with a little less nervousness.

"And how much if there is a connection?"

"$200."

I pause for a second while I consider the cost. $200 is a lot of money. I did have the money available in my checking account but this would really cut into my vacation fund. But after a moment I realize that this was important. I had just spent the last five months working the brotha over like a piece of tough meat. I needed to know if it was worth it.

"Ok. Do you come to me or do I come to you?"

"You come to me, sweetie."

I do a quick evaluation of how drunk I am and then agree. She then gives me her address and I give her a time.

I think back to a sheet that came with my driver's license renewal forms. I remembered that a person of my weight could handle three glasses of alcohol before becoming too drunk to drive. So I fix myself another drink, shoot it back and hop into the shower.

"So what's going on?" the brotha asks.

"We're going to test out your new size. I'm going to go get a massage and if we like her and she likes us then we're going to get ourselves some pussy."

"Oh, ok."

You know, ever since my discovery of 5% spandex, boxer brief trunks, the brotha has been much easier to deal with. He didn't say much. He didn't ask for much. He didn't even drink much. It's kind of like when you have an uncontrollable dog and you put a choke collar on it. After a few yanks, they calm right down. I guess that's just the magic of spandex. I wondered what women were talking about when they said that.

I got to the intersection that Julia had mentioned, and then called her again.

"I'm here," I say, very relaxed from the alcohol. "Where should I go?"

"Drive down the street and you should see the Tango building. I'm in room 306. Just come up."

"I'll be there in a second."

I drove down the street a little further and the building was on my left. It was a nice building and it being a Saturday night there were a lot of college students hanging out in front. I park the car and step up to the door. It's locked and there is an entry box beside it. I lean over in my drunken state and try to figure out what I'm looking at. Even in my sober state I can never figure those things out, so drunk I have no chance.

After a second, one of the college students apologizes to me when he sees me struggling with the box. He opens the door for me.

"Thanks," I say back, before entering and looking for the elevator.

The building is pretty big and it takes me a while of snaking around the building before I find 306. Standing in front of the door I do a quick evaluation of my sobriety and state of mind. I decide that I am too drunk to stand up straight for too long, but not drunk enough to slur. I also decide that I am not nervous at all. In fact, I'm really looking forward to taking the brotha out.

The woman who answers the door isn't Asian at all. I would describe her as Cuban or Puerto Rican. Or maybe she's Dominican. Either way she's not Asian and she has what looks like 'C' cups. But at this point I'm way too drunk to care so I say hello and walk in.

"Did you find it ok?" she asks in a voice that doesn't have any nervousness at all.

"Oh yeah, it was easy. Nice place."

"Thanks."

I look around her studio apartment. It was a small, empty apartment and in the living room was a massage table illuminated by candles. In the space that separated her living room from her bedroom was a large piece of furniture that was nothing but cubby holes. And in the cubby holes were an endless supply of stylish shoes.

"So is this your Manolo Blahnik shrine?"

Julia laughs. I knew that watching that episode of 'Sex in the City' would come in handy someday.

"No, I was married and my husband used to give me shoes."

"So at what point in the marriage did you realize that he was gay?"

Julia laughs again. "That's funny because my family thought he was gay too. No, he just thought that women loved shoes, so he bought them."

I walk over to the shrine and pick a shoe up. "So, he just showed up one day with this shoe."

"Actually yes, he bought me that pair."

It's surprising to me, but for the next thirty minutes Julia and I just stand around the apartment talking. I didn't expect to be able to stand for two much less thirty minutes so I start to think that she's from Haiti and that her place is reinforced by voodoo. But I'm drunk, so what do I know.

"So, why are you still dressed?" she says playfully.

I quickly whip off my shirt and say "what shirt?" I know that it isn't exactly what she said, but I'm just proud that I'm not doing the drunk weave and tripping on my tongue. And when Julia laughed it's just an added bonus.

I then take off my shoes and pants. I turn back to Julia and she is still dressed, staring at me.

"Don't tell me that you're one of those guys that leaves their socks on. That's so weird."

Actually I'm not. I just had to slow down because the floor started to move when I leaned over to step out of my pants. Once the floor straightened up I slipped off my socks and then stepped out of my boxer brief trunks.

I turn back toward Julia and she is now standing in a cute pair of underwear that shows off her firm, worked out body. I see her take a quick peek down at the brotha and I examine her face for a reaction. I can't find any. Without looking down, I rub my hand on the brotha and realize that he is completely soft. From all of the guys in the changing room, I knew that the brotha was at least as big as the rest of them when soft so I didn't feel too bad.

"Do you mind using an oil I brought?" I ask her.

"No, what did you bring?"

I go back to my pants pocket and pull out a small bottle and hand it to her. She reads the label.

"Stein's Baseball Glove Oil."

"I seem to respond well to it."

"Ok."

I get on the massage table face down. She lifts her 5'7", small framed body onto the table with me and then sits on my butt. She then rubs my shoulders and it feels great.

"I like your body," she says in a soft voice.

"Thanks. I really like yours too," I reply back, enjoying what's going on too much to open my eyes.

"Your eyes are pretty closed. I mean, not that they aren't open," she says, back-pedaling.

I smile. "Thanks." I took that as a genuine compliment because girls had told me that before. They say that I have really long eyelashes and I assume that that's what she's referring to.

After working my neck and lower back, she then puts her knee in between my legs and massages the back of my thighs.

"I like legs and you have really nice legs."

"Thanks." I have to admit that I really liked what she was saying.

"You have really nice legs. I really like your body," she says again as her voice cracks a bit.

After she touches every inch of my back side, I feel her climb off the table.

"You can turn over if you want," she says in the same nervous voice that I first heard on the phone.

I open my eyes and turn over. I am still drunk and very relaxed, but the brotha is standing straight up in the air. I turn to the side and I see Julia standing waist level next to the table. She is naked and absolutely beautiful. Her twenty-seven-year-old 'C's' are firm and perfect. Her butt sticks out a little bit and her light tan complexion is flawless from head to toe.

"So what's your favorite sexual position?" she asks as she rubs the area around my cock.

I think for a second and then say, "I like it when you're on top."

She then takes a hold of the brotha. And with her soft, small hands around him, I hear the brotha say "passive protest!" He then goes limp in her hands.

My eyes shoot open so hard that my eyeballs almost slip out. I look down at Julia and she is staring curiously at the brotha.

The brotha is looking back at her and in an evil, spiteful voice he says, "passive fuckin' protest."

"Did your dick just say passive fuckin' protest to me?" Julia asks.

"I got to go to the bathroom," I say, as I slide from under her and head to the only door in the apartment.

When the door is closed and the lights are on I look down at the brotha with a look that says I'm about to become a eunuch. "You betta get your head out of your balls and straighten up."

"Passive fuckin' protest," he says again with a spirit that I hadn't seen in while.

"You think I'm playing?" I say in a hushed but intense voice. "You think I'm playin'?" I say again, losing control of my volume. "If you don't get your dick up…"

"What you think I'm just gonna sit around and do whatever you say? You think you control me? You don't control me. I control you!"

"If you don't get up right now, I'm gonna feed you to the fan. You want me to feed you to the fan?"

"Don't fuck with me. You don't know who you're fuckin' with," the brotha says with a little fear in his voice.

"I'm drunk as fuck right now and mad as hell. I'll feed you to the fan so fast that your balls will spin."

"Don't you fuckin' feed me to the fan!" the brotha yells back in fear.

"I'll feed you to the fan right now! You want me to do it. I'll go home and do it right now."

"Don't you fuckin' do. Don't you fuckin' do it!"

"Is everything alright in there?" Julia says in a way that tells the brotha and me that she has her ear to the door.

"We're fine," the brotha and I say in unison. I look down at the brotha and give him a look that tells him to shut up.

"Is there someone in there with you, sweetie?" Julia asks with caution.

"No, no. I'm just… um… washing my hands," I flinch, because even in my drunken state I know it's a bad lie.

"Ok," Julia replies back.

"Am I gonna feed you to the fan when I get home?" I ask the brotha in a very determined, yet soft voice.

"It's all good man. It's all good."

"Then get up."

I watch as the brotha returns to a fully hard position. "And stay up. And you don't fuck with me. You stay up." I give the brotha one more harsh look and then slowly open the door.

When I leave the bathroom Julia is standing right next to the door.

"I didn't hear the water running," Julia says apprehensively.

"Oh, it turns out that I didn't have to."

Julia doesn't reply. Instead she just stares at me wondering what will happen next. I look at her very still, naked body and then I look down at the brotha who is standing at full attention. I think for a second if there is anything that I could say to return things back to the way it was before 'the brotha show,' but my drunken mind draws a blank.

I then walk past Julia and sit on the edge of the massage table. Julia then stands in front of me but just a little too far to casually touch.

"What's goin' on sweetie?"

Her voice is surprisingly compassionate and her tone sparks something in me. Unable to filter what I'm saying I speak. "I'm having a problem with my junk. It has a mind of its own and now it just doesn't want to cooperate."

I look up into Julia's eyes and I see the softest and most beautiful pair of eyes staring back. "That's ok sweetie. We could take our time. Are you ok with that?"

Speechless I shake my head 'yes' and with her light push I lay back down on the massage table. She takes the brotha into her hands and with the glove oil she massages the brotha. It feels really great.

"When you get really hard, your head gets big. I like that," Julia says in a comforting voice. "I really do like your body."

I look over at the beautiful goddess standing beside the massage table. From the angle that I'm at I can see her nipples sticking out and they are hard. I can also see her face and she reminds me of a woman on heat. Her mouth is slightly open and she is very focused on the brotha.

"You know I don't think I'm going to go to clubs anymore," Julia continues. "The last time I went it was to a gay club with my friend and a woman practically stuck her finger in my pussy."

That thought really turned me on so I lifted my hand up to rub her stomach with the outside of my pointing finger. I only touch her for a second before she takes my hand and places in on her ass. Still thinking about her story in the club I slide my finger on the inside of her ass cheek and follow the crack down to her pussy.

With my finger I can tell that she is shaved. I can also tell that the lips of her pussy are swollen. I lightly brush her lips with my finger and then I slowly narrow down on her clit. She is a skinny girl so I have to navigate her pelvis bone but eventually I find it. After a few seconds there I slide my finger back and slowly push it into her wet pussy. She's pretty tight so it takes some pushing before my finger pops in. She moans.

I keep moving my fingers, trying to get as deep as possible. When I finally get my middle finger down to the knuckle she tilts her head back.

"Did you say that you like it when I'm on top?" she asks.

"Yeah" is all I can say back.

She gently pulls away from me and my finger slides out of her. She takes a few steps into her bedroom and comes back with a condom. She looks at me as she tears it open with her teeth and all I can think about is how much I am enjoying what is going on.

She places the condom on the brotha and rolls it down. She then works her way back onto the table and I watch as she positions herself over me. She then slowly lowers herself down, stopping when her pussy makes contact with the brotha.

The condom makes everything a little less sensitive for me but I can feel the pressure as she makes a couple of attempts to get the brotha inside of her. With her right hand guiding the brotha she makes another attempt. On this try the brotha pops in and she arches her back in what looks like pain.

'I'm big,' I think. 'She can barely take me.'

The thought alone is enough to get me close to the finish line. But I manage to hold off long enough for her to work the brotha all of the way into her. Once she's sitting on my pelvis she lifts back up slowly. She is clearly struggling with my size and I couldn't be happier. After she gets up and down two more times I can't hold it any longer and the brotha spits up.

When she feels the brotha flinching inside of her she stops and braces herself. After the flinching stops she continues to sit there for another few seconds and then she slowly works the brotha out of her. With her knees on either side of my hips and her hands on my shoulders, her long hair touches my chest. Without awkwardness I look up into her eyes and her face looks tired and satisfied.

Looking up at her I wonder if she is expecting me to say something, but when I decide not to I realize how good it feels to just look up into her eyes. And then, after what feels like not long enough, she speaks.

"I'll get that for you."

She then walks her hands down my body until she is sitting on her heels. Like an expert she rolls the condom off the brotha, ties a knot into the end of it and heads to the bathroom.

I am very comfortable lying on the table and that doesn't change when she returns with a few baby wipes. She very quickly wipes me off and tosses the cloth into a bin in the corner of the room.

"You can wipe your finger off on the table cloth. It's clean."

I wonder what she's talking about and then remember that I had my finger inside of her. The memory feels good.

Julia then stands at the side of the table and I look into her face to see if she's anxious for me to leave. I find no evidence so I continue to lay there.

"My best friend says that black guys only have sex when they want to."

I think for a second about how I should respond but she cuts off my thought.

"But I guess that I'm the same way. Only I like to have sex all of the time," she says with a smile.

"How big was your husband?" I ask her, wondering why she had such a hard time with me.

"He was average sized. We used to have sex all of the time. My favorite is when we had sex six times. I was so tender afterwards that I could barely touch my pussy," she says with a laugh.

Just then she did something that I didn't expect. She very gently slipped her soft small hand into mine. The feeling that I had in that moment was like nothing I had ever felt before. It was intimate in some way.

"What's your favorite type of guy?" I ask, wanting to know what she was thinking.

"I like black guys and Japanese guys. My husband was from Turkey. I was the black sheep of the family... And at the same time, the smartest one," she says with another laugh. "My husband took my family on this big fishing trip once. I speared this 25-pound grouper, swam him up to the boat, and dragged it in. Later that night I skinned him and fried him up for dinner," she said, laughing again.

I look into the eyes of this 110-pound, slim woman trying to see if she's exaggerating. "What were you using?" I ask.

"A Hawaiian sling. I got him right between the eyes," she said, smiling.

I sit up and as I do she lets go of my hand and touches my shoulder for support. With me sitting up she backs up for a second in case I wanted to go, but when she saw me settle she stepped back into reach.

"You are a very interesting woman," I say, surprised at the amazing beauty standing in front of me. She smiles back and an unfamiliar look comes over her face.

Julia then pokes me in the chest and says, "You like me," in a tone that says that she just figured it out.

I am caught off guard by this statement. But instead of remaining quiet and instead of playing it cool, I say the first thing that comes to mind. "I do like you." I process what I said after I say it and the surprise that was in my inflection was well placed. When I called her, I didn't expect to like her. All I was expecting was to take the brotha out for a test drive. That's all I wanted. But the truth was that somehow she had gotten under my skin. She had affected me is some way that I couldn't explain. And now I needed to get out of there.

Julia giggled a little bit and then stepped back when I made a move forward. I then slipped back into my clothes and peeked back to watch her put on her tight tee-shirt and then her snug sweatpants. When she put her pants on without panties it turned me on.

While she was still facing the other direction I took the $200 out of my pocket and put it onto her breakfast nook. When she walked towards me I pointed at the money and she barely acknowledged my gesture. She then, without a word, slipped her arms around me, placed her face into the space between my neck and shoulder and held me. I expected the hug to last a second, but when she didn't immediately let go, I knew that the hug was meant to be something special. I then closed my eyes and breathed her in.

I didn't know what to say as I walked toward the door so I said that we had to do it again. She didn't reply and before I knew it there was a closed door between her and me. I snaked back through the hallways still having the smell of her on my hands. I casually lifted one hand to my nose and smelled the acidic smell of her pussy. I smelled the other hand and recognized the flowery smell of her place.

They both turned me on, but I didn't want to enjoy the smell of her there, in her building. Instead I waited until I got home. I got undressed and lay in bed. I brought the hand with the smell of her pussy to my nose. I wrapped my large hand around my face until all I could smell was her. With my left I then stroked the brotha who wasn't quite up for it so quickly after such a short time.

I breathed in and then stroked. I breathed in and then I stroked. And as I could feel the spit working its way through the brotha I felt something that I had never felt before. In those moments between inhales and strokes a door opened in my mind. For a brief second it was like I couldn't breathe. It was like I was falling naked through a cool breeze and every part of me was suddenly alive.

And just as quickly as the feeling came, it left and the brotha spit up his limited juices onto my stomach.

"What was that?" I muttered to myself.

I laid there for a moment trying to remember what I had felt. And when the memory was locked in, I got up and cleaned myself off. I then sat naked on the edge of the bed wondering what I should do next. I picked up my phone and stared at it in my hands. I flipped it open and texted a few words to Julia on the chance that she might have texting on her phone.

'I'm sure all of your guys say this afterwards, but I had a really great time with you. Save my number and if you ever want to use it, I would be open to hearing from you,' I write.

I send it off, expecting never to hear from her again. But a minute later my phone beeps and my heart drops. I open it up and read the message. It says, 'Not all of my guys say it. It's funny, I have a song stuck in my head, Bad Romance. LOL.'

I type a smiley face back, slip on a pair of boxer brief trunks and get into bed. It was a good day and I never wanted to forget it.

Chapter 7
How to Last Longer in Bed

The next morning I felt as great as a person who had too much to drink the night before could feel. I was smiling when I brushed my teeth and if my head hadn't felt so cloudy I would have sung in the shower. The brotha on the other hand was quiet. I didn't encourage him to speak by looking at him, but he also didn't ask to be pleasured in the shower.

Something had come over me last night when the brotha pulled what he did. And I think that I really would have driven home and fed him to the fan. Maybe the brotha sensed my sincerity. Maybe he was now a little afraid of me. 'How great would it be if I had a brotha that would do what I said instead of being a dick all the time?' I thought. But as great as the thought was, I could never imagine that I would ever get that.

When I got to work everything was as it usually was except Chip silently watched me. I knew that I was going to talk to him at some point, but the truth was that I didn't know what to say. I didn't know if I wanted to share my incredible experience with anyone, much less Chip.

Chip had made an effort to get me laid. And no matter how unsuccessful that attempt was, it was still worthy of acknowledgement. Now, I could acknowledge it by telling him that I called his girl and she turned out to be a dragon lady who was afraid of black men. Or, I could say that she then gave me the number of a girl that was beyond anything that I ever hoped for.

But again, if I told him how much I liked Julia, I'm sure he would ask me why I liked her so much. And to explain that, I would have to explain the brotha and my penis enlargement. Not only is that something that I don't want to discuss with someone I worked with, but Chip was hung like a mule, a thick, Puerto Rican mule. I didn't want to have to admit my inferiority to him. The balance of power between the two of us could too easily switch.

"You look like you had a good night," Rose said from the chair opposite my own.

"Yeah, I had a great night," I replied.

I definitely wasn't going to say too much to Rose. Rose and I were going to sleep together, and I didn't want to pee in the pool by mentioning last night.

"What did you do?" she asked cheerfully.

"Ya know, I just stayed in and watched TV. It was a very relaxing night."

"Wow, what was on TV?" she continued.

'Oh no,' I thought. 'This questioning is getting too detailed. I wasn't prepared for this.'

"A little bit of this. A little bit of that," I say, hoping to end the conversation there.

"You almost look like you got laid," Rose said with a smile.

'How the hell did she guess that?' I wondered.

Rose had never struck me as being observant so suddenly I got very self-conscious. There was something about me that screamed I had had sex and I didn't have a clue as to what it was.

"I love sex," I said without thinking.

"You did get laid!"

'Damn, that is not what I was hoping would happen,' I thought.

I didn't know a lot about women. I didn't know how they thought or what they wanted. I didn't know how to dress for them or where to take them. I didn't know how to please them or even where to find them. As far as I knew, when I went into my house at night, they all flew back to their hive and fed off the stray guys that didn't make it home in time.

But one thing that I did know was that, no matter how curious she was, and no matter how big her smile was while asking me that question, if I told her that I had just paid for sex and it was better than anything I had ever had in my life, I was never going to get to bury my face in Rose's pollen and play motorboat with it. And this boy needed to shoot his stinger into some Rose-flavored honey.

"Nah, I wish I did though. No, I just sat at home alone," I said.

"I wasn't doing anything either. You should have called me," Rose said with a continued smile.

"Yeah I should have. Maybe the next time I will."

"No, maybe. Just call me."

"Ok, I will," I say with a smile while handing the till over to Rose.

Rose takes the till and leaves. I watch her body as she turns away knowing that I was going to be able to see her naked soon. I wondered what secrets her twenty years held. Rose had a round face and round hips. I imagined that underneath her shirt she also had a slightly round belly. Not a big one, but a soft one that made small mounds when she bent over. Her body wasn't going to be like Julia's fit, toned body. Rose's body was going to be more like a woman's, or more precisely, like a twenty-year-old girl's. Naked, Rose would look like those statues from a long time ago.

I leaned back in my chair and remembered my time with Julia the night before. Everything about it was so great. I thought about how there was nothing about it that I would change.

And then I remembered the actual sex. As I played it back and forth in my mind something that I hadn't thought about before became apparent. 'I didn't last very long during sex,' I thought. 'After I got all of the way inside of her, I don't think I even lasted 30 seconds. That's not good!'

My thought was interrupted by a knock on the door.

"Come in."

The door opened and it was Brian.

"Hey what's up man," I said, trying to get my mind back onto work.

"Hi. I wanted to drop off my resume."

"Oh. Come in. Have a seat."

Brian handed me his resume. And as much as I tried to focus on the page, the only thing I could see were three blocks of words surrounded by a lot of creatively arranged line spacing. After what seemed like an appropriate amount of time I rested the page onto my desk and turned to Brian.

"So, how's your girl doing?" I asked.

"Still pregnant," Brian said with a smile.

"Yeah, I could only imagine." I looked around the room looking for either something to say or a way out. "Umm, I don't really know what's available. As you know, these stores are run through the corporate office and what they do is determined by store sales divided by this district's marketing expenditures with the community's activities being a determining factor."

"What do you mean?" Brian asked.

I look back down at Brian and he has a very confused look on his face.

"The corporate office gives us our budgets to hire and give raises based on their profit margin for each store."

"Oh," Brian says.

"And what determines a store's profits, excluding rent and utilities, is how much they spend on advertising. And what they do there is determine which stores benefit from the local commercials or newspaper advertising and then divide the cost for the advertising among all of the stores.

And if there are an extra number of sporting leagues in the community around the store, corporate adds to our payroll budget so that we can accommodate the extra foot traffic."

"Ok," Brian adds, trying to take it all in.

"I say all that to say that I have to check with corporate to figure out if I can be allocated additional funds for an assistant manager."

"I appreciate that."

"Hey, you earned it. Now it's just a question of whether or not it can be worked into the budget."

"So is there anything that I should do?" Brian asks.

"No, just hang out. I'll figure out my plan and once I've spoken to them I'll let you know. Cool?"

"Ben, I really appreciate this."

"Cool."

Brian gets up and shakes my hand. Usually I would have made fun of him for being so formal, but I could see that he was nervous and that it meant a great deal to him, so I play along. And when he opens the door to leave I see Chip standing on the other side of it, waiting.

When Brian is gone Chip sticks his head in.

"Can I come in?"

"Yeah man."

I'm not sure what topic he wants to discuss so I let him do his thing. He comes in, closes the door quietly, sits in the seat opposite me and leans forward slightly.

"What happened?" he asks.

"Nothing," I decide to say. "She wasn't into me."

"What do you mean?" he says disappointedly.

"She said black men are too big for her."

"Really?" Chip says, leaning back in his chair.

"Yeah. Have you ever been with her?" I ask, very curious to know the answer.

"No, my buddy told me about her. He said she was a cute little Asian with a nice ass, so I thought you'd like her."

"Maybe, but I never even met her."

"So like, she told you this on the phone?"

"Yeah."

"And she didn't give you like a reference or something?"

'Crap,' I thought. 'He really does know how this stuff works.'

"Yeah, she gave me a number."

"Did you call it?"

'Crap,' I thought.

"Ahhh, yeah."

"And what happened?"

'Crap,' I thought.

"Listen, let me ask you something. How long do you usually last when you're fuckin' someone?" I ask Chip.

"I don't know, maybe about twenty or thirty minutes. Why?"

'Fuckin' Puerto Rican mule,' I think to myself.

"Just curious," I say, really not wanting to explain.

"What? Did something go wrong?" Chip asks.

"No, I was just curious. No, nothing went wrong. I was just trying to figure some stuff out."

"So you didn't hook up with anyone last night?"

"No. After I spoke to her on the phone I decided to just watch TV."

"I'm sorry man. Do you want me to find you someone else?"

"Naw, that's cool. It was a stupid idea. But you know what, I really appreciate you tryin'."

"It was nothin' man. Any time you're looking for someone, let me know. I know a bunch of girls. You just tell me what you want, and I'll find it for you."

"That's cool man. I don't think I will but thanks."

"No problem man."

Chip gets up and grabs the knob. "Just let me know." Chip closes the door behind him.

'He's a pimp! That's why he so tired at night. He works as a fuckin' pimp,' I realize with a flash. 'No wonder he thinks fifty bucks is fifty bucks, it's probably because his motto is "the bitch better have my money".'

As disturbing as it is that I went to a pimp to be set up with one of his hookers, I had more important things to worry about. I had to turn thirty seconds into thirty minutes and I had to do it before Rose lost her bloom. And by bloom I mean 'big puffy one for old Ben and the brotha.'

Instead of refocusing on the audit, I decided to do a little surfing online. While looking around I remember Cristian and RateABull.com. I go there and take a look again at his featured videos. When I click on the 'more' button I see a video that I had noticed before but hadn't considered watching. It was called 'How to Last Longer in Bed.'

I stared down at the link for a while before looking up at the door to my office. 'What are the odds that someone will walk by and hear it?' I wonder. 'It's too high,' I decide. So my good judgment gets the better of me and I decide to wait until I get home.

After work I head to the gym for what is a great day on the bench. I was able to increase my bench press and lateral chest pulls by five pounds. And more than anything I felt really strong. Overall, I was in a great mood so when I got into the changing room I stripped down, threw the towel over my shoulder, slid on my shower shoes, and headed to the steam room.

As usual the gym was busy, but unlike usual the steam room was packed. In the entire space there were only two places to sit. And what's worse was that everyone was wearing a towel. So, me walking in with the brotha dangling in the breeze had to be annoying to everyone there. I remembered when it was the other way around. There had been many times when I was sitting in the steam room and some big dicked naked guy would walk in. I hated it. But now that it's the other way around, I could barely remember why I was so annoyed.

Even so, I realized that my liberation day could have been better timed. As it was, I had to sit between an older Asian man in a towel and some twenty-five-year-old gym novice white dude, who was actually wearing his shorts.

After a few minutes I decide that I had made my point, but I couldn't get myself to leave. I could still remember when the places were reversed and the naked guy would walk out two minutes after he walked in. My first thought was always that the toweled people shamed him into leaving. I didn't want everyone to think that about me. I wanted them to know that I was ok with my nudity, and that I only left because I was ready.

I decided to wait everyone out. Often in the steam room a person comes in for a quick steam and then they leave. Other times a person comes in for a medium length steam and then they take a cold shower and come back for another round. That is what I usually do. But I have also done the third option. I have sat in the steam room until I felt like I was going to pass out.

Today I might have to do that again. I had decided that the only way that I could make sure that everyone in the room knew that I wasn't self conscious was to not leave until everyone that had been there before me left. I was still feeling really pumped from my workout and this little bit of competition felt like a great way to end the day.

The guy next to me in the gym shorts was the first one to leave. That's no surprise. He was wearing shorts. He wasn't ready for prime time.

Next out was a fat, hairy, Greek looking guy who was sitting on the upper level in the back left corner. He looked like he had been in there for a while so there was no shame in him leaving.

Next out were the pair of thirty-year-old guys. It didn't look like they were together, but leaving a steam room is often like the tour de France. Drafting behind the guy in the breakaway is the easiest way to leave the pack. You don't want to be the guy that everyone stares at as you leave so you wait for someone to get up and as soon as they reach for the door you get up and slip out too.

Everyone else left one by one while other people arrived. When the newbies stepped in, they scanned the room like usual. Me sitting there towel free told them that this was a clothing optional steam room and if they didn't like it they could leave. Some did but only after sitting for a second so I couldn't really say if it was because of me.

After what felt like twenty minutes the room had completely recycled itself. Everyone had left at least once except for one person, the Asian man sitting next to me. The truth was that this was what I was afraid of. Asian steamers are like Kenyan runners; they both hold a lot of rice and they go forever.

When I had walked in the Asian guy was sitting with his eyes closed. That is never a good sign in this type of competition. What it means was that he didn't care about the steam. What he was trying to do was talk to his ancestors, so hallucination was the goal. I have always been the type that left before the hallucinations began. But who knows what would be necessary to pull out the victory tonight.

As time slowly ticked on I thought about the brotha. He was surprisingly quiet through this whole thing. In the past he would have been up and looking around. He would be making inappropriate sounds under his breath. And he would be more excited about getting out than I was.

This time though, he just hung there. I looked down a couple of times to check on him and I found him laying there quietly with his head on the bench tile. I decided to take this time to figure out what I was going to say to him when we got home. I closed my eyes and thought about it.

I was pretty drunk last night and I said a few things that perhaps I shouldn't have. But drinking doesn't turn you into someone else. It just lowers your guard and allows the true you to come out. The truth is that I have been angry towards him for a long time. If I'm really honest about it I would say that there were times, many times, when I hated him.

He's such a fucking dictator. Ever since I was fifteen years old, he has held my sex life hostage. I couldn't even make a move on some chick without wondering what the brotha would think about her. Would he like her, or would he end up humiliating me again. If I was really honest with myself, he was the reason that I was alone. How could you get close to someone when there are three people in the relationship and one of them is a real dick?

And as I thought about it, I realized that there was a part of me that hoped that the brotha would've acted up again last night. I really wanted to feed him to the fan. I really wanted to show him who was boss. I wanted to be rid of him, but I didn't want him to be off somewhere drinking and having a good time. I wanted him to be dead.

I wanted to make him suffer for what he had done to me over the years. I wanted to watch him die. And if I were willing to entertain the thoughts that I often hid away, I would say that there were times when, if I had a knife, the task would already be done. His randomness made my life unbearable and something had to be done.

When I opened my eyes again, the Asian guy was gone. I'm not sure when he left, but it must have been a while ago. In his place next to me now sat a naked man. In my quick peek over I saw that he was a muscular, hairy white guy in his mid-30's. And when I peeked over he took that opportunity to try and meet my eyes.

'Ok, time to go,' I thought.

I then stood up and took a few steps to the door. I could feel everyone's eyes stare at me as I did. I grabbed my towel hanging on the hook outside the doors and then took a quick shower.

The muscular, hairy white guy followed me out. He then put himself in the shower opposite mine and faced outwards toward me as he turned on the water. I figured that it would best to ignore him. After I got my body temperature back down, I toweled off, wrapped up, and was gone.

The muscular, hairy white guy must have gotten the message because I never saw him enter the changing area. I then thought about the brotha again because this guy wasn't small. In every instance in the past this is where the brotha would have embarrassed me. This time he didn't even budge. Clearly something was up.

When I arrived home I took my time in making dinner. I was out of leftovers, so I took the chicken from the fridge, sprinkled it with season-all salt, dipped it in breading, put it in a baking pan and popped it into the oven. Without a word I slipped off my pants so that the brotha could see the TV. We then both watched it but I was the only one to laugh when something funny happened.

When dinner was done I heated up some ramen noodles and sat down to eat. I was surprised by how good it tasted. Most nights I took much more time and used many more ingredients. But this time with almost no effort I had made something really good.

Full from dinner, I pushed my chair away from the dining room table. The TV was still on, but I wasn't watching it. Instead I looked around the room. The room was a collection of items from the last ten years of my life.

There was a black leather couch and love seat that sat in front of a 47-inch flat screen TV. In the cabinet that the TV sat on was a Sony receiver that I had bought ten years ago, and the Tivo box. The walls were pretty bare. There was nothing above the TV, but above the couch was a photo that I had taken on a trip to the Smoky Mountains.

Although I wasn't supposed to, once I had entered Smoky Mountain Park, I pulled over to the side of the road and took a hike. Eventually I had made it to a clearing in front of a lake with the mountains in the background. I was so struck by the beauty of what I saw that I took a picture. The picture came out so well that I blew it up and put it on the wall.

There wasn't much to the living room and dining room. I was taught well by my mother to keep my surroundings clean. And the lesson stuck so well that that was how I kept my house. I rarely bought anything that I didn't need. And when there was something that I wanted I went through a very long thought process before I decided to buy it.

What that meant was that the house always had an emptiness to it. I had visited the houses of my friends back home and they were all filled with stuff. In fact it was hard to get around in their houses because of all of the stuff. But mine was very different. My house looked like a showroom house. Anyone could be living here. And except for the photos on the wall, none of which had any people in it, there was nothing of me anywhere in the place.

The office was the only room in the house that broke away from the emptiness. The office contained pictures of family and friends. I had made sure to include one picture of everyone that meant something to me. There was even a picture of my father. The one that I decided to pin up was the one with him and me mowing the lawn.

When I was about seven years old, things still seemed to be good in my household. I can remember me being a happy kid. And to me, mowing the lawn was a rite of passage. The lawn mower was a scary thing. It had a fast spinning blade that my father showed me one day to teach me to keep my hands away from it. So sometimes when my father mowed the lawn, I would follow him around the yard. The picture was of one of those times. Both he and I were smiling in the picture.

But other than the pin board with all the pictures, the office matched the rest of the house. The walls were sparse. And the colors, which matched the rest of the house, would probably be described as neutral.

I didn't even have a DVD or music collection that would set my place apart from someone else's. I think that if I got drunk and woke up in an abandoned building, it might take me three days before I realized. And even then, the only giveaway would be that my shows weren't being recorded on the Tivo. I hadn't really noticed just how empty the place was until that very moment. But now that I had noticed it, like the letter grades that the health department made restaurants post in their windows, it was hard to ignore.

"I'm not happy," the brotha said, breaking the silence.

I let a moment go by before answering. "You mean you're still unhappy. Because the last time we talked about this, you said that you were unhappy because you felt small. You're not small anymore, so what you're saying is that you're still unhappy."

"Yeah, I'm still unhappy. I thought that it was my size making me unhappy. And in the beginning I was really happy. But as I got bigger, my joy didn't increase. And then when I started to realize that my happiness wasn't growing with my size, I started to feel unhappy again.

And you're right. What I tried to do last night was an asshole thing to do. I don't know what I was thinking. I guess in my mind, I wasn't happy, so I didn't want you to be happy either. You were right to want to feed me to the fan. And I wouldn't blame you if you still did it. I'm just a fucked up little shit and if I could go away and never come back, I would."

This was not how I expected this to go. Once again he had surprised me by being humble and rational. I didn't know how to respond to that. He was a little shit, and a cock blocker and everything else that he thought he was. And I did hate him for everything he has said to me over the years and everything that he has done. But something told me that if I let him, he really would go away and never come back. And as much as I hated him, and in my heart I really did hate him, I didn't think that I could live without him.

"You know what brotha, you have been the biggest little shit that I have ever met. And there is a part of me that really hates you for everything that you have put me through all these years. But what am I supposed to do with that? We're stuck with each other. We're here in this right now. You're you and I'm me. Where is either of us gonna go?

And you know what? I'm not happy either. But I'm not happy because of you. If you would just stop being such a dick, maybe I could be. Maybe I could find someone. Maybe I could go out at night and meet people and have a normal life. Maybe I could have friends."

"You think that I'm the reason you don't have friends?" the brotha asked softly.

"Yeah, you're the fuckin' reason! I never know what you're gonna do. I don't trust you around anyone. I don't know when you're going to speak up or do anything. I just feel tense all the time. Why don't you just give me a fuckin' break? Why don't you, for once in my life, just give me a fuckin' break!"

"If you want me to go I will," the brotha said sadly.

"And stop that 'I'll just go' shit! You know you can't go anywhere. That's what I'm talking about when I talk about bein' all tense around people. How am I supposed to relax if at any point I know that you could be gone. Stop being such a shit. Stop bein' such a fuckin' shit! Please. Please!"

"Alright," the brotha said back quietly.

"Thank you!" I said without giving an inch. "And if I choose to be with someone just let me do it. Please, just shut up and let me do it. Let me have that. You have already taken away so much from me. Just let me have that."

"Alright," the brotha said again in a soft voice while staring at the floor.

"Thank you," I said calming down.

Those were the last words that we said to each other that day. After that I cleared my plate, but it in the dishwasher and moved to my office. I hadn't forgotten my endurance problem and my upcoming time with Rose. I had to figure out how I could get myself to last longer and I had to watch Cristian's video.

I kind of wished that things hadn't gone down like they did with the brotha because I was hoping that this was something that we could do together. But the tension between us was so tight you could play it like a guitar and I wasn't about to start up the band.

Though there were still things that I wondered. I wondered what the brotha's experience was like last night. I know for me, physically speaking, it wasn't like the last times I had had sex. The last times it felt like so much more than it did this time. This time I had to watch Julia moving up and down on me to know that she was there. The last time the brotha could feel the breeze move as the woman approached me.

What I really wanted to ask the brotha was if he had noticed the same. It could be possible that all of that was in my head, but Cristian did say in his video that a loss of sensitivity was probable. I guess he played it down so much that I didn't think that I would be able to notice it. But I did notice it, and I'm wondering if the brotha noticed it too.

I typed RateABull.com into the browser and the site popped back up. I went through a couple of the advice center questions wondering if I could lend assistance to anyone else and when I didn't find anything I had expertise on, I moved on to the featured video section. There I clicked on the 'more' button and the complete list appeared. I scrolled down until I saw what I was looking for. The link read 'How to Last Longer in Bed & PC Exercises' and I clicked on it.

With the brotha quietly hanging by I watched the video. On it Cristian talked directly to the camera in front of a series of walls and doors. He said:

"My name is Cristian, Cris-tee-in and this is my vlog. How to last longer in bed. Well there are two things you need to focus on if you want to last longer; there is the physical aspect, and there is the mental aspect. Let's talk about the physical aspect first because that's easiest."

Here in the video Cristian's head slid to one side of the screen. A black background filled the other side of the screen and the heading 'Physical Technique' appeared.

"The things that allow you to ejaculate or cum are the PC muscles. They're the muscles that… when you orgasm it's the shooting muscle that flexes back and forth. If you have weak PC muscles, you will not be able to control when you orgasm. You'll feel it coming and there will be nothing you can do to stop it and you'll just shoot on through.

So what you can do to strengthen those muscles is a trick… when you're peeing, when you're urinating… and this is every time you pee… when you go to pee, and you get the full flow going, clench back and stop the flow. Get it to stop completely without dripping or anything. Do that for five seconds, and once those five seconds are over, you let go and allow the pee to start flowing again. And once it flows for a bit longer, you clench again and stop it, and you hold that for five seconds. You do that seven times, every time you pee and it will help you to strengthen the PC muscles and it will help you to be able to control when you orgasm.

When you first start it, it will take you a little while to actually get used to it and you won't be able to stop it off completely. But once you do and you can do it seven times without peeing, then you know your PC muscles are there and that's no longer a problem.

Now, the mental aspect. We all know why we come too quickly. It is because it feels really good and there's no stopping it. But that's not true. Here are a couple of things we can do, first of all, and this is the best possible thing you can do: You stop when you feel it approaching; not when it's about to hit, but when you feel it approaching, you stop intercourse and if necessary, you pull out. You remove the sensation away from your penis and that allows you to come back down to normal. If you pull out and then come, you've waited too late.

So you pull out when you feel it coming, and then you do other things. You kiss, you caress, you maybe give some oral sex. You give it for a while and then once you feel you are back down to normal, then you start up again. That's one thing.

The second thing you can do, and that you should always do is wear a condom, and not the extra sensitive ones. Use the non-extra sensitive ones. This will give you at least another thirty seconds or so, maybe up to a minute before you come. But you should be wearing a condom anyway, so I hope you are.

The third thing you should do is start having intercourse later. So let's say that you start off kissing, start off caressing, and you start off giving her oral sex. And you get her to the point where she is close to coming herself. And then once you are entering you're timed up because you're ready to go, she's ready to go and there it is. You wouldn't realize that you haven't lasted long and she wouldn't realize that you haven't lasted long because you both are coming at the same time.

The fourth thing is, and this really is the fourth resort, if you feel this could help, before you actually date, an hour or two before you actually have sex, masturbate. That will take some of the charge out of it so that when you are actually having sex you'll be able to last a little while longer and maybe that'll be long enough.

Something else you can do, and this doesn't always work well for me, but this is standard: Mental distraction. It's the old thing of 'think of someone you know naked.' Make it someone in your family, someone you can never find attractive and that will help you to go longer. Or maybe do math. Do math in your head. Do your 7's times tables, or your 6 times tables or the 9 times tables. You know, do the hard ones.

Also, what you can try and do is take the tip of your tongue, this is when you start to kind of feel the orgasm coming, take the tip of your tongue and place it on the roof of your mouth. Holding it there distracts you a little bit. It takes you out of the moment and holding it there allows you to go for a little longer.

And this is something else you can do, it's pretty strong and I guarantee that if you do it, you will last longer. It is the jelqing technique that I talk about in my 'How to Enlarge your Penis' video. What it does is it desensitizes your penis a little bit because of all of the stretching. And I guarantee you, if you do it, not only will you get longer and thicker, but you will be able to last longer in bed.

So these are some of the techniques you can do. You can go to RateABull.com to check out the rest of the techniques, also how to enlarge your penis, and also how men can have multiple orgasms. So check out RateABull.com, and drop me a line and tell me what you think."

I leaned back in my chair thinking about what I just saw. Certainly what Cristian said about jelqing making your penis less sensitive was true. But even with that, I still came very quickly with Julia. When I was having sex with her I didn't try to last longer. I was simply there having sex, and then I felt it, and then I came. I guess if I would have tried anything at all I would have lasted longer.

Julia didn't seem to mind how quickly I came. In fact, she seemed to have a problem with my size. Because of that problem I got the impression that she was happy that I came quickly. But I'm sure that other women might not be so happy.

I rewound the video to a place where all of the techniques were listed on the screen.

Physical Techniques:
- *PC muscle exercises*

Mental Techniques:
- *Pull out early*
- *Use a thicker condom*
- *Start intercourse later*
- *Masturbate before sex*
- *Mental distractions*
- *Tongue touching*
- *Jelqing*

Most of them were things that would be done during sex or right before having sex. The only things that could be done in preparation for sex were the jelqing and the PC muscle exercises. I had already done the jelqing, so that meant that the only thing left to do were the PC exercises.

I typed PC muscles into Wikipedia and read that the PC muscle is a hammock-like muscle, found in both sexes, that stretches from the pubic bone to the coccyx (tail bone), forming the floor of the pelvic cavity and supporting the pelvic organs. Its function is to control urine flow and to contract during orgasm. PC muscle exercises are a set of exercises designed to strengthen and give voluntary control over the pubococcygeus (or PC) muscles.

I then looked at the diagram to get a full sense of where it was.

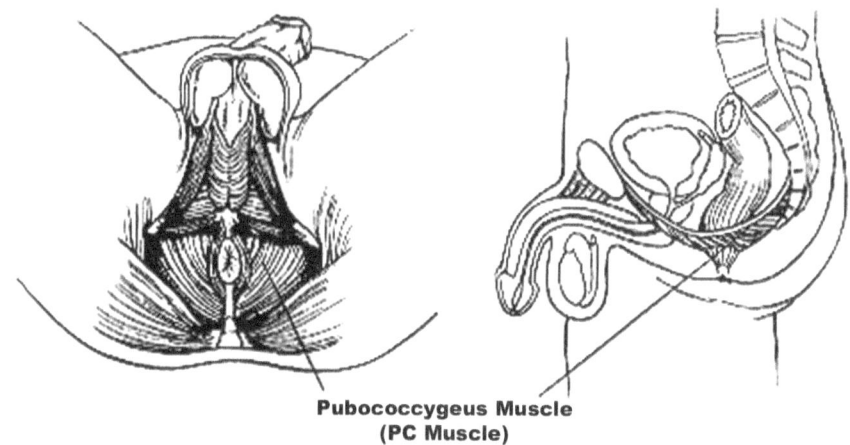

**Pubococcygeus Muscle
(PC Muscle)**

If I was going to try to do PC muscle exercises I was going to need the brotha's help. He had as much control of this part of the body as I did. And if he wanted to be a dick about it, he could prevent me from taking control of those muscles during the exercises.

'There is only one way to find out,' I thought.

I got up from the computer and went into the bathroom. I stood in front of the toilet and took hold of the brotha. I closed my eyes and felt the pee as it made its way down the brotha. Once the pee started flowing with a strong stream, I clenched. When I did the brotha let out a groan. The feeling stung a little and I couldn't cut off the stream completely.

I tried again and the brotha groaned again. I tried five more times but wasn't able to completely stop the pee from flowing. This was clearly going to be a challenge. But what was more important than whether or not it would work, was the fact that the brotha was going to let me do it. I think that we had finally reached a place in our relationship where I was in control. It seemed like he was going to let me drive my life and it felt good.

Chapter 8
The G-Spot &
How to Help a Woman have an Orgasm

With the audit at work quickly approaching my preparation had entered another phase. And with Brian hoping to become an assistant manager, I decided to bring Brian into the process. With the store practically empty, I found Brian where he could usually be found, sitting on the bench press bench furthest away from the door.

"Hey Brian, you want to help me with something?" I said loudly across the practically empty store.

Brian nodded his head in agreement and then walked towards me. Brian and I had different ways of doing things. Brian was quiet and passive. I'm not sure how I was in social situations, but when it came to running the store I was purposefully loud and demanding. The reason why was because I wanted to establish dominance over the people that worked under me. I was the alpha dog in this situation and I wanted everyone to know it.

I wondered how Brian would handle the same situations. I didn't doubt whether or not he could handle the books or any of the other tasks that came with management. What I wondered was whether or not he could handle the people management part.

"Rose, we're going to be in back if you need us," I yelled to Rose as she watched the only customer in the store leave.

"Ok," she yelled back.

"So every year I like to get as prepared as I can for the audit," I said, turning to Brian. "Part of what they'll be doing in the audit is counting inventory so that they can reconcile their books." I led Brian into the storage room.

"Wait, what does that mean?" Brian injected.

"Well, they know that they ordered 50 exercise bicycles this year for this branch. They also know that we sold 47. That means that there should be three left in inventory."

"Solve for 'x'. Gotcha."

"What?"

"You want to do a check to make sure that there are three in inventory ahead of the audit," Brian explained.

"Exactly."

"Do you do that with every item in the store?" Brian asked with concern in his voice.

"No, no, just the big ticket items. If we come up a bottle or two short of resin, then that's just marked off as a loss. Small items can go missing. And when the cost of the item is a dollar or two, no one really cares. What they care about are the benches, and the bicycles, and the hundred dollar sneakers and that stuff."

"Got it."

We entered the storage room and made our way to the last row.

"I'm going to give you these pages. Only count the items on the sheet. Put a check mark if your count matches the sheet. Put a minus sign in front of the amount of missing items and a plus mark in front of the number of extra inventory."

"I can guess why there might be some missing, but why would we have extra?" Brian asked.

"Returns that may not have been reentered into the system. Items put on layaway and never picked up. Inventory transfers from other branches that might not have been registered correctly at corporate. In those cases they will show up as missing inventory somewhere else or as an instance where register receipts don't match end of day deposits. The problem is that since there are two different shifts run by two different managers, figuring out the discrepancy is a bastard."

Brian smiles. "Yeah, I could imagine."

"But, if I can solve some of the problems before the auditors get here, this branch looks like the best run branch in the state. And I get an end of year bonus."

"Oh, managers get end of year bonuses?"

"Senior managers do."

"Oh, ok."

Brian looks over the sheet and then heads to the center of the row. I watch as he moves around the items on the shelves. 'His personality may not be made for people management but I bet that he is crazy detailed,' I think.

I checked off a few items on my list and then I took another look at Brian. He had worked his way to the far end of the shelves. I looked for an item that was near him and then I headed down.

"So how's your girl doing?" I asked, breaking the silence.

He lets out a sound that shows his frustration and then finishes off the count. "She's driving me nuts."

"Is she having a lot of cravings and stuff?" I ask.

"No, but she really wants me to get a promotion. We talk about money every day and she is always up my crawl about all the things wrong with me."

"Sounds pleasant," I add.

Brian chuckles. "I'm going to be honest with you. I like having to work late, because I don't know how much I could take her hormones."

'I knew it!' I think. "But everything's cool between you two, right?"

"Yeah, I guess. I'm just glad that you've been so cool about this whole promotion thing. Because she made me promise that if I didn't get it, I would have to get another job."

I wasn't sure how to take that. Was Brian threatening me? Was he saying that if he didn't get a promotion he would leave? "Where would you go if you left here?"

"I have a buddy that works at Disney in the grounds department. He said that there were always openings there."

"Would you want to work outside all day?" I ask.

"No, I would hate it. But their pay is better than here and they get benefits."

"Oh, ok."

"Right now my girl's all about making me into the person that she wants me to be."

"And you're ok with it?" I ask, knowing that his passive personality probably couldn't stop her if he tried.

"I don't know. I just figure it's the hormones, right?"

"No, it's not," I add, returning to my list.

"What do you mean?" he asks, completely focused on me now.

"Guys meet women and they want them to stay the same. Women meet men and imagine what they could turn them into."

Brian takes a long pause where he blankly stares at his list. "That's not bad, right? I mean, aren't the guys that succeed, the ones that have a strong woman behind them?"

"I think that it probably takes all types."

"Yeah, I guess," Brian says, returning to the shelves.

A few minutes go by before I ask what I truly wanted to ask him. "So where did you meet her anyway?"

"In a bar. My buddy from Disney and I were at Toppers and we saw her and her friends at a table. We asked them if we could join them at their table."

"Just like that, huh?" I ask, amazed at the simplicity.

"Yeah, pretty much."

"So did you guys hook up that night?" I ask casually.

"Hell no. I had to ask her out twice before she even went out with me. And even then she kept saying how she wasn't sure about me. We had to go out about five times before we had sex."

"That's a long ass time," I say, not liking what I hear.

"Yeah it is. But she's pregnant now, so I guess I win," Brian says with a smile and a knowing look.

I break out into laughter and when Brian joins me I know that he's kidding. I have to admit, that was very funny. His joke causes me to think back to when I helped Brian to realize that she might be pregnant and he covered my office with puke. That wasn't a 'oh, I'm so happy puke.' That was clearly a 'oh, did you say that you were going to ram that hot poker up the hole in my penis, puke.' In both cases the body contractions and the heaving look the same. But being the expert in body language that I am, I didn't miss the subtle differences.

In either case, he had answered the question that I needed answering. He had met his girl in a bar. Bars were hard for me. Bars were best when you were hanging with someone else and I didn't really have anyone else that I could go trolling with. I needed to meet someone new to test out my lasting longer techniques and Julia was a little expensive. And, after all, the way she struggled with my new massive size, I don't think my lasting longer was something that she wanted to explore.

During lunch I grabbed some McDonalds and ate it in my office. I knew that there was one place where I could find quick hook ups and it was just a click away. I navigate to Craigslist and click on the women seeking men section. There weren't very many women looking for men in Orlando, so I decided to respond to all of them. Most of the pictures were of girls who didn't share my love of fitness. And all the ones that described themselves as average or slender seemed to have kids. But I wasn't looking for someone to love. Someone to fuck would do just fine.

It took two weeks before the first of them ended up in my bed. Hers was the ad with the heading that read 'WF with tons of baggage looking for WM to help me dump it.' Apparently being a white male wasn't required.

During our first phone call she told me that she had kids and was in the middle of a custody battle with her ex. When I suggested a little sexual healing her response was "God yes!" After that it was just a matter of arranging between her kids' schedule and her ex's bouts of his own special brand of crazy. During dinner she told me that she didn't think that she could ever date a black guy long term so I decided to save my money on dessert. Instead we would have that extra twenty minutes for the long lasting loving that I would give her. But looking back on it, I guess we had time for coffee because I only ended up needing ten minutes.

When the brotha didn't complain about the woman after a few days, I decided to set up another date. The next one to be introduced to the brotha was a woman whose ad read 'Sick of playing this game… bout to throw in the towel… help me out.' She was clearly looking for something more than I was offering. But I considered her warned when I said that I was looking for someone that I could have good times with; then if it leads to more, even better.

I was willing to toss this fish back, but at the end of the night she asked me about my house. I offered to show her it. When I showed her the bedroom she rolled herself onto my bed. She had mentioned in her ad about how she liked to cuddle, so maybe she thought that that was what she could get. But all of that went out the window when she reached down and slipped her hand into my pants.

She was pretty young. Her ad said 21, but I wouldn't be surprised if she was only 20. She clearly didn't have much experience with sex and for the most part she just laid there. As inexperienced as she was, she took the brotha pretty well. There wasn't much easing necessary and there wasn't any hesitation once he was in.

With her I was able to try out the tongue touching technique. It didn't work. But I also pulled out before I got too close and that worked. When I was out I did a little kissing and some oral sex and then when I felt like I might lose the brotha's attention, I started up again. That technique extended our time by about thirty minutes and I considered my experiment a success.

The only problem with this girl was that I had to drop her home and she didn't want to leave. Since I knew that there was no getting her out of my bed, I invited her to stay the night. Laying there with her naked pale body on mine I couldn't help but think of Julia. I wondered what she was doing and who she was doing it with. As great as my performance was with Tanya, or at least I think that was her name, it wasn't like my time with Julia.

There was something special that happened with Julia. There was a connection that I felt with Julia. And there was a freedom that I felt with Julia that I didn't experience with these last two girls. It was almost like Julia and I were the same type of person, so there was no need to pretend to be anyone else.

It was work being with these last two girls. I had to remember to do the tongue thing and the pull out thing, and I had to worry about how she was responding to everything. Maybe that is the difference in being with someone you pay for and getting it for the cost of a dinner. But even if it is I would prefer to pay.

I figured that one thing I could do to work around my having to always monitor how the girl was doing was to try one of Cristian's other techniques. Cristian had suggested that if you waited until the girl was just about ready to blow before you started to fuck, it wouldn't matter how long you lasted because you would both come together. This was worth trying.

I couldn't get any more of the Craigslist girls to meet up under my terms, so I had to step things up and post my own ad. I tried to be as honest as I could without scaring anyone off. I mentioned I was a fun guy and that I was looking for a fun girl. I mentioned my larger size, and man did it feel good to be able to post that. I mentioned who I was open to and what I was interested in doing. I hoped that that would be enough.

After two days passed without a response, I posted it again. The first woman to respond was a woman in her forties. I would have responded to her except she was large enough that I was sure the brotha would hate me forever for bringing the two together.

The next one after that was the winner. She was an upper-forties white woman with a two baby body. She wouldn't be my pick if I had the choice, but I didn't have a choice so she was it.

Sex with her was a surprise. She wasn't a twenty-one-year-old girl who just laid there. This woman was all over the place. With both of her hands on my nipples and my cock in her mouth I felt something slide into my ass which I had to assume was her big toe. And I'm not going to lie to you, I dug it. Midway through what she was doing, I had to check for an Adam's apple but not finding one, I can say it felt good.

This woman wasn't hard to bring to the edge. I flipped her onto her back, pushed her knees to the side of her face and let my tongue do the talking. It was like her clit was a switch. I swear it only took a minute before she was ready to blow. And then when I slipped a rubber on and did a couple of pumps we both came shooting together. But I got to say her contractions were so tight that for a while I thought that she would cut the brotha in two. Afterwards she described what klegel exercises were and it made sense. Klegel exercises were PC muscle exercises for women. Apparently the exercises work.

Still, as great of a time as I had with Joan, it wasn't like Julia. First off, I felt really inexperienced next to Joan, and secondly Joan didn't make me laugh. The inexperienced part I could do something about because Cristian had a few videos on RateABull about different sexual positions. But the laughing part couldn't be changed. Joan was a nice woman, but she wore the experiences of her life on her like those shoulder pads from the 80s, a decade I'm sure she remembered well.

After two weeks where I didn't get any responses from my Craigslist ad, I considered whether it was time to stem the Rose. Rose had continued to flirt with me at work and every time she got the opportunity she suggested that I give her a call when I was bored. There was one more of Cristian's videos that I wanted to watch before I did, so the night before my day off I scheduled a little Cristian and me time.

Before Rose left work that day I asked her what she would be doing the next night. She excitedly told me that she had no plans and then I hinted that I may call. It made me feel good when I saw her become red. It told me that she really wanted me.

'Ahh, white people,' I thought, 'so easy to read.'

Hell, from how red she turned, it seemed like I could have had her right there in my office. But no, there was that video, and I wanted her to think I was a superstar.

It was a gym day so I did my usual workout, but decided to skip the steam room. I made it home a little earlier than usual, but then had to cook dinner since I was completely out of leftovers. Usually when I cooked I made a week's worth of food and then ate it until it was gone. However, this week I had been feeling a little hungry, so second dinners were necessary and enjoyed.

I had a package of chicken thighs in the fridge thawed out so I flipped through my mental rolodex of chicken recipes. Curry chicken was off the menu, because I didn't want to take the chance of sweating with Rose and smelling like an India restaurant. Orange Garlic Chicken was off as well because garlic was just as bad. I decided to stick the chicken in the broiler and then after forty minutes spread a little Sweet Ray's barbeque sauce on it. I loved that stuff and who wouldn't want to smell like Sweet Ray.

While the chicken cooked I got undressed and parked myself in front of the computer. The brotha had actually been quiet for a while. The only thing he ever said now-a-days was "Can I have a large drink?" And since he asked for so little I always got him one without argument.

Over the weeks the request for drinks got very consistent. So instead of him having to ask for it, I just made him a tumbler full of vodka cranberry, and gave it to him after dinner. The brotha had always been a heavy drinker, so I didn't worry too much about him. And if the drinks were what was keeping him from trying to control my life, I had no problem with keeping the drinks coming. Vodka was only $8 a bottle and Cranberry juice was only $4. Two bottles a week were a small price to pay for my freedom.

"Can I get my drink now," I heard the brotha say as I was getting comfortable.

I looked at the clock. It was only 8:15. I usually didn't make his drink until about 10. It was a little early for him. But again, who am I to question what works?

I got back up and prepared the drink.

"And can you ease up on the cranberry juice. I think it's watering it down."

It was interesting that he would say that, because I had made his drink exactly the same way with the exact same proportions everyday. But again, if the brotha wanted it a little stronger, then that's what he'll get.

I mix the drink and do a 50/50 mix. I sipped it to check it and it was way too strong for me. But if I put in even a dash more of juice it would pretty much be what I made before.

I walked back to the computer and propped the tumbler between the brotha's balls and the chair. I helped the brotha into the glass and navigated to RateABull.com. I scrolled down the featured video section and I found the link called: How to find the G-spot Orgasm. I looked down to make sure the brotha wasn't silently drowning and then I clicked on.

The video was above a lot of comments from other members. Most of the comments were saying how well Cristian's technique had worked, so I got excited about watching it. I scrolled back up to the video and got comfortable. Here was what the video said:

"Hello. My name is Cristian, Cris-tee-in, Cristian. And this is my vlog. The G-spot; where is it; and how to help a woman have an orgasm. Ok. You know there are benefits to being with both guys and with women. You really get a good perspective on what people like, all of them."

"What?" I paused the video.

I started the video again to make sure that I'd heard what I did. I caught a look at the brotha out of the corner of my eye and he was also up and paying attention. I leaned back in my chair and considered what I heard. Cristian, with all of his videos, had become a kind of hero to me. Because of his height and his issues I saw him as someone just like me. Now I felt a little disturbed in the comparison. How could I really take sex advice from a guy that has been with other men? That would be really gay.

Justin from work was the only gay person I knew, and I kind of liked it that way. Ok, maybe the brotha was gay too. But ever since I discovered spandex I've been able to keep that issue in my pants. But now, if I continued to watch this video I would be doing something that I didn't feel comfortable doing. I would be endorsing the behavior. I'm not sure if I was willing to do that.

"Aren't you going to watch the video?" the brotha said with an echo generated from the almost empty glass.

"What's the matter?" the brotha asked when I didn't answer.

I stared at Cristian's frozen face and looked for the gayness in it. The closer I looked the more I picked up on his lips. He kind of had gay lips. And his eyebrows, I guess they weren't exactly gay, but they were at least bi-curious. These were two features that I hadn't noticed before. But now that I saw them, they were hard to ignore. Cristian is a very good looking dude, and that on its own should have told me something.

"Aren't you going to play the video?" the brotha asked again.

"Yeah," I finally said. "I was just thinking about something.

I pushed the play button and the video continued.

"So, since I've had some insecurities in my life I have done a hell of a lot of research on what women want, what they enjoy, what works. And of course I had a chance to use it multiple times and see what does work and their responses to it. So now I'm going to share it with you so you can skip over all of those years of trying to find out for yourself, and just kind of go in there with a game plan the first time out.

First, a couple of notes. The most important sexual organ on a woman? What? The brain. Because the feeling of anticipation, feeling safe, feeling secure, feeling satisfied, they're all arousal things. The beginning of sex starts in the brain for a woman. It does in a man too but in a different way. But it's all about setup. It's all about foreplay and preparation (Cristian says with a big smile, a big gay smile).

Ahh, the largest sex organ for a woman, for a man too? The skin. The skin becomes very sensitive when aroused. Touching anywhere on the skin heightens the sexual experience.

Ok, quick, the erogenous zones, the areas that when you are aroused become extremely sensitive. What are they? There are seven of them: lips, neck, nipples, the areola area, lower back, anus, vagina and behind the knee. Those are the seven. So if ever you're looking for something to do when you're making out and you're trying to find something new, work those areas with your tongue. She will love it if you're with a girl. He will love it if you're with a guy... or however you want to match yourselves up there.

Ok, now, techniques. This is the technique that I've researched and tested and works very well. Here's what I do. Oh, and rule of thumb, twenty minutes of foreplay. You can't do that all the time. That's like ideal, but men just don't work like that. But if one night you decide it's her night and it's all going to be about her enjoyment and tomorrow's your night, this is what you should do for her night.

So you're kissing and you leave the lips. What you do is work your way down the body. From the lips to the neck, it's kissing, kissing, kissing, and then you get to the breasts. Ok, you work some time on that.

Here's what I like to do there. Caressing. You start off caressing with the hands, light massage of the breast type-of-thing. Then you go and you start kissing. Let's say you start on the right breast. You start kissing, getting closer to the areola. Then you take your tongue and you lick just outside the darker part of the areola in circles. Then you go to the other breast. You do the same thing just outside the areola.

Then what you do is go back to the first breast and work the areola, not touching the nipple, just the areola. You work the outside of the areola slowly working your way in because this is a very sensitive part. It is even more sensitive on a woman than a man. And you keep doing this without touching the nipple.

But then you go back to the left breast. And instead of using your tongue, you use your finger and slowly trace a circle just outside the areola getting wider with each pass getting further away from the nipple.

This is called the 'teasing technique' because what you are trying to do is build up anticipation and build up desire. You want her to say in her mind, why the hell aren't you working the other nipple? Touch me, goddamn it. Touch me! This is what you want, a building up of desire.

So you're working the breast with your finger and you go back to the right breast. Now what you do is start sucking on the nipple. You caress it with your tongue. You work it around with your lips. You're very gentle with it. And then again you go back to the other breast and you work outside the areola with your finger teasing away.

Then you go back to the right breast, the first breast, and you blow your hot breath over the nipple. So in essence what you're doing is you're giving one breast, one nipple, warmth. And you go to the other nipple and you blow very lightly over the top of the nipple so it feels more like a cool breeze as opposed to the warmth of the first one.

You've now worked the breast a while. So what you do is work your way down from the breast very slowly. If your hands are dry it becomes very smooth to the touch. And at about this point she should be aroused, which means that her nipples should be hardened and her other parts would be engorged as well. But this will also make her skin very sensitive. So if your fingers are dry, they will rub very softly over her body and she'll love it. And what you're simply doing is working your way back down now.

So you work your way, rubbing very lightly with the finger tips down the stomach, down the sides, and into the pubic region. The part where the leg touches the pubic area, where the hair is, is very sensitive. So you want to work your way very lightly with the fingers or kissing your way down there and spreading her legs open. And what you want to do is work your tongue outside the lips of the vagina. The lips are the parts on the outside. And I did not know this for a long, long time but when a woman becomes aroused, not only do the nipples become hard, but the lips become swollen and look more fleshy. When they're not aroused, it looks more like skin hanging there.

So when she becomes aroused, and she should be at this point, you stay away from the actual lips and you circle the whole vagina area with your tongue. Very slowly you go around the outside while not touching the lips. And you circle in moving closer and closer to the lips until now you are finally rubbing your tongue against the lips.

The clitoris is of course close to the front of a woman. It is in a slit which is closer to the front. When you are circling, you miss that and circle outwards around it. You miss that and then come back to the lips.

When a women become aroused they release a fluid to make sex easier. It should be coming out at this point so what you can do is very lightly rub your tongue across the top of the clitoris. The clitoris should be aroused and sticking out at this point, or at least not far hidden within the lips. And if it is, you can pull the lips apart a little bit or work it apart with your tongue. And what you do is rub the top of the clitoris with your tongue. You do it just once like you're licking a lollipop.

Then you back off and use your finger, or perhaps your thumb, and you rub her lips while you continue to lick her clitoris. You do it a little more and a little heavier. And as you go on you start to insert a finger into her vagina. Your middle finger is probably the best one because you have more control. Meanwhile you continue to licking her clitoris with your tongue.

Now, a lot of women don't have orgasms at all with intercourse. However, with oral sex more women do, a lot more women do because it just feels better to them. The clitoris is their penis. It is their most sensitive sexual organ. So the harder you rub on the clitoris the more enjoyable it is

As you're pushing on the clitoris working it around in circles, you are adding more and more pressure. At the same time you are inserting your finger into her vagina. And let's say she was lying on her stomach, the g-spot would be an inch to an inch and a half on the inside wall of her vagina on the part which is closest to the bed. She has to be aroused for you to find it, but what you'll find is a bean type of thing, an inch and a half in there. And there is some skin over a lot of nerves. And when you touch it, it should be very sensitive… so I'm told.

None of the women that I've been with have had a 'Oh don't touch there, it's too sensitive' reaction. Maybe I haven't worked it hard enough to get that reaction, but you don't want that reaction. You just want them to enjoy it with heightened pleasure. So you can rub lightly on it, and if there's no over-the-top response you can keep doing that. But you want to do different things, so mostly you want to work around that bean area.

And if you work that bean area while your tongue is applying a lot of pressure in circles around the clitoris, you will mostly likely get the 'writhing affect.' The writing affect is when a woman rocks her body very sharply from left to right. I've gotten that a couple of times, and it is because you are working the two most pleasurable areas of a woman's body at once. And if you do this long enough, if your neck holds out… Ladies, this gets tiring so if he stops you know why… if you do it long enough, she will have a very, very large orgasm.

Does this work? Well, I have had a woman do a 500 mile booty call for another go-round. And the great thing is that the second time, it took her about four minutes to get from first kiss to orgasm and it we didn't even get to intercourse. I was like 'wait, wait we're going to keep going right?' So, there you go, it does work.

Now here's another thing you can try, but you have to work this out. You have to judge it before you try anything like this. I was told that if a woman is close to the point of orgasm, she will get a lot of pleasure if someone inserts a lubricated finger into her anus. Why? Because it is one of those erogenous zones.

You can try it. I was told it in front of a woman. The guy turned to her and said, 'Well, have you ever had that done?' And she started blushing and said 'yeah.' He then asked if she liked it and she said 'YEAH!'

So you can try that. I've never done it. But see what happens. Have fun and explore.

But that is where the g-spot is. And that is how you help a woman, because a guy can't give a woman an orgasm, he can only help her achieve one on her own. That is how you help a woman have an orgasm.

You can thank me later for this great advice. I prefer cash. So when you're out enjoying it. And people are saying that you are so great because of it, in your mind, you can just go, 'that was Cristian. Thanks a lot man.'

That's it for now. I'm sure that I'm going to come up with something interesting for next time, so I'll talk to you later. Bye bye.

When the video went black I continued to stare at the screen with my mouth open. After a moment the only thing I could say was "He is a sex god!"

"I'd do him," the brotha added.

"That's not funny," I quickly told the brotha.

"I'd split him like a tree," the brotha continued.

"How do you split a tree?" I ask turning to the brotha.

"Instead of swinging the axe horizontally, you swing it vertically. And if you swing it hard enough you can split the tree. I would axe him like a tree."

At this point I'm sure that he's just saying these things to make me feel uncomfortable.

"I'd bang him like a tree."

"How drunk are you?"

"Really drunk," he says back without giving it a second thought.

"I was thinking about inviting Rose over tomorrow night. What do you think?"

"Oh, I like her. I'd split her like a bush."

"A rose bush?"

"I was making a pubic hair reference but if you want to go there you can."

"Well, you'll get the chance because I talked to her about it today and she was really into coming by."

"I will prune her like a bush. See now if your thumb turns green people will think that it's because of your gardening metaphors."

"Could you possibly hold off drinking tomorrow?" I ask the brotha.

"You know at night when you're sleeping I go around and play with your ass."

'Oh god! I hate him so much,' I think. "You're not going to do anything to ruin it tomorrow, are you? Because I really like her and I'm hoping that, maybe, we could have something long term."

"You want to make her your girlfriend," the brotha said tauntingly.

"Yeah maybe. You're not going to do anything to ruin it tomorrow?"

"Ben?"

I don't reply.

"Ben?"

"What?"

"Do you love me?" the brotha asks.

I hope that he doesn't see the look on my face as I lower my forehead into my hand. "Yeah I love you."

"No, I'm not going to do anything to ruin it tomorrow."

"Thanks. I really appreciate it."

"Your finger's green from sticking it in your bum hole," the brotha says with a laugh. And as he laughs, I again consider how much I truly hate him. After that, I grab dinner.

Chapter 9
Ben, the Brotha and a Rose Bush

The next morning, in spite of how drunk he was the night before, the brotha woke up early. In fact he was up before me and in my half dream state I started grinding him against the bed.

"Oh yeah," I heard muffled through all the cloth.

His voice pulled me completely away and I rolled face up.

"Hey, why did you stop? I was liking that, the brotha said through my trunks."

I didn't bother to answer. Instead I got out of bed and took a piss. As I did I remembered what getting up was like six months before. I remembered how every morning I had to dig around for the brotha and how I would worry about losing him because he had retracted so far into my body. It felt good to stick my hand in my underwear every morning and know he would be there. My new size felt good.

After the pee, the brotha spoke up again. "So are we banging the bush today?"

I still didn't feel like talking. It took me a good fifteen minutes before my brain connected to my mouth. However in the old days, if I didn't reply when he asked me a question there was usually hell to pay. This new dynamic that we had was great. But I wondered if it would hold if I continued to ignore him.

I tried to engage my mouth and failed on the first attempt. I was going to say 'that is the plan,' but it spontaneously aborted on launch.

"Am I going to give her the old in out?" the brotha asked again.

'Wow, he is talkative today,' I thought. And then it hit me. "Are you still drunk?" There I got it out. It probably shouldn't have been my first words on a day that I was counting on his cooperation, but there it was.

"No, I'm not drunk. Does a brotha have to be drunk to feel good? Can't a brotha just feel good?" the brotha said, with building anger.

It was early so I couldn't think of what I could say to calm him back down, but I didn't need to. In a moment he was again calm.

"Do you think I'm still drunk?" The brotha paused and considered. "I think I'm still drunk. You fuckin' asshole. You got me drunk."

"I didn't make you drink it."

"Yeah but you made it for me. And you want to know how I know you made it for me? I got no opposable thumbs, you poop chute. Now I'm going to be all hungover when Rose gets here!"

I paused for a second. I had no idea that he would care so much about Rose coming over. "Brotha, you never told me that you were interested in Rose."

"Well I am you fuckin' piss factory. Now I'm gonna be all weak and Rose is gonna think I'm a lame ass piss spitter that can't get hard in a block of ice."

"Wait, I don't know what that means," I say, confused.

"It means you need to get me sober and I mean now."

"You know, I could just reschedule if it means that much to you."

"No, no. It took a fuckin' year for your sorry ass to invite her over here. I'm not gonna let your appetite for pillows ruin it now."

"What does that even mean?" I ask, confused again.

"I'm trying to say that you like it up the ass and your latent homosexual feelings have been screwing me over from trying to dive head first into Rose's bush."

"Wow!" I think normally that statement would have rolled off my back. But it hits you differently after you spent a few minutes with someone's toe up your ass. And it's even more different after you admit to yourself that you liked it.

"You need to shut your drunk ass up!" I say, preparing for a fight.

"What? Listen here you granny fuckin' mother fucker, when I need your shit I'll look under your granny's toe nails. Until then you better recognize."

"Recognize what, huh? Recognize that you are probably the biggest dick that anyone could be around. Recognize that if two other dicks stood on top of each other and then swallowed another dick, they couldn't be as big of a dick as you? Is that what you want me to recognize."

"Oh, fuck no. OH-FUCK-NO!"

That is the last straw for me. This is it for the two of us. I pull down my trunks and look him straight in the eye.

"Or what?" I say with all of my anger floating on the surface. "What you gonna do? What you gonna do? Nothing. You know why? You got no opposable thumbs motha fucka."

At that point the brotha did something that I genuinely didn't expect. He somehow managed to retract himself into my body. And after what felt like a smurf swimming through my insides, he poked his head out of my ass.

"How you like me now motha fucka? How you like me now?" the brotha yelled between spits.

It is hard for me to describe what it feels like emotionally to have your own brotha poking ass-backwards out of your ass. Imagine thirty feet of rough twine, a cheese grater and a hairless puppy...

"Don't you ever underestimate me," the brotha said, interrupting my moment of thoughtful horror. "You may think you run this show, but you don't run it. I run all up in here. You hear me? I run it."

If a tree falls in the woods with its own dick sticking out of its ass, does its silent screams of horror make a sound.

"I will fuck you up motha fucka. You hear me? I will fuck..."

That's really all I heard. The next thing I knew was waking up a few hours later with my spandex boxer briefs around my ankles and a look of terror Charlie-horsed on my face. This was not how I imagined my day off going.

I look down to see if what now only existed in my memory really happened. And to my surprise, I see the brotha looking back at me.

"I think I may have crossed a line," the brotha says apologetically.

I'm too groggy to really know what's going on. That high pitched noise is still buzzing and I'm still way too scared to move any part of my body.

"But in all fairness to me, I was still drunk from a drink that you made for me. Yes, maybe I have a little problem with alcohol.

Maybe I drink a little more than I should. But I would like for you to consider what it's like being me.

Don't you think that I know that you hate me? I've known that you've hated me for a long time. I probably knew before you did. And even so, I have had to wake up each day knowing that you do.

You never touch me unless I ask you to touch me. You were so goddamned ashamed of me for so fuckin' long that I don't know how to feel good about myself anymore. And you care about me so little that you are willing to stick me in anything that moves. And then it always turns out that when there is someone that I start to feel connected to, I never see them again."

"I don't see them again because of you," I say, still lying in the same position as I was, but listening much more closely now.

"No, you got it wrong. You may blame me, but it's because of you. In the last few weeks you slept with four different women. Not one did you even bother to call back. That's not because of me. Yeah, I might have done some shitty things to you in the past. But your not-calling-them-back wasn't because of me.

The reason that we live here alone is not because of me. The fact that you never grab a beer with friends after work isn't because of me. The fact that we live in the coldest, emptiest house on earth isn't because of me. Yet you hate me as if it was. You hate me like, if it wasn't for me, your life would be perfect. Here's a little truth for ya, it wouldn't be. But yet I have to share this fucked up world that you created for us, take the blame for it and then just deal with it.

So yeah, I crossed a line. I drank too much and I crossed a line. But I want you to consider how your choices may have affected the both of us. And I want you to consider that I'm still here. I could have left. I thought about leaving. I considered leaving, but I'm still here."

I heard what the brotha had said. And the thought of it all made me feel very flush. I looked across the room at the fan to see if it's on.

"No, not the fan. Please not the fan!"

"I'm not gonna stick you in the fan. I'm just a little hot that's all."

"Oh. Because I'm gonna be honest with you. I was a little worried there," the brotha said with a toothless smile.

I take this moment of silence to move my body searching for sudden jolts of pain. When nothing comes I roll over and think about what the brotha said. He was right; he had definitely crossed a line. But a few of the other things might have been right as well. To be more precise I would have to say all of it was right.

"So, do you still think that I should invite Rose over?" I ask the brotha while staring at the bumps on the gravel-patterned ceiling.

"What do you think? You think that the three of us could still have some fun tonight? Do you think you could forgive me?" the brotha asks.

"Forgive is a little strong," I say with a smile. "But I think we could have some fun."

"You think that she might be someone that might get a second call?" the brotha asks with another smile.

"Well we work together so I won't have to call her back," I add with a chuckle.

"Right."

I sit up, slowly preparing for a pain in my ass that never comes. I then reach down to my ankles and pull up my underwear. I look over at the clock and see that it is already 3:45 pm. It's way too late for breakfast and almost too late for lunch. But I'm feeling so light-headed that I didn't care what the meal was called, I just needed something to eat.

In the kitchen I scan my options. Egg salad takes too long. Tuna salad takes too long. The only thing that requires a minimum amount of time and energy is cup-a-noodle soup. So I put a cup of water in the microwave and cook it up.

With the brotha firmly on board I was again excited about Rose coming over. And with everything that I had learned in Cristian's video, I was ready for anything that came. I was considering using Cristian's sexual technique, but that required a time commitment that I wasn't sure I liked. Even so, it might be a good introductory session. It would be a good primer that made the paint last longer.

At five o'clock I gave Rose a call. I knew that she would still be at work, but I wanted to catch her before she had to decide how she was going to spend her night.

"Hello, this is Rose," she said formally.

"Hello, this is Ben," I replied playfully.

"Hello, yes. Can you hold on a moment please?"

"Sure. Go ahead."

I had seen Rose answer personal calls before at work and this was always the way that she responded when she had a customer in front of her. I'm guessing that she thought that this response sounded more professional. And I guess she's right. It certainly beat 'Hey bitch, what's up?' so I give her credit for that.

"I'm sorry I had a customer in front of me," Rose said when she came back.

"That's ok. Has it been busy there?"

"Not really. You know, it's the same old Friday."

"Hm. So I was thinking about it. I was wondering if you would like to come over for a home cooked meal?"

"Who's cooking?" she asked playfully.

"I'm cooking! Who else do you think?" I asked, pretending to be insulted.

"Well, I don't know. You eat a lot of KFC for lunch so I figured that you didn't know how to cook."

"Are you kidding? I'm a chef de jour. I can cook like the wind. You wouldn't even know what hit you."

"You mean like food poisoning?" Rose said with a tone that made it clear that she was smiling.

"Oh see now I'm offended. Maybe I'll take back my invitation," I said, genuinely a little hurt this time.

"Oh no. No I'm just teasing you. I would love to come over," Rose said graciously. "What's your address and what time should I come by?"

I gave her the address and told her to come by at 8:30. I figured that that would be enough time for me to do some shopping, and get the meal almost done. I wanted her to see me at the stove cooking the meal because I had read that a man that cooks for a woman is considered a turn on by most women. I'm sure that she didn't need any other reason to have sex with me, but it never hurts to double down when you know you have a winning hand.

I decided to make my best recipe for Rose. It was a twice-cooked chicken that I discovered about ten years earlier when I was looking for a new way to enjoy fried chicken. What you do is season the chicken and then dip it in a flour, parmesan cheese, and seasoned salt mixture. And then you dip the chicken in an egg and honey mixture and then dip it again in the flour mixture. After that you fry it.

Although you fry the chicken at a medium low heat, you don't have to worry if it isn't completely cooked. Because once the coating has nicely browned, you take the chicken out and set it aside. When all of the chicken is done you then put a can of tomato sauce into a large pan, add onions, brown sugar, salt and pepper. After the sauce mixture has heated up, you put the fried chicken into it and cook it for 30 to 45 minutes. It's a lot of work, but the chicken is so good afterwards that it just slides off the bone.

For dessert I bought a chocolate mousse that looked really good on the box. I wasn't going to experiment with making a dessert as well. I didn't feel that I needed the seduction that came with baking. I figured that as long as the dessert was chocolate, it would take care of itself.

After I set the chicken to stew, I hopped in the shower.

"Are you feeling good, Ben?" the brotha asked me.

"Yeah I am. I'm thinkin' that she could be the one."

"The one?" the brotha asked surprised.

"Could be."

There was still a part of me that thought that the brotha was planning something. I had experienced so many years of psychological abuse from him that it wouldn't surprise me if all of this was just a long form con to get me in the perfect position to really fuck me up the ass.

But still I decided to take him at his word. I decided to take his gestures of encouragement for what they were. If I was going to believe that I could change my life, then I had to believe that the brotha was capable of changing his.

When the doorbell rang, I have to admit I had a flash of nervousness. I had opened a bottle of wine and I had the first five minutes of arrival set. When I opened the door I greeted her with a kiss on the cheek which I thought to be the perfect transitional greeting. We had barely touched each other before so that seemed more appropriate than just grabbing her boob.

I started off by showing her around my living room. I pointed out all of the pictures and gave the stories behind them. She was particularly interested in a picture that I had hanging opposite the entrance to the kitchen. It was a picture I took once on a visit to the Bahamas.

The picture was one of the three pictures in my beach series. The two on either side of it were of empty beaches with blue skies. But the picture that intrigued her was the one that I took from behind the marsh-like plants that grew above the shoreline.

I had put that picture in the center of the series because it reminded me of being in jail. It was as if there was someone trapped in a cage just a few feet from the glory of heaven. And to me it felt like a bit of cruel torture that the person looking out could watch the wonder and not be able to join in. It was the depth that I saw in the picture that made me want to feature it. But when Rose asked me about it, I simply replied "isn't it cool?" She agreed and then followed me into the kitchen.

In the kitchen I poured her a glass of white wine.

"Oh, do you have any red wine? I like red," Rose added.

"Actually, we're having chicken so I only got white. You know, red with red meat, and white with everything else."

"Oh ok. I like white too," she replied.

After a bit of work talk I directed her to sit down and the meal began. I took her plate and dished her up some white rice and then added a piece of chicken and poured a little of the sauce on the side. I did the same for me and then served it to her.

"Oh my god, it looks so good. What is it?"

"It doesn't have a name so I like to call it Chicken Ben."

"Oh my god, it tastes so good too."

"And you thought I couldn't cook," I say jokingly.

"No, no, I was just joking," she said more defensively than I had picked up on on the phone. "I was really just joking."

"I know. I'm just playing with you."

"Oh ok. Sometimes I don't know if you're playing or not," Rose said returning to the meal.

I thought about what she had just said. I had always thought that Rose and I had a playful relationship. At no point did I get the impression that she couldn't tell if I was joking. I always assumed that she just got me. 'Hmmm,' I thought.

The meal was a real success and although she said she was full I still got her to try the dessert. I knew that I shouldn't force food on her, but I really wanted her to experience all of what I had planned for her.

"And with dessert I have something special." I go to the fridge and pull out a bottle of something that I had been saving. "Have you ever had plum wine?"

"No," Rose replied curiously.

"I tried it once at my mother's place and then had to go and get a bottle. But I never had a good reason to drink it. I think that this night is special enough," I said with as much charm as possible.

"Oh, you're so sweet. But I don't know how much more I can eat."

I have to admit, this disappointed me. I looked down at the bottle and then considered putting it back. I know that she was full, but this was my special moment. This was the experience that I was waiting for to enjoy this thing that was special to me. But if she couldn't enjoy it too, what was the point?

"I mean I could have a little, I guess," Rose said breaking my thoughts about the bottle.

I looked up at Rose and wondered if I should share it with Rose. But after only a moment I knew that I had to at that point. There was something a little awkward about the dinner, and I didn't need to make it any more awkward by acting like a little bitch.

I forced a smile and poured two glasses of wine. After I took a sip I remembered how sweet and filling the wine was. And when I watched Rose take a sip I knew that that was all she was going to take.

After a bite of the dessert she declared herself too full to eat another bite. So while our food digested she asked me about the house. I told her the story about how I found it and bought it and she listened intently. As I looked over into her eyes I could see a little something extra looking back. There was contentment about her. She was more than just full, she was ready. So when I told her the story about how I had decided on one of the bowling ball beds from the commercials, she asked to know more.

"You know, it's one of those beds from the commercial where the couple puts a glass of wine on the bed and then drops the bowling ball."

"I don't know that commercial," Rose said.

"Yeah, it's supposed to keep the glass from spilling when the ball drops."

"Then let's go test it out," Rose added while grabbing her glass of wine.

'I guess the wine was put to good use after all,' I thought.

I lead her back to the bedroom and once in, I looked back at Rose and she was bright red. 'Ah, white people,' I thought. Rose climbed onto the bed and placed her glass on the bed in front of her.

"Ok, jump on the bed."

I stood on the bed bounced around a little. Each time I did the glass tipped over completely disproving the commercial.

"Maybe it isn't a bowling ball bed," I admitted, confused.

"Maybe it's bowling ball defective," Rose added.

"Yeah."

There was something erotic about me standing on the bed looking down at Rose, who lay at my feet. I felt very dominant over her. And when I looked into her eyes I could see that the look in her eyes, the tilt of her neck, the position of her shoulders and the openness of her hips all screamed 'take me'.

As I got on top of her she relaxed onto her back. Her head was tilted back waiting for a kiss so I gave her one. While I kissed her I put one hand on her breast and she rested her hands gently on my side.

I wasn't a big fan of how she held me. She held me like she wasn't really there. She held me like she felt obligated to touch me while I did what I did. That didn't turn me on.

I then kissed my way to her ear and as I did, I slid my hand down her side. It was disappointing to me when I found her leg lying flatly on the bed. The image that it put in my head was that I was making out with a mannequin or a really lifelike sex doll.

At that point I decided to use Cristian's sexual technique. I figured that that would turn her on. And once I found that switch she would jump on me like a cat.

I moved from her ear to her neck. And then after I pulled off her shirt and bra I moved from her neck to her breasts. Like Cristian said I pleasured one and then teased the other. I looked up at her face a couple of time and watched as she relaxed with her eyes closed and a smile on her face.

After about ten minutes I kissed my way down her flat twenty-year-old tummy to the button on her jeans. I unbuttoned, unzipped and slipped her pants off. I stuck my tongue under the waistline of her panties for a moment before trying to fit my face into them and pulling them off with my hands.

I was surprised to find that Rose was completely shaved. I found it very appealing. And without a word or a touch the still Rose spread her legs giving me easy access to her swollen pussy.

I continued to kiss and circle and please as Cristian suggested and when I finally slipped my finger into her, the finger slid right in. With varying degrees of pressure I lapped on her clit. It wasn't much bigger than a breast nipple but it was hard and ready to go.

I searched around a little bit for Rose's g-spot. She was clearly aroused so I knew that it would be there. And then when I found a rough patch on Rose's upper vaginal wall, I knew I found it. It was about two inches in, just as Cristian had said. And it was not until I started lightly rubbing that spot that she began to shift her head from the left to the right.

Finding the right spot I pushed down even harder with my tongue. She lifted her arms above her head and arched her back. She continued to rock her head when the little groans started. She was having an orgasm and when she finally clamped her thighs around my face all I could do was stop. She locked my face there for a second and in that moment I realized that I couldn't breathe. My nose and mouth were full of her flesh and I just counted the seconds until she let go.

When she relaxed she returned to her pre-orgasmic position. In fact, it was like nothing had happened at all. I began to slip my finger out of her when her pussy took a death grip on it. Within the grip I could feel her throbbing. Her pussy was making what seemed like involuntary contractions and in between those throbs was when I inched my finger further and further out.

With it out I moved my finger to her clit. But as soon as I touched it her hand came flying over to push it away. I moved my finger back knowing that I was going to have to get off in some way but she immediately pushed it off again.

I reached under the bed where I kept a condom and slipped it over the brotha. I then climbed up the bed until the brotha was in line with her pussy. I reached down and slid the brotha into her pussy. Her warm throbbing pussy felt good.

After a few strokes she reached down her hand and stopped my motion. I gave it a few seconds and then started up again. This time she grabbed me around the waist and held me very tightly. The grip was so tight that I couldn't move my hips. Clearly she was trying to stop me from fucking her and finally I got the picture.

I lay there hard inside of her for the next five minutes. Every so often I would flex the brotha just to see if he was still hard and she tightened her pussy in response. It was amazing how willing the brotha was to stay with it. After ten minutes it was still the same. The brotha was still hard and Rose's pussy was still flexing in response. Out of all of the things that had happened that night, Rose's pussy flexing in response to mine was the best. It made me feel like I was with someone instead of a lifeless doll.

As I lay there my mind went to Julia. I wondered what she was doing that night. Was she having sex with someone else? Was she also thinking of me? Julia might have allowed me to have sex with her for money, but there was something about the time that I spent with Julia. It felt more real than this entire night. With Julia our conversation was flowing and deep. And what was more, Julia got me. Her eyes were compassionate and she got me.

Julia was the last thing I thought about before Rose spoke.

"Why don't you have a girlfriend?" Rose asked.

I thought about all of the possible reasons why and then I felt the brotha shrink his way out of Rose.

"Bye," Rose said in response.

"I guess I haven't found the right person," was my response.

I wondered if Rose understood what I was saying. I had never found the right person and I still hadn't. Rose was great. She was cool and had a hot little body. But there was something missing from my experience with her. It was something I hadn't even experienced until my time with Julia. But now that I had, there was no going back.

When I saw that Rose had no intention in leaving, I rolled over and spooned her. That was the position that we had when she fell asleep. Afterwards I quietly got up, had a piss and jacked off in the bathroom. It wasn't a great night, but it was the night that I had wanted. The only question was how I was going to handle it tomorrow.

As quietly as I got out, I climbed back into bed. I got comfortable on the other side when I felt Rose roll over and spoon me. I guess I had woken her up. 'Oh well,' I thought. 'I hope she can get back to sleep.' After that I was out.

Chapter 10
Escorts Need Love Too

Before I opened my eyes the next morning I remembered that Rose was next to me. The thought didn't make me feel any better or worse than any other morning. When I finally did open my eyes, I looked directly into the face of Rose, who was looking back at me.

"Good morning," Rose said with a fully awake voice. "I didn't want to wake you up."

"Morning," I replied, trying to shake the rattles out of my voice.

"I had fun last night," Rose offered up.

I didn't reply. Instead I closed my eyes again and saw how close I was to going back asleep.

"You awake?" Rose continued.

"Yeah," I replied, knowing that I had gotten all the sleep I was going to get.

"I have to go get ready for work," Rose said, trying to get me to wake up.

"Ok," I said, trying to pull my thoughts together. I opened my eyes to find out if she was suggesting a morning sex session. But when she didn't make a move I knew that she just wanted to go.

I rolled onto my back for a moment to clear my head and then I rolled back towards Rose. She was still naked. I loved finding naked women in my bed the next morning. It always felt like the night before and the morning after were two separate experiences. And when I saw the naked woman from the night before in the light of day, it was like seeing a completely different naked body.

I liked Rose's breasts. They were the most perfect size B/C's that you could ever see. She had small areolas, which I also liked. And her skin was flawless. I remembered why I wanted so much to slide inside of her. Unfortunately it was everything that led up to sliding in her that was a disappointment. And now lying naked with her after a night of awkward sex, I didn't have anything to say to her.

"Did you have fun last night?" Rose finally asked, breaking the silence.

"I had fun," I replied as I reached out and gently squeezed her breast.

"I want to do it again. Do you?" Rose asked.

"Yeah."

I leaned over Rose to kiss her and I could feel the brotha reaching over as well.

Rose pushed me back and said "No, I mean soon. I don't have time. I have to go to work."

"I'm the boss, I'll let you be late."

"No, Ben. I have to go."

I again rolled onto my back and this time I looked down and saw that the brotha had pitched a tent. 'Great, now I'm going to have to jack off again,' I think.

Rose slips out from under the sheets and sits on the edge of the bed. I look at her pale naked back. It is so perfect looking that I have to reach out and touch it. I like touching Rose's body so I pull myself closer, slide my hand around her and cradle her breast. I like holding her breast in my hand so I pull myself even closer and kiss her back.

As if I wasn't even there she slips on her panties. When she stands I fall away from her back and onto the bed. She doesn't face me again until she is completely dressed. She is still very cute dressed but I liked her better naked.

"Are you going to walk me out?"

I slide the sheets off of me and I can feel that the brotha is still up. I see as Rose checks out the brotha.

"Just in case I needed to go again," I say. Rose doesn't respond.

I get out of bed. Still naked and erect I walk her to the front door. I unlock the door and let her out. Before she leaves she throws her arms around my shoulders and kisses me.

"I really had a great time," she says.

"Me too," I say back, feeling obligated to respond.

"Good," she says with a smile before leaving.

With the door closed behind her I look down at the brotha. "Did you have a good time?"

"At what?" the brotha asks. "I didn't do anything."

"Just be happy because I did a lot and it didn't make it any better."

When I arrived at work everything was as it usually was. Rose looked at me smiling, Brian sat on the store window sill staring, and Chip was in his usual place trying to catch a nap.

"Good morning," Rose said without any indication of what happened the night before.

"Morning," I replied in kind.

As I unlocked the door and turned on the lights I could feel Brian staring at me. I thought that Rose might have told him about her plans the day before so I decided to ignore him. As I walked back to the office I looked back at Brian and when he saw me looking he quickly turned his attention to the weight benches. And as I entered my office I notice as Brian straightened up the already straightened equipment.

"Hey," Rose says to me in a way that reminds me of a cat. Her voice even had the same tone as a meow.

"Hey. Did you tell Brian that you were coming by my place yesterday?"

"No, why?"

"No, he's just looking at me kind of strange."

"No, I would prefer to keep what we do between us. So when do you want to do it again?"

I look at Rose's sweet round face and blue highlighted hair and fall silent. The truth is that I didn't know what to say. What I have decided is that we have work chemistry. It's a surface level chemistry that doesn't go much deeper than that. It was clear last night. But on the other hand she has a smokin' hot body, so there's that.

"Soon," I say, remembering what she had said to me earlier.

"Ok," she says with surprising acceptance.

By this point I have retrieved the till and I hand it to her. Looking down at the till, Rose smiles and walks out. I really thought that Rose would be hurt or offended by my suggestion of 'soon.' But apparently I had nothing to worry about.

Moments after Rose left there was another knock on the door.

"Come in."

Brian pokes his head in.

"Do you have a moment?"

"Sure man, come in," I say. Brian sits and I ask him, "So, what's up?"

"I was wondering if you found out anything about my promotion?" Brian asks, looking very nervous.

"No, not yet. I have made the formal request and they are evaluating."

"Do you know when they might get back to you?" Brian asks.

"Honestly, I'm not sure. This is about parting with their money, so I imagine that they're not going to rush it. But don't worry, I made a great case for you so it shouldn't be a problem."

"Umm, ok. But here's the thing. Remember I was telling you about the grounds keeping job at Disney?"

"Yeah, you said that you would hate it," I said, reminding him.

"Yeah, I probably will. But I applied for the job a few months ago and they got back to me yesterday. My girl really wanted me to take it so I did."

"I thought you were going to wait for the assistant manager position here?"

"I was, and I really wanted to take it, but even with the promotion I would still be making less here and with the baby coming I need to make all of the money I can."

"No, I can understand that." I let the thought flow through me for a second. As strange as it sounds I kind of considered Brian to be my best friend. Certainly things had changed once his girl got pregnant, but before that I thought that we had a good flow at work. Now with him going I felt kind of lost.

"I don't know what to say, man."

"I don't want to leave. It's just the money."

"No, I get it. You need more money. I understand. So how long can you give us here?"

"Is it cool if I leave at the end of the week? Disney wants me to start on Monday."

"Well today's Thursday. You have Friday off and all that's left is Saturday."

"Yeah."

I feel the need to rub my face with my hand. The warmth of my hand comforts me. "You know what? Take Saturday off as well. I'll pay you for it. Consider it a paid personal day. I'm sure that you have a few things that you need to do before you start your new job."

"Seriously?" Brian asked, not sounding excited about the offer.

"Yeah man. You've been putting in a lot of overtime and extra work. It's not a problem. We don't live to work, we work to live. Enjoy the time."

"Ok, thanks."

"Yeah," I say, still rubbing my face. There's a pause so I ask "is there anything else."

"No, that's it," he says a little quieter than normal.

"Ok," I respond back.

Brian then gets up, and steps outside. "Do you want me to close it?" Brian asks.

"Please."

After the door closes I sit for a second. When I think he has walked far enough away I get up and lock the door. I then sit back down and think about how ridiculous it would be if I cried. I then spin my chair to face the wall, put my face in my hands and my elbows on my knees. And once the thought of Brian leaving hits me again I begin to sob. And when I say sob, I don't mean that tears rolled down my face. I mean that my body shook and snot rolled out of my nose.

'This is ridiculous,' I thought to myself as the feeling started to pass. 'All I did was think about Brian leaving.' And as the thought came back I lost control again. I don't know why I did. I couldn't explain it if I tried. All I know was that Brian was leaving and again I was going to be alone. It's a crazy thought because Brian and I barely hung out together after work. But there it was. He was leaving and I was a pussy. There was no other way of explaining it.

I didn't have a reason to leave my office until lunch. And all I did then was make a beeline to the door with a quick "I'm going to lunch" to Rose. When I came back in an hour I said even less. Finally it was six o'clock and Rose came in and delivered the till to me. She wasn't going to say anything to me so I spoke to her.

"You know it's Brian's last day today?"

"Yeah, he told me," she replied, offering nothing else.

"Ok," I said before turning to balance the receipts.

Rose left without another word and a few minutes later Brian peeked in.

"Hey" he said, breaking my concentration.

"Oh, hey man," I said getting up. "So are you looking forward to the new life you're gonna have?"

"No," Brian said abruptly with a knowing smile. "But you know, I just wanted to thank you for everything. I really liked working here. And you were great to work with. You really made things…" Brian looked around for the word, "fun."

"Thanks man. I tried." I let the silence develop in the room before I spoke again. "So am I going to see you around?"

"Definitely. We should grab a drink or something."

"Yeah, it sounds cool."

"Ok then. My ride's here so I have to go."

"Ok. Good luck man."

"Thanks." And then Brian left.

After that I quickly finished up with the receipts and I was gone. Mercifully it was a gym day and although I knew my workout would suck, it was better than going home. Although after a few sets I learned that it wasn't much better than going home. I couldn't complete my full reps of any exercise. And even the steam room felt unfulfilling. I think I transferred from the steam room to the cold shower more than I had any other time. But in spite of the effort, I couldn't feel the rush I usually got.

When I got home the place felt emptier than usual. I immediately turned on the TV when I stepped in the door and warmed up some leftovers. But even as I ate I couldn't stop thinking about where else I could be. And after more thought I remembered the bar in the Grand Hotel.

The Grand Hotel was the largest hotel near the Orlando airport. Because of Disney it was always full and just past the lobby was a restaurant bar. The bar stayed open until two and everyone in Orlando knew that if you were looking to hook up with a tired traveler, this was the bar to go to. So I shaved, got dressed up and headed out.

Whenever I went on vacation, hotels felt like a wonderful place, but visiting the hotels around Orlando always made me feel a bit uncomfortable. It always felt like there was something artificial about the experience. And as I walked through the lobby I couldn't help but think that everyone there knew what I was after. But at this point, I couldn't really get myself up for caring.

The restaurant was a large room. When it was full, it must have taken seven waiters to service it. But now, after ten, I would be surprised if there were more than two. From what I was told they stopped selling food at eleven, but the bar got hopping just before that.

When I walked in, the bar was still pretty empty. There were only a few people sitting at the bar, and all of them were men. As I made my way to the bar I recognized one of the guys. I wasn't sure so I headed over and the way he leaned over the bar confirmed it for me.

"Chip?"

Chip turned around and an uncomfortable moment followed.

"Hey Ben. You hang out here?" Chip said awkwardly.

"I figured that I would give it a try. Do you mind if I sit down?" I say, sliding onto the bar chair.

"No, go ahead."

I looked at his drink and noticed that it was almost empty. "Do you want another one?"

Chip looked down at his glass. "Sure man."

"Can I get a vodka cranberry and whatever he's drinking," I say to the bartender. "So did you hear that today was Brian's last day?"

"Yeah, I heard."

"You think you can handle the section by yourself for a while?" I ask, making conversation.

"I'll try, but there's only one of me."

"Understood."

An awkward silence follows and I am relieved when the drinks arrive. I give the bartender my debit card and then he goes away. Looking for something to say, I think back to him and Jasmine. I start thinking about what it must be like for a pimp. And before I realize it I ask.

"So I know why you're always so tired when you get to work. I know what you do at night."

"Yeah?" Chip asks with a look of fear covering his face.

I leaned into Chip. "Yeah, you're a…"

"You don't have to say it. I know what I am. Are you gonna fire me?"

"No. You are on time every morning. You get along fine with everyone, and you do your job without question. So as long as that world doesn't interfere with our world then we don't have a problem. Cool?"

Chip looks at me with an amazing amount of gratitude. "Yeah, it's cool. That's very cool of you man."

"No problem man." I think for a second and then I have to know more. "So when did you start?"

Chip looks back at the bartender who is out of earshot and then leans in a little closer to me. "When I was nineteen."

"Really?" I ask very surprised.

"Yeah, I was with this guy and he kind of introduced me to the idea. We were together for a while and then he asked me if I wanted to make some money."

It was odd the way he used the word 'together.' He almost made it sound like they were dating. But he was Puerto Rican so English wasn't his first language. The incorrect usage of words had to be allowed.

"In the beginning he would set things up for me and then he would take a cut. And then after a while I ditched him and worked for myself."

I was having a very hard time following this conversation. 'Why would a pimp have a pimp?' I thought. 'Am I missing something?' "So how did you find your first girl?"

"My first girl? In a bar. She was an older lady that was hanging around me. But mostly I see guys."

'Oh my god, he's a male escort.' The thought freezes me in my tracks. 'Oh my god, he fucks guys for money!' I can't stop thinking.

"You ok, man?" Chip asks me.

But I can't answer. I'm too busy reinterpreting every conversation that we ever had. 'Wait, he started at nineteen? What the fuck? He has sex with guys for money! What the fuck!'

"You knew that I was into guys too, right?" Chip asked, confused.

"Yeah man. How could I not."

"I didn't realize I was that obvious," Chip said, looking down at his drink.

"No, it's not that you're obvious. I just had a feeling that's all. Wait, so are you saying that you won the Justin bet?"

"Yeah, I won it," Chip says with a smile.

'Fuck! This is just getting worse and worse!' "Well, you know that the bet is void if you don't have proof?"

"I know."

'Damn that was close,' I think. "So is that what you were doing here tonight? Waiting for someone?"

"Yeah. The bartender is ok with it as long as he gets a cut."

I look up at the bartender. "Seriously? I wouldn't have thought."

"Yeah, I'm sure there are a lot of things that you wouldn't have thought," Chip says with a smile.

"I guess so." A silence develops between us again. "You're 26 right?"

"Yeah."

"So you've been doing this for seven years?" I ask.

"Yeah."

"Then why did you start working at the store?"

"Things slowed down for me. I'm an old man now. No one wants to be with an old man," Chip said with more heart than I had ever seen him display.

"Twenty-six is old?"

"It is in what I do. When I was twenty I used to make five grand a week sometimes."

"Seriously?"

"Yeah."

"That's a hard way to make your money though."

"It's ok."

"I don't get it. What do you do when the guy is fat and hairy?"

"I charge them more," Chip said with refreshed bravado.

"But you could go through with it?" I ask.

"Yeah, it's money you know. But most people are pretty cool. I like to get to know them a little, you know. It makes me feel good."

"You ever had a girlfriend?" I ask.

"Yeah."

"What happened?"

"She was supposed to be out of town and she came back early. She had a key to my place and she came in and found a bunch of gay porn around. So she left."

"Have you had a girlfriend since?"

"No. Girlfriends are hard doing what I do."

Although there was a part of me that really didn't want to know, there was the other part that really had to ask. "Any boyfriends?"

"A few. But they all wanted me to stop doing what I was doing so it didn't last."

"So why didn't you just stop."

"The money man. And I enjoyed it. It's like an addiction sometimes. I need to cum three times a day sometimes. And I just like having someone there, you know. Sometimes when I leave one person, I'm thinking about who else I can find on the drive home. You know what I mean?"

"I don't, man," I say coldly. But the truth was that I did. I didn't know what it was like to be him or to be gay or whatever he was. But there was something about the way that he described driving home and needing more that felt very familiar to me.

A long silence developed between the two of us where I finished one drink and ordered another. I no longer felt uncomfortable sitting next to Chip. In fact, it was starting to feel nice. I thought about what I was going to say next before I said it.

"Ya know, I wasn't completely honest with you about the woman you set me up with."

"No?" Chip says without much emotion.

"No."

"Then what happened?"

"I called her up like I told you and she said that she didn't see black guys."

"Yeah, I'm sorry about that, man."

"That's cool. But I told you that she didn't give me a reference when she did."

"Yeah?"

"Yeah. And I called her and we met up."

"How was it?" Chip asked genuinely interested.

"It was really nice." I looked up at Chip and Chip looked down at his drink. "It was so nice that I wondered if she really liked me." Chip doesn't respond. "Do you think that's possible? Did you ever develop feelings for anyone that you were with?"

"I don't know man. That's deep." A moment goes by where it looks like Chip is lost in thought. "Yeah. Yeah, I did."

"What happened?" I ask softly.

"She was about twenty-eight. She was married. She had two kids. And I couldn't help it. As soon as I met her I fell in love. But she had two kids, ya know. We saw each other a couple of times and then she never called me again. The rule is that you don't fall in love with your clients. And I try to stick to it. But sometimes you're only human, ya know."

"So what do you do when you feel something for someone and you're working?"

"I block it out. I try and numb myself. It's only sometimes when it slips out and you don't see it coming when it's a problem. But you cope, ya know."

"Yeah, I know. Ya cope."

Another silence develops between the two of us until Chip breaks it.

"You should call her. What does she call herself?"

"Oh right, it's probably not her real name. The name she told me was Julia."

"No, I don't know her. But if you think that you felt something with her, you should call her. Feeling stuff is hard. And if you felt something with her, you should definitely call."

"You think so?" I asked, unsure of what I wanted him to say.

"Yeah. Call."

Chip shoots back the last of his drink and then gets up. "I'm gonna go. I'm not into this shit tonight."

"Heading home?" I ask as I watch a restlessness overtake Chip.

"Somethin' like that." Chip turns around and heads out. "I'll see you tomorrow."

I sit at the bar a while longer until I have the courage to take my phone out. I had saved her number to my address book under the name Julia Mass. The 'Mass' was for massage. Thinking more about it, I decided that this wasn't the place to call Julia, so unlike Chip I close out my bar tab and head home.

Without turning on many lights I head to my bedroom. I lie down on the bed face up and talk to the brotha.

"I know that you really liked Rose."

"I did."

"I really liked Julia."

"Julia is a whore."

"I know. But when I was with her I felt accepted. I felt like I could tell her anything."

"That's what you were paying her for."

"I know. But would you mind if I found out for sure?"

"I think you should call," the brotha says. "And thanks for asking."

I pull out my phone and look at Julia Mass's number again. I take a moment to think of what I will say and I call. When I hear the third ring I think that it's going to voicemail, but at the last second Julia answers. No one says hello on the other end so I do.

"Hello?" I say a little confused.

"Hello," Julia says back, in a tone that says that she expects me to start talking.

"Hi Julia, this is Ben. I don't know if you remember me, but I'm a very tall, black guy. We met up a few weeks back."

"Sure I remember you. How are you?" she asks, really sounding like she remembers me.

"I'm good. How are you?" I ask in reply as if on instinct.

"I'm good," she replies. "What are you looking for tonight?"

This was a good question. It was to the point.

"Actually, I was thinking about the time we had, and I really liked it."

"Oh, I liked it too."

"But I mean I really liked it. I have been with a number of women and I never had as great of a time as I had with you." Julia doesn't reply. "And here's the thing, I would like to go out on a date with you. If you would prefer to keep our relationship professional then I'm okay with that. But I want to get to know you and I would like to spend time with you on a non-professional basis."

Julia remains quiet on the other end of the phone. And at that moment I start to think about how many other guys must have called her asking to spend time with her for free. And suddenly I feel very foolish.

"I'm only asking because during the time we spent together I felt like we had a connection. And I don't usually feel like that. If you didn't feel the same then that's fine. But I did. And because I did I would like to see if there could be more between us."

I listen to the silence a little while longer. "Are you still there?" I ask.

"I don't know. I tried dating someone without charging them and they got very demanding and tried to get me to quit what I was doing and stuff."

I thought about what she said and I could understand how that could happen. Dating someone that was also with other guys would be very hard. And for the first time I considered what it would be like. I didn't know if I could do it.

"Are you still there?" Julia asked.

"No, I'm here. I'm just listening to what you're saying. I could see how that could happen. That must have sucked for you. How about this, no matter what, I promise to accept you for who you are. And no matter what you say, I promise not to freak out. I just felt like we had some type of connection. I felt that for that brief moment you got me and accepted me. So I would never pay you back by for accepting me by not accepting you.

I know this must be a strange call. But I've been thinking about you. When something happens to me, I wonder what you are doing at the same moment. And I want to know more about who you are. I just want to get to know you."

There is another little pause before she says, "you do huh?"

"Yeah, but only if you do too. I only want to get to know you if you want to know me too."

I stop talking and the line goes quiet again. At this point I start to wonder what I am getting myself into. I start to think about Rose and the way I left it with her. I even think about Brian and his girl. Everything else seemed easier than what I was trying to do with Julia.

I then remember what Chip had said. Chip had implied that Julia wasn't even her real name. "Is Julia your real name?" I ask.

"No dear," she replies back in a way that makes me feel foolish for thinking that it might have been.

"So what is it?"

"How about this, I need $200 to pay my phone bill. You give me the money for that, pick me up, take me out for dinner, we have a few laughs, and then you take me home safe and sound. And if you are a gentleman, then when you leave I will give you my real name and number."

"Oh, do you have another number that your friends call you on?" I asked, really not understanding the way it worked.

"Yes dear," she says in a way that gives me the impression that she is laughing at me.

The line goes quiet again as I considered her offer. I didn't want to become her sugar daddy. At the same time this is what she was offering. If I said no, then I don't think we would have anything else to say to each other.

"I'm serious," Julia said, taking her turn at breaking the silence.

"I know." Another moment goes by before I respond. "Ok. When did you want to get together?"

"Did you want to meet tomorrow?" Julia, or whatever her real name is, asks.

"Yeah, let's do it tomorrow. Should I pick you up at 8:30?"

"Yeah, that's good. Do you remember where I am?" she asks.

"I do." I consider what I have agreed to do and in spite of the fact that it will really dip into my savings I decide that this was one of the things in life that was worth the expense. "I'm looking forward to it."

"Ok," she says back. "Call me tomorrow, before you come."

"Why, you want the option to change your mind?" I say kiddingly.

"No dear," she says in a way that makes me feel like I'm talking to a hooker.

"You can call me Ben."

"Ok, Ben. I just want to make sure that you're still coming."

"You think I'm gonna crap out on you?" I say with a smile.

"Well, you sound like you could be a little full of crap, so I don't know," she says with a smile back.

With that I start to remember why I liked her to begin with. "No, no," I say. "Here is a good way to tell if I'm talking crap."

"Your lips move," she says, interrupting me.

"No. I was going to say…"

"You're awake?" she injects again.

"No."

"You're horny?"

"A little bit, but let me tell you how you could know I'm talking crap."

"I wasn't asking you if you were horny," whatever her name is says.

"Oh, I thought you were turned on by what I was saying and you were trying to get in my pants again," I say as an obvious joke.

"Hmm, I can see that you're gonna be trouble. I don't know if I want to go out with you if you're going to be trouble," she says flirtatiously.

"Nope, it's too late now. You already agreed. You can't take it back," I say.

Julia laughs.

"Besides, if you canceled on me now, you would break my heart in two," I say in the same joking tone.

"Break it in two, huh?"

"Snap it in two," I say, still joking.

"Ok, I guess I don't want to do that… yet," she says with a smile in her voice.

"Oh see, now I see that you're trouble. You're the one that's trouble."

"Maybe I am," she says with obvious flirtation in her voice. "Call me tomorrow."

"Ok, bye."

"Bye now."

I hang up the phone and roll over.

"That sounded like it went well," the brotha said from down below.

"Yeah it did."

"Are you glad you called?" the brotha asked.

"I think I am. Do you think I'm doing the right thing?" I ask the brotha.

"You just asked a hooker out on a date. What could possibly go wrong there?" the brotha says without humor. "And what are you going to do about Rose?"

"Hmmm," I say, considering everything that had happened that day. "I'll think of something."

"Yeah, because you know how much women like being fucked by you," the brotha says with a chuckle.

"Don't be an asshole."

"I'm a dick. Get it right."

I roll over and smile.

Chapter 11
How Big is Too Big?

When I arrived at work the next day all of the things that were the same were now different. Brian wasn't sitting on the window sill waiting. Rose was not trying to catch my gaze to give me her usual smile. And Chip wasn't sitting in the corner trying to get his last few minutes of sleep.

Instead Chip was now sitting in the window sill and he seemed not to be able to stop looking at me. It was odd how in one day my entire world had changed. It was disturbing. The one thing that always told me that I was living my life, was its consistency. And now a whole lot of it was different.

I unlocked the door and instead of Chip heading for the back, he strolled over to his section and started straightening the benches. When Rose walked through the door it seemed that she didn't know what to do with herself. First she walked around the clothing section waiting for me to reach behind the counter to turn on the lights. And once I headed back to my office she went behind the counter and started moving the key chains and bottle openers around.

I continued on my usual routine and headed back into the office. I grabbed the till and counted out the money from the safe. When the hour hit and Rose still didn't come in to collect it, I took the till out to her. The only thing I could think to say when I gave it to her was "Here you go." And she replied with "Thanks." That was all she said to me all day.

Chip on the other hand was different. While the entire day would often go by without talking to him, he came looking for me today.

"Come in," I replied to his knocking.
"Hey, can I come in?" he asked.
"Sure," I replied, wondering what he would want to talk about.

Without having to ask he closed the door behind him and then sat down in front of me.

"Did you call?" Chip asked.

I started to wonder whether or not I would regret talking to him about Julia. Chip represented an overlap between work and my personal life that I didn't like. You would think that that would have happened when I stuck the brotha into Rose, but I didn't feel that was the case. No, what I had spoken to Chip about felt much more personal to me than anything that had happened with Rose. And here he was about to pick at it like any itchy scab.

"Yeah, I called," I replied in a cautious way.

"How'd it go?"

I considered whether or not I should tell him. But in the end I decided that he could be helpful to me because he knew things about Julia's world that I could never understand on my own.

"I think it went well. She asked me to pay her to go to dinner with me, but she said that if I was a gentleman afterwards she would give me her real name and number."

"That's good," he said.

"Is it? Because I wasn't sure."

"Yeah, as long as she gives you her real name and number. Did you tell her that you didn't want to see her as a client?"

"Yeah."

"And what did she say?"

"She didn't say much, actually. She was quiet a lot in the beginning. But then after a little while she came up with this deal."

"I can tell you this. I've been doing this a long time. And I have met a lot of people that wanted to date me for free. And you always consider it. I might decide not to, but it's because I don't like them enough. And when I don't want to date them I always try to keep them as a client so I try to make things as clear as I can while not trying to insult them.

So what I usually say is that I like the way things are now. Or I just say that I don't like to date my clients."

"How do they respond?"

"Sometimes I see them again. Sometimes they get pissed. It's different. But she offered to give you everything. That's good."

"Yeah as long as I pay her for it," I add with a smile.

"You don't get it. It's money," Chip said without further explanation.

"Meaning what?"

"Money is everything. How much you can charge for your time matters when you do this. I used to charge $300 an hour when I was younger. Now I have to charge $150. And it hurt, man. I almost couldn't take it."

"Why did you lower your price?" I asked, confused.

"Because no one was willing to pay my fee anymore and I didn't have any other options. That's when I applied here. It wasn't until I started working here that I felt better about lowering my price. I don't think that you should look at it like she is charging you to go out with her."

"How should I look at it then?"

Chip thought for a moment. "Think of it like you're telling her how much you like her. If you wanted to impress a girl, wouldn't you take her to a nice restaurant and spend a lot of money on her?"

"Maybe."

"Well it's the same thing. This business is funny, man. You know exactly how much you're worth at every moment. It's tough."

"It's tough if you don't like what the price is."

"Yeah, it's fucked up," Chip said, sliding back in the chair.

I looked at Chip shrinking in front of me, and it is like I am seeing him for the first time. I never realized how small Chip was until that very moment. Chip was pretty thin. It wasn't that he was boney, but that he lacked muscle tone. Chip had a narrow face and a relatively small body frame. Chip was a kid really, not so much in age or experience, but in something that I couldn't explain.

Talking to Chip was like talking to an eight-year-old buddy that had experienced way more than an eight-year-old should. But the funny part about it was that I liked it. And for the first time since I met Chip, I liked him. Sitting across from me, Chip seemed more like a normal guy than he ever had before.

When he first started working here I thought of him as one of those lazy Puerto Ricans. Then I thought of him as a sexual stud. After that he was a dirty pimp and hooker. But now he was a guy that wasn't very different than me. In fact, there was a part of me that wanted to protect his innocence. That's kind of funny if you think about it, but it was true.

"Have you ever considered quitting all together?" I ask.

"Yeah, a lot. But it's not like I have a lot of skills. I was glad to get this job."

He was right. I remember seeing his resume for the first time. There was almost nothing on it. I only hired him because he presented himself well. Something told me that he was not going to cause problems, and quietly do what he was asked. And I was right. That is exactly the person that I got. But I considered myself to be a good judge of character as it relates to work. Other people wouldn't have looked at him so favorably.

"I should get back to the floor."

"Yeah ok. We have a shipment of benches coming in tomorrow. Do you want me to bring in someone to build the benches or can you handle it if I cover the floor?"

"Whatever you want."

"Ok. I'll let you know tomorrow."

"Cool."

As Chip got up to leave there was a knock on the door. Looking at me for approval Chip opened the door. Rose stuck her head in and with an annoyed tone to her voice said "There's someone asking questions about one of the machines. Is there anyone working in there today?"

"Yeah, I was just heading out."

Chip passed by Rose and neither of them looked at each other. Afterwards Rose shot me a look that I couldn't interrupt, but told me that she wasn't happy. As I looked back at Rose I knew I should have had something to say, but I couldn't figure out what. So instead I stared at her as she looked back at me.

This continued until she simply turned and closed the door behind her. Rose was a situation that I was going to have to address. And as soon as I figured out how, I was going to do it. Until then I turned my attention to my date with Julia and everything that could follow.

At the end of the day Rose dropped off the till and left without a word. But where as she would usually be gone by the time I left, when I went to the parking lot I saw Rose and Chip engaged in what could almost be described as a heated discussion. I wasn't even aware that they spoke outside of work, so this seemed strange to me.

As I passed by, I heard Chip say "good luck tonight." I looked back at him and he was offering a genuine smile. I wished that he hadn't said it in front of Rose, but I knew the wish was genuine so I let it pass. Having driven to work this morning I looked at the two of them again as I drove away. The discussion seemed a little more intimate than I expected. It wasn't like they were touching each other. But there was something about it that seemed personal.

I also looked to see if Rose had reacted to Chip's good luck wish. It was tough to tell, but I think that she had. Maybe it was in the way she stood or the look on her face. I couldn't tell exactly how, but if I had to guess I would say that Rose knew that the luck had to do with another woman.

'I have to deal with this whole Rose thing,' I thought. 'But it's not going to be today.'

It was a gym day, but I decided to skip the gym so that I could prepare for tonight. It wasn't like I had to get a haircut or anything. But Chip had made me understand that this was going to be my opportunity to impress Julia. And if that was the case, I had to spend some time thinking about where I was going to take her. All day I was thinking that I was going to take her to the Grand Hotel restaurant bar. But just as I was leaving for the day I remembered that that was where Chip did business and the same could have been true for her. Taking her there on our date might be a little awkward.

Once I hopped online at home I found another place that was both close and nice. Carib was a Caribbean restaurant that looked fun, nicer. It maybe wasn't as impressive as the Grand Hotel's restaurant, but unlike there I was sure that she would like the food. And besides, since she was from somewhere in the Caribbean, I figured that it would show that I was paying attention when she told me about herself.

I was a little nervous when I called her to let her know I was about to leave to pick her up. I want to say that she was surprised that I was actually coming, but I don't know if that would be the best way of describing her reaction. Afterwards I looked down at the brotha and said, "are you up for this?"

"I'm up for anything," was his reply. And it made me feel good that he was so gung-ho about it.

My nervousness only increased when I arrived at her place. I didn't know if I should go up to her door or wait for her in the car.

But I remembered the building's buzzing system so either way I had to call her to let her know I was here.

Just as she picked up the phone I considered that I should have brought something. But then I realized that I had. I'd brought $200. And that looked better than flowers or a bottle of wine.

"Hello?" Julia answered the phone.

"Hi, should I come up?" I ask.

"I'm sorry who is this?" she asked as if she wasn't expecting anyone.

This takes me back for a second, and for that second I'm not sure how to reply.

"Ummm…"

"I'm just kidding Ben. Come on, you have to loosen up if you want to be with me."

"No, I knew you were joking, I just couldn't think of what to say."

The truth was that I didn't know she was joking. I was kind of planning my retreat.

"Should I come up?" I asked, trying to move on from that embarrassing moment.

"No, I'll come down."

"Ok, I'm out front."

When she stepped out of her building I was very relieved. Because even though I would have gone out with her no matter what, I didn't remember what she looked like dressed. I was a little concerned that she would dress like a prostitute. But no, she was wearing a one piece dress that came down to mid-thigh. It wasn't loud or slutty. It was hot, and showed off her body very well.

As she stood on the doorstep scanning the cars, I remembered just how beautiful she was. This is a woman that could have any guy she wanted, and the thought of that made me stop for a second.

'I'm just fooling myself,' I thought. 'This is a woman that would only be with a rich man. I can't afford a woman like this.'

But even with those thoughts I couldn't stop myself from getting out of the car and waving to her.

'Well, if this is the only date I was going to get with her, I may as well have fun,' I decided. 'And I'm gonna do this up old school.'

She smiles at me and heads over when she sees me waving. I then cross around and open her car door. She gets in and I close the door behind her. When I get in I put both hands on the steering wheel and then turn to look at her.

"Hello, person whose name I don't know," I say.

She laughs.

"Hello," she says with a smile.

"Do you mind if I tell you that when I saw you standing up there, I thought you were so beautiful that I almost didn't get out of the car?"

She laughs again, but this time I think it's from embarrassment. "Why wouldn't you get out of the car? All you have to do is stick your hands in your pockets. That's what you guys do, right."

I start to blush as much as a black man can blush. "No, not because of that. But by the way…" I then point up and down her body with my finger. "All of that, smokin'."

She laughs again.

"No, it's because I thought, 'why would someone as beautiful as that be interested in someone like me?'"

"Well, I'll tell you at the end of the night if you're lucky. But you're doing really well so far."

I probably should have said something in reply, but I couldn't get myself to speak. I just turned, started the car and pulled off. This is a little embarrassing to admit but as we drove to the restaurant my heart was racing. I was nervous. I started to reconsider my brand of deodorant and my choice to only wear one layer of shirts.

'Two layers of shirts,' I thought. 'My tee-shirt that said 'Kiss my Momma' would have been perfect. Why didn't I go with 'Kiss my Momma?'

As the silence grew I realized that I had to speak. I knew that I didn't want to ask her about work. And work was always my first question. Without it I couldn't lead into my work and all of the other topics that I knew very well.

What that meant was that I was going to have to think on my feet. Thinking on my feet was never one of my strengths. Of course, neither was thinking in bed. I would like to say that I was more of a man of action, but most people didn't consider jackin' the brotha off in the shower in the morning much of an action.

"Hey, I have a question for you," I said, thinking of something to say at last.

"Ok."

"When you're spear fishing and you corner a fish. And you're looking into the fish's beady little eyes. Do you have a catch phrase that you say before you pull the trigger?"

Whatever her name is laughs again.

"There are so many things wrong with what you just asked. First off fish have big round eyes not beady little ones. There is no trigger on a Hawaiian sling, which is what I used. And third, everyone knows that when spear fishing the phrase you use is 'Say hello to my little friend.'"

When she made the Scarface reference, I was sure that I creamed my pants a little. I was so sure that later in the trip, when she looked out the side window, I checked the brotha for wetness.

I smile back at her and stay composed. "Well, I'm trying to figure out if you're a woman that likes the classics or if you like to mix it up a bit. But no, I see that you're a little old school. That's cool."

"No, I'm a classic girl," she says with a smile.

I look at her and smile back, but there was clearly more to that statement than I understood. I think she was trying to tell me something, but hell if I knew what it was. Oh, well. It was probably important.

When we got to the restaurant she told me that she had been there before and had liked it. It felt good when she complimented me. Later on after we ordered we started discussing our families. Or more accurately, I asked her about her family and then dodged the question when she asked it back.

But it seemed that I didn't trick her. In fact, I saw her face distort when I used my usual dodging technique.

"No, tell me about your family," she said.

I can't say whether it was because of who I spent most of my time with, but I didn't talk about my family much. But to be fair, the brotha had heard most of it first hand, so there wasn't much to add. So when I finally thought about talking about my family, I didn't know where to begin.

"I don't know where my father is," I said.

"What happened?" she asked, seeming genuinely concerned.

"A couple days after my sister turned eighteen, he left and I never heard from him again."

"Do you know where he went?"

"I think he came to Orlando."

"So is that why you came here?"

"No, the fact that I'm here is a coincidence. My friend wanted to move here. I just came with him."

"Do you still live with your friend?"

"No, he moved back to Beloit a few years ago."

"But you stayed?" she annoyingly pointed out. With that statement I started to wonder how much I really liked her.

"Yeah, because I had a job that I didn't want to leave. What, are you trying to get rid of me already?" I said trying to change the topic.

"No, I'm just interested," she said gently.

When I saw how genuine she was being, I decided to play along. "My father stopped acting like a father when I turned about fifteen years old. I mean, he was there, but he may as well have not been. I would go into his TV room and say 'dad' and he wouldn't even turn around. So when he finally left, it really wasn't that big of a change."

"And still you followed him here?"

"I told you I didn't follow him here. My friend wanted to come here."

"And you stayed while your friend went back."

"Yes."

I looked into Julia's eyes and considered ending the date right then. I was clearly not the type of guy that she would ever be with, and she was starting to be more trouble than she was worth. So I was taken back with what she said next.

"When I was fifteen, my mother left my father. Before she left I thought my mother and I were close. But she moved in with the guy she was seeing and then I barely ever saw her again. When she first moved out she told me that I could move in with her, but at the last minute my father said I couldn't. I hated him for a long time after that.

Two years later I tried to move in with my mother again, but this time she said I couldn't. And the way she said it made me think that it was her idea the first time too. I figured that my father had done something to cause her to say that to me. I lived with him, but I hated him. I just hated him for so long."

I got the feeling from this that she was trying to relate it to my story in some way, but I didn't see it.

"Is that when you took up spear fishing? So that you could have your revenge; you could release some of your anger?"

"Yeah, with every fish I imagine my father's face and then I aim for between the eyes," she said with a straight face.

I wasn't sure if she was joking or not, but either way the image was disturbing. I started to see her as Lora Croft in a wet suit, but not in the sexy fem-bot way. It was more like the 'my nipples are hard because I spend my day killing men' way.

We talked less once the meal came. I had the Nassau Grouper, and she had the stew conch. After that we both had dessert and then the night was over. I drove her back to her place in silence. I have to admit that I was feeling a lot of sadness about the fact that I would never see her again. She really was a very interesting, fun, sexy woman. But it was because she was very interesting, fun and sexy that I knew that this was it. This is fuckin' hard to admit, but I knew that I wasn't man enough for her.

All of those things that makes a man a man, I was not. I didn't have a lot of money. I liked my job, but I knew it wasn't the type of job that women liked. All I had was the brotha, and up until recently he wasn't very impressive either. The statement was a tough one, but a real one. I just wasn't good enough. She could never love me.

When I parked in front of her building I wasn't sure what came next. I imagined that I would pay her and she would either give me or not give me her name and number. But when I reached for my wallet she stopped me.

"Not here," she said. "Come up with me."

'I can understand that,' I thought. 'She doesn't want to give her neighbors any hint about what she does.'

When she didn't make a move for the door, I realized that she wanted me to open the door for her.

"Hold on, don't move," I said to her as I rushed out my door.

I opened the door for her and she climbed out with a smile.

"Thank you."

I followed her to her door and then up the elevator to her apartment. I had been drunk the last time I was there so now being sober I somehow expected the hallways to look different. They didn't.

I got to the door and she signaled for me to follow her in. Exchanging money is always a very tricky thing. Handing money to someone made it feel like you were paying for something. But putting money somewhere for someone to find always felt more like a thank you. And expressing thanks never felt wrong.

"I'm going to the bathroom. I'll be right back," she said before stepping out for a minute.

I took that opportunity to place the money on her counter, the same place I had before. And when she came out I watched her eyes to see if she saw it. And when I never saw her look down I pointed. She neither acknowledged my pointing nor followed my finger.

"Would you like a glass of wine?" she asked.

With the business part of our evening done, I thought about the wine. "Sure, I'd love a glass."

"My father stocked me up on wine the last time he came to visit me," she said.

"Is he a collector?" I asked.

She laughed. "No, he got me a lot of liquors as well. He just got me wine because he knew that I liked wine."

She poured out two glasses, handed me one and led me to her bedroom. When she sat on the bed, I wondered what she was doing. This felt a whole lot like she wanted to sleep with me, but I remembered very well that she said that she would give me her information only if I was a gentleman. I had thought that that meant that I couldn't have sex with her. But I guess that there were only two options in her place for sitting, the dining room table and the bed. And this one was nicer.

"So, was there something that you wanted to know?" she asked me with a smile on her face.

"Are you going to tell me?" I ask, trying to get my mind back into a playful mindset.

"Maybe if you asked nicely."

'Nicely? What does nicely mean?' I thought.

I decided that no matter what I did, this wasn't going to work out. So, yes there was something that I wanted to know, and it wasn't her name and number.

"You're asking me what I want to know?" I said moving in a little closer to her. "I want to know…" My words drifted off as I leaned in to kiss her. At first her lips were rigid. It was almost like I could hear her scream 'how dare you' in her mind.

But within a second her lips loosened and when my hand held the small of her back, her body let go. I felt as her mouth opened slightly inviting my tongue to enter it. It felt warm inside her mouth and our two tongues twisted and touched each other. When the juices filled my mouth I tilted my head up to swallow. I had thought this would be the end of it but using her lips, she tilted my head back down and her mouth opened again.

The brotha was up and listening everything that was going on. And as he pulled at my pants I reached down to adjust him. She must have thought that I was reaching for her pussy because she quickly lifted her hands and rested them on my chest. I don't know if that was supposed to block my access to her, but what it felt like was that I was holding a delicate little girl in my hands. And in response the little girl was shyly resisting.

I closed my mouth and she did the same. I then started to pull away before heading back in for a few more kisses on the lips. Then with the last one I completely pulled away and opened my eyes.

The woman that I was looking at seemed so innocent. And in spite of my leaning back she didn't remove her hands from my chest. I focused on her hands to judge the pressure. They weren't pushing me away. They were just placed there. And as I thought about it again, her touching my chest felt good.

"You…" her first attempt at speaking was interrupted by something in her thought. If I didn't know better I would have thought that she was fighting back tears. However, that would have been ridiculous.

"Did you want to know something else?" she said before losing her voice at the end.

'Was there something else that I wanted to know?' I thought. 'Yes, I decided. I wanted to know what it felt like to make love to her like I loved her. That is really what I wanted to know.'

And when I looked down into her eyes, I couldn't help to see what she must have looked like as an eight-year-old child. Her eyes were so wide, and bright and shiny. And I couldn't tell, but maybe there was a little fear in them. I didn't have the time or energy to figure out what that was all about. So instead I looked down into those childlike eyes and replied.

"Yes, there is something else that I want to know."

But as I leaned in to kiss her, she leaned back. And at the pace that I was moving I didn't catch up to her lips until she had her back on the bed. And then once I did, she was trapped. She was now the delicate little girl that I had trapped on the bed between my two arms and there was nothing she could do about it.

I kissed her again, and she kissed me back. I reached up and held one of her breasts. She arched her back to push it deeper into my hand. That's when I became sure that she wanted me. She wanted me to be there. She wanted me to kiss her. And she wanted me to make love to her.

I let go her breast and then slid my hands down her side. When I found the bottom of her dress, it had ridden up to an inch below her panty line.

'That's what she was doing in the bathroom,' I thought. 'She was putting on panties. She definitely didn't have a panty line under that dress before. Wow,' I thought. 'She had decided that her dress was coming off by the time she entered the apartment.'

The thought of her sexual assertiveness excited the brotha even more. And I suddenly found her thigh warmer to touch. I slipped my hand under the folds in her dress and felt the flesh of her almost bare hips. I loved it. I felt like that barely bare flesh was mine to do with what I liked. And what I liked was to free them even more.

I put both of my hands onto the sides of her dress and she lifted her hips to help me slide it off. I pulled the dress the length of her body and I was surprised to realize that even though she had put on panties, she hadn't put on a bra.

'Man, I like this girl,' I thought, trying to contain myself.

To extend the experience I move my lips down to her beautiful 'C's'. I use my tongue to trace around the edge of her areola. And with my free hand I held her other bare breast.

After a few minutes of moving from one nipple to the other I kiss my way down to her underwear. I grip either side of her tiny panties and her hip raises to also allow these to slip off. Once her underwear is off I see that her pussy lips are already swollen and there is moisture developing where the pussy walls touch. And when I use my tongue to dig through her flesh to find her clit, her juices are very tangy to taste.

It doesn't take much manipulation with my tongue before she starts to moan. And when her shoulders start rocking from one side to another I decide that she is ready to be entered.

"Do you have a condom?" I ask from down below.

Without a word she quickly reaches into her nightstand and pulls one out. I kiss back up her body as I reach for it and line the brotha up with her pussy. I rip it open and slide the condom on. I then press the brotha on the opening of her pussy and her hands go flying down to guide his way in.

She uses one hand to grip the brotha and another to hold back my stomach so I can't push in too quickly. Feeling her hands there, I release some of my strength and allow the brotha's pushing against her pussy wall to hold me up. And when I do this the brotha enters with a pop. She almost slides her way up the bed trying to make sure that I didn't go in too far.

I go to push in again, and again she slides up the bed. I then rest my free hand on the bed just above her shoulder trying to prevent her from moving further. And once I have her locked there, I push again. This time she squeals, but not with pleasure, but with discomfort.

Her pussy is tight around the brotha. It is almost tight enough to be uncomfortable. But even with that tightness I push in even further.

"Oww," she says.

I look up at her and wonder why she is reacting with pain. This is what she does. There is no way that my size could be giving her problems. Even Rose, as small as she was, didn't have a problem with my size. I decided that she was pretending to make me feel better so I play along.

I get a little more aggressive with her and she stops making a sound. Instead a painful look covers her face. Her game is turning me on so all I could do is push a few more times before I am ready for the brotha to spit up. I consider whether I should pull out and extend the experience. But I decided that it would be better for her if I stopped.

I give a moan to let her know that I'm close, and she echoes a moan back telling me that she's ready. I speed up the pumps and she grips tighter onto the brotha with her hands. Her face turns red. When I cum, I close my eyes and feel the throbbing of the brotha inside of her. And as soon as my pulses slow down she slides up on the bed again pulling the brotha out of her.

Looking down into her face I see something that I didn't expect to see, relief. This confuses me. But continuing to play along I lie next to her and hold her head in my hand. She doesn't move. She lays there like a child. And I comfort her like a man.

We lay in silence for what feels like a long while. I knew that she would want me to go, but I didn't know how long I should stay.

"Are you ok?" I ask.

"Yeah," she replies back.

"What's the biggest guy you ever had?" I ask, looking for some type of explanation for her reaction.

"About nine, I think."

"Really?" I ask more confused than I was before.

"Yeah, I haven't had sex in a while."

"Have you had sex since me?" I ask.

"No. I usually don't have sex. I'm kind of small."

"Then how did you take the nine?" I ask, curious.

"It hurt a lot. That's why I like to give massages. I was only with you that time because I liked you so much. You're really big."

"I'm not that big," I say, a little embarrassed that I had to admit it.

"You're bigger than most guys I've seen, and I've seen a few."

It made me feel good, when she said that. It felt good to feel big. It felt good to feel that I was almost too big for her. But what didn't feel good was the amount of restrictions she gave me when fucking her.

"You really know how to work your tongue," she said. "I liked that."

"Yeah?" I said, hoping that she would say the same thing about my dick. But she never said it.

"Did you still want to know my name?" she asked softly.

"What's your name?" I asked as if she had never prompted me.

"It's Kelly."

"Nice to meet you Kelly. I'm Ben," I say before falling silent for a while.

I again wondered how long she was going to allow me to lie there. I felt very comfortable next to her. In fact, I think that I could've fallen asleep holding her if she let me. But I knew I couldn't. Kelly was an expensive girl. Her time was expensive. Her tastes were expensive. And I wasn't enough of a man for her. So instead of wondering when she was going to ask me to leave, I sat up to leave.

Kelly got up with me when I did. Unlike when she led me to the bed her movements were now unsure. The beautiful creature sat wide-eyed further from me on the bed than she had been all night. There was almost a sadness in her eyes. I didn't know where that sadness was coming from, but I imagined that it had something to do with me.

'She regrets me being here,' I thought. 'She regrets this whole thing.'

I got dressed. And as I reached for my shirt, Kelly finally got off the bed and headed to the bathroom. When she came back, she was wearing a pair of tight sweatpants and she was putting on a t-shirt.

Fully dressed I stared at the beautiful creature in front of me. I loved standing with her. I loved talking to her and I didn't want this night to end.

"What?" she said looking back at me.

I thought about telling her how beautiful she was. I thought about saying how great of a time I had. But neither of those things came out.

"I miss my dad," instead came out.

"What we just did reminded you of your dad?" she said with the first sign of a laugh that I had heard from this new girl, Kelly.

"No. I don't know why I said that. It just came out. I was actually thinking about something else."

"I miss my dad," she repeats with a laugh. "That a new one. At least you didn't say that you missed your mom, otherwise I would have been really worried."

I laugh back and then finally see why my comment made Kelly laugh.

"Right. What, you don't like my pillow talk. That doesn't turn you on?"

We both laugh.

"Ooo, spank me daddy," she says mockingly back.

Once the laughter stops and we are again silent I think about leaving.

"So, can I see you again?" I ask.

"Do you want to see me again?" she asked in a way that sounded like a serious question.

With her playfulness gone I started to wonder if we were back to the business part of the night.

"I had a great time. I would love to see you in a non-professional way," I say.

"Let me give you my other number and why don't you give me a call and we'll see," she said with a smile.

She turned around and wrote it down on a piece of paper and handed it to me. I took it from her in such a way that my finger tips brushed lightly across the back of her hand. I can tell she felt it because she got still when I touched her.

"Did you really have a problem with my size?" I asked her, trying to figure out if I was going to call her again.

In that moment the face of her eight-year-old came back. She softly nodded her head yes in reply. "But usually I can do things and it doesn't hurt as much."

"It hurt?" I asked surprised to hear her use that word.

"A little."

I thought back to how her face twisted when I was fucking her. If I took what she was displaying as real, that wasn't the face of someone experiencing a little pain. She was experiencing a lot.

This was a surprising turn of events. The last thing that I expected from the prostitute that I had twice paid to have sex with was for her to not be able to take my new size. I especially didn't expect this because all of the other girls that I fucked in between my time with Kelly hadn't had a problem at all. There was a part of me that continued to wonder if she was just trying to make me feel good.

"I'll be ready for you the next time though," she added, breaking another silence.

"I hope so," I said. I don't know why I said it. It was just another one of those things that slipped out.

I walked over to the door with her right behind me. I turn one more time before I leave and I kiss Kelly on the lips.

'Wouldn't it be something if she cried after I left. What would that mean?' I thought. I don't know why I thought that. The only thing I can guess would be the strange look Kelly had in her eyes.

I leave her place and walk to the car wondering if I should see her again. By the time I got to the car I still hadn't decided. When I arrived home, the thought still hadn't ended. And when I got into bed I hadn't made any further progress.

'How was it possible that she could find my size too big?' It didn't seem possible. 'And if she did find me too big, how could I be with her? And should I even think about being with her considering how poorly I measured up to her?'

None of these questions were answered by the time I fell asleep. All I knew was that I had spent the night with the most perfect woman for me and still there were things that kept me away; that thought kept me quiet. And surprisingly, the brotha didn't have anything to say either.

'I miss my dad,' I thought again. 'Why am I thinking about him now?' I wondered as I drifted off to sleep.

Chapter 12
Why You Shouldn't Screw a Rose Bush

When I woke up the next day, the brotha was quiet as usual. It had been a while since we had had our latest blow up, but ever since then things had been good between us. At least things felt good between us. He was a tricky dick. The last time things seemed good it ended with him sticking head first out of my ass.

But now with all of his silence, I wanted to hear what he had to say. I didn't think that I would ever encourage him to speak up, but here I was. So in the shower I spoke up.

"So what did you think of last night?" I asked.

"That was one tight pussy," the brotha said before anything else. "I thought that I fell asleep and you had put me into some type of sausage press. It was like you were trying to peel back my skin or something."

"Seriously, it was that bad?" I asked, not knowing if he was serious.

"It was tight. And not in the 'goddamn, I got myself a tight one, tight.' It was more like the 'holy crap, I can't feel my balls,' tight."

"So you didn't like her?" I ask the brotha, a little disappointed.

"Well, she seemed cool except for her vice grip pussy."

"Yeah, she seemed cool," I said, not knowing what else to say.

I returned to the business of showering before the brotha spoke up again.

"Did you like her?" the brotha asked me.

I thought for a moment. "Goddamn, killer gram!" I said when the realization finally took hold. "Yeah, I did. She was so fuckin' cool! And I don't know what it is about her, but fuck."

"So are you gonna call her?" the brotha asked.

"For what though? So she could fuck with my head? I can't take care of her. I can't support her. Fuck, I can't even please her."

"She seemed to be pretty pleased when you had your tongue stuck up her hole."

"Yeah, but…" I stopped there because the thought was almost too fucked up to say aloud.

"What?" the brotha asked.

"It doesn't matter."

"No, what were you gonna to say; that if I didn't convince you to make me bigger you would be fine now?"

I didn't reply. That wasn't what I was going to say, but it was close.

"I just can't stop fuckin' up your life, can I?" the brotha said, without another word.

"I was there too so it wasn't just you," I said under my breath.

This was a tough thought. In his video Cristian had talked about how women had different sized vaginas. But after everything that you see on TV and movies, it's hard to believe anything other than 'bigger is better.' And I guess if there are guys with very small penises, there must also be women with very small vaginas. I guess it makes sense; I just never thought that I would meet any of them.

Of course, if that was the only thing that I had to worry about, that would be one thing. But if I wanted to be with Kelly, I would have to find a way to make more money. If I could make the brotha bigger, there had to be a way to increase the size of my bank account.

I decided to drive into work, and pulling in I could see that the new normal had been established. Chip was now the one waiting on the window sill and Rose was the one looking away as I approached.

"Morning," Chip said, more awake than anytime I'd seen him.

"Morning," I said back. I then looked over at Rose and what I caught looked more like a sneer at my exchange with Chip.

Today when I opened the door, Rose made her way into the storage area. I figured that I would have to deliver the till to her. But when it was ready Rose knocked on the door.

"Is it ready?" Rose asked.

"Here you go."

I knew that I should have said more. After the moment passed I realized that that would have been the time to talk to her. I still wasn't sure what I would say, but anything was better than nothing.

The problem was that I didn't know if what I had with Kelly was going anywhere, so I wanted to not completely end the possibility of Rose and me. Ok, I realize that keeping Rose in my back pocket might be a little unfair to Rose, but I would think that the alternative was even more unfair.

This is what I was thinking about when Susan from the corporate office gave me a call. Susan was the overweight forty-year-old woman who handled budget approvals. It was her that I spoke to about the assistant manager position for Brian.

"We are going to approve your request," Susan said.

"That's great. One problem. Brian's last day is today." His last day was actually a few days ago, but this was the severance I had approved for him as a departing gift.

"Well, isn't that a kick in the rear?" Susan said with a smile in her voice. "Well, you have approval for an assistant manager. So if you want to hire someone into that position you can."

"Would it be a problem if I promoted from within and then hired an entry level person?"

"If you have someone else, then go ahead. We trust you here," Susan said with another smile.

It always felt good that I had the trust of corporate. Maybe there was a way to move up here and make this the new job that Kelly would respect.

When I got off the phone with Susan I called Chip into my office.

"How did it go last night?" was the first thing that Chip asked.

"It's hard to tell. I had a good time, and she seemed to have a good time."

"Did she give you her real name and stuff?"

"Yeah, but I don't know. There are a few more problems than I first thought."

"Like what?" Chip asked with a look of real concern on his face.

"She's an expensive woman. I don't think I could afford her."

"Oh, she still wants you to pay?" Chip asked, disappointed.

"No, I mean in general. She seems like the type of woman that cares about how much you make."

"Oh, that's too bad."

My chest hurt a little when Chip gave me his sympathy. Until Chip said it, it didn't feel real. But his quick understanding of my situation told me that it wasn't all in my head. It told me that I probably wouldn't be able to be the man that she wanted. I have to admit that the idea hurt a little.

"Well, that's the way it goes sometimes, I guess. But that's not really why I called you in here."

Chip sat up in his chair a little more. "Ok, what's up?"

"Remember when you told me that you would give up your side job if you got a more secure opportunity here?"

"I guess," Chip said with a little hesitation.

"Were you serious?"

"Yeah, why?" he asked, confused.

"Here's the thing. Before Brian left he had asked to be made an assistant manager. Corporate just told me that they approved the position but he's gone. I now have to fill that position. I can hire someone from the outside or hire from within. I think that you would have the skills to do the job, but I'm not sure if you would act like you wanted it. Do you know what I mean?"

"You mean like smile a lot and stuff?"

"No. I mean, not arriving to work sleepy, not sleeping in the storage room before work, not sleeping with the other employees. I'm basically hoping that you leave your other life behind and focus on this new one."

"Oh."

"Now, what you do on your own time, is your business. But what I'm giving you is a chance to start a new life if you want it."

Chip didn't speak. He just sat there. Within the silent minute that would pass, he sometimes looked at me, and sometimes looked away. Part of the time was spent looking down, and the rest looking up. I hadn't expected this to be such a hard decision for him. And after the minute of silence passed I was the first one to speak.

"What are you thinking?"

"Have you ever, and you probably haven't, but have you ever been sitting home alone watching TV. And something comes on, it doesn't have to be sexual, it could be like a commercial with a dad watching his kid play football or something. And after it comes on, you get a really strong desire to have sex?

Wait, that sounds weird. That sounds like I have a thing for kids or something. I don't. But still, for whatever reason you just have to have sex."

"I'm not sure," I say.

"I do. And I get that a lot. Except just having sex doesn't satisfy it. The only thing that makes it go away is when someone pays me for sex. You know what I mean? Of course you don't know what I mean. But you know what I mean?"

"So you're thinking that you won't be able to stop having sex for money?" I ask, confused.

"What if I can't? Because I've tried before, and it's too strong. I can't."

"Like I said, I can't stop you from doing anything that you do on your own time. But if I offered you the position, it would be so that you can stop. I think that you can do the job, but so can a lot of people. I would be doing it to help you do something that I thought you wanted."

"I do want it. I just don't know if I can stop. Sometimes I'm just sitting at home and everything feels completely normal. And I don't know what happens, but all I know is that I just need it. I just fuckin' need it. Maybe I'm possessed by the devil, ya know," he said with a nervous laugh.

Listening to Chip, I began to realize that I was biting off more than I could chew when offering to help him. But still, even with this latest bit of information I still couldn't help but see him as a sweet guy. For months he silently walked into the shop, took his naps and did his work.

So now it amazed me just how deep and open he was. Chip was a complete human being. He wasn't just a guy that worked in retail, or just a male escort. He had dreams, and problems, and hopes, and fears just like the rest of us. And unlike many of us, Chip was sweet, whatever that meant.

"If I slipped one night, would you fire me?"

"I wouldn't fire you for something you did on your free time. But if I offered you the position, I want your word that you would make a real effort. And not just a half-assed thing, I mean, I would want you to do everything you could to succeed. Could you do that?"

"I'm scared man," Chip said with a smile.

"Now, there's a lot that comes with the job, and you will have to learn a lot. Are you up for that?"

"Yeah, yeah, I'm up for that," Chip says with a smile.

"Are you excited?" I ask.

"Yeah, I'm excited."

If I had known everything that I now knew, I don't know if I would have offered him the job. But it was out there and there was no taking it back now. "Ok, then congratulations Mr. Assistant Manager."

Chip shook my hand excitedly, and in spite of my second thoughts it felt good to see him so happy.

"I'm thinking that the position would start officially on Monday, and that is when I'll start to train you."

"Thank you, Ben. I'm nervous," he says with a smile.

"You're excited," I said correcting him.

"Right."

"Ok, that's it. I'll talk to you later."

What followed over the next week was surprising to say the least. You never know when you're standing in quicksand until you're ankle deep. And by that point the ground isn't firm enough to shift your weight and pull your feet out.

I don't know where the turning point was. Every time I think of one event that seems to have set it all into motion, I remember another that set that into motion and then the thought starts all over again. One thing I do know is that once Chip left my office, I called corporate and told them who I had chosen. I don't think that there was anything inflammatory there.

The next thing I knew Rose came into my office and she was mad. Hopping mad.

"You made Chip an assistant manager?" she yelled.

"Yeah. Why?" I asked, very confused by her reaction.

"Oh, this is great. It wasn't enough that you fucked with my head once, you had to promote Chip as well? Fuckin' great!" Rose barked back not lowering her voice at all.

I had never heard Rose curse before. I knew that she was capable of it, but she had always been in a great mood whenever I saw her. Even when she talked about the guy that gave her VD, there was still a lightness about her. But man, now I kind of wish I had given her VD. Maybe she wouldn't be making such a scene at work.

"You want to close the door?" I said calmly.

Rose closes the door behind her and then makes up for it by yelling louder. "Why are you such an asshole?" Rose yelled.

"Woah! Where did this come from?" I ask, confused as hell.

"You're such a fuckin' asshole! You're such a fuckin' asshole!" she kept saying. And when she started crying I began to believe that this had something to do with me. Perhaps it had to do with us sleeping together and then me not bringing it up for the last couple of days. And if that was the case, I think I could see why she might be upset.

That being the case I felt like I should say something about it, but I wondered if there might be an easier time in the future to bring it up. She was already crying. Our conversation probably wouldn't have gone well.

"Do you need to take the rest of the day off?" I asked, hoping that she would stop crying.

"Do I need to take the rest of the day off?" she yelled back. And there was something about the way that she yelled it that told me that that wasn't the right thing to say.

"I quit, you fuckin' asshole. Do you want to talk about that? I quit."

She then turned around and slammed my office door behind her. By the time I recovered enough from her yelling, I only saw her backside leaving the store. She always had a really sweet backside and I remembered how much better it looked naked.

Rose left the store without ever looking back. She walked straight to her car and didn't even look back to reverse. She grazed an older woman and her son, but they were both alright so I guess there was no harm done.

Walking to the front of the store to watch as she drove away I couldn't help but think about how I was of two minds about this. On one hand, I was down two employees in a week, both of whom I really liked. On the other hand, I would never have to say to her, 'no, it's not you, it's me.' And that relief has to account for something. If only it were that clean.

Chip approached me at the front door and told me that he had told her.

"I didn't know that she would freak out like that. I thought she would be happy or something," Chip said.

"You know what, I didn't see it coming either."

"I think I know why she freaked though," Chip said.

I looked at Chip and my heart hurt. One of the only good things about Rose telling me off and storming out was that no one would have to know that we slept together. Clearly it wasn't my best decision. "Really, why do you think?"

Chip just looked at me for a second with a guilty look on his face. Remember when you said that I shouldn't sleep with anyone that worked here?"

"Yeah," I said, not liking where he was going.

"A few months ago we slept together and she got all weird about it."

'Wow,' I thought. 'Is there anyone that he hadn't slept with in the store?'

"The other day out of nowhere she asked me if I wanted to get together again. In fact, remember when you saw us talking in the parking lot when you were leaving to meet up with Julia? That's what she was saying. I didn't think it would be cool, because of how freaky she acted the first time."

"Freaky?"

"Yeah, she was weird about being in the same room with me and stuff. She was over it though. So I don't understand why she went all psycho like that."

"I do," I say after putting it all together.

"How come?"

"I don't know. I just want to say that this is why I said that you shouldn't have sex with people at work."

"I know. That's cool, not again."

"Good."

I went back behind the cash register and finished off the day there.

That night I considered calling Kelly. But each time I did I jacked off the brotha instead and the thought quickly passed. But after the brotha started to become too sore to touch I began to consider it again.

My hesitation came from when I asked myself why I would want to put myself through it. Kelly really was great. She was pretty. She was hot in fact. She made me laugh, and there was something about her that made me want to talk about things that I had never talked about. But Kelly was a person that had sex for a living. And even if what she usually did with guys didn't count as sex, she still jacked people off every day. All of that comparison could never end well for me in the long run.

And on top of that, she was an expensive girl. I'm sure that the first time that she, let's say, has one of those Disney executives on her table and he discovers how great she was, she would be his. And no matter how much I liked her, or how much I made her laugh, I wouldn't be able to compete with what he had. I was just a manager of a sports store, and my only hope would be some type of promotion.

So after pushing through one last jack off I went to sleep. I have to admit that it was a little amazing to me that I didn't feel the need to think about Rose and what happened at work. I can't explain why she didn't come up in my thoughts. I liked Rose, just like I liked Brian. Well, I guess I liked Brian a little more, but I gave her the old brotherly in and out, so that counts for something too.

But even with that, Rose's leaving didn't make me feel anything. I wasn't happy. I wasn't sad. I was just focused on Kelly and why I shouldn't call. Oh, and I was trying to figure out if jacking off enough would cause the brotha to spit sawdust. And the short answer to that one is no, sawdust will never come out. I think the little sticky chunks that did come out were parts of the inside of my balls that the brotha dry heaved up. But there was no sawdust.

I got to say though, that I was surprised that the brotha didn't even speak up then. He was suspiciously quiet during this entire thing. It wasn't like him to be so quiet.

The next morning when I went to work, Tina was waiting for me. She was one of the night cashiers. I saw her come in as I left and she told me that she was looking for a few extra hours. It was perfect timing.

After giving Tina the till and before it got busy I thought about Rose for the first time. I started to feel bad for her. I considered that I had done something wrong in not talking to her after we had sex. After all, that might have had something to do with why she quit.

I considered the idea that I should call her up and apologize. Maybe if I did I could convince her to come back. I knew that she didn't want to leave. I knew that she liked working here. I guess it would be a little strange to work under two people she had had sex with, but it wasn't like it was at the same time or anything. Neither of us cared.

It was the generous mood that I was in when my phone rang.

"This is Ben," I said, not expecting who it was.

"Hi, this is Susan from corporate."

"Hi Susan. What's up?" I said, not liking the timing of her call.

"Listen, I'm sitting here with Rose and I thought that I would bring you into the conversation."

"Ok," I said as the sweat beaded on my forehead.

"What she's telling me is that she's quitting. And that it's because you have created a sexual environment that she doesn't feel comfortable in."

"Ok," I say, while screaming at the top of my lungs in my mind.

"She's saying that you initiated a game called 'How gay is he?' And the object was to get one of your other employees to do things that would show how gay he was. Is this true?"

Ya know, as Susan said it aloud, I have to admit, the game did not sound good.

"And Rose is saying that someone bet that he was so gay," Susan continued uncomfortably, "that he would sleep with one of the guys that worked there. And then he had sex with the person in question. Is this true?"

Yeah, it looked bad. "Susan, I can't really say what happens between my employees when they are not at work."

"Did you tell the contestant in question that they would have to supply proof, if he had sex with him? And did you suggest that they have sex in front of one of the security cameras?" Susan said in a way that made it clear that she was grossed out by what she was saying.

It's funny because I don't remember ever telling Rose that I had tried to get Justin to jack off to Madonna where the security camera could capture it. Susan was too close to have made it up, so I must have told Rose at some point. I'm just grateful that Rose didn't actually tell her that I suggested it so that I could win the bet. Because if she'd mentioned that, I would really come off looking bad.

But, clearly Rose was there at corporate because she wanted to get back at me. She was pissed and I don't blame her. I should have spoken to her about our time together. None of this probably would have happened if I had just talked to her about what we had done. And realizing all of that told me what I had to do next. I had to admit my mistake.

"Susan, I think that all of this could be cleared up if I just told you something. Rose and I, both being adults, had sex together. And…"

"Ben, stop talking. Just stop talking. Stop talking."

"But I need to tell you what happened."

"Ss-top. Just stop. I'll call you back. Just wait there. Don't go anywhere. I'll call you back." With that Susan hung up.

The fact that she cut me off and told me to shut up told me that I may have said something wrong. It was always hard to tell with Susan, but that was my guess. After an hour of sitting in my office I left the door open and stood outside the door scanning the store.

From his section Chip caught my glance. And when he did, he walked over to me.

"Tell me, does Justin know about the bet that we had on him?" I asked Chip, hoping that Chip would know.

"No, he doesn't know. He would probably quit if he knew. He's really uncomfortable about being gay and he could barely admit it to me even though, well you know. He and I did stuff. That's why I never collected my winnings. If it got back to him that it was a part of the bet he would really be hurt."

I guess Chip was a better person than I gave him credit for. Because let's be real, 50 bucks is 50 bucks.

"Rose is at corporate right now and she told Susan about our little bet. And from what I can tell, she did not make it sound good."

"Crap, I told her I slept with Justin."

"And again, this is why you don't sleep with people at work," I said like a hypocrite.

"Do you think she mentioned that to Susan? You think they're gonna fire me?"

"She definitely mentioned it to Susan, but I don't know if she mentioned you by name, so you might be safe."

"What about you?" Chip asked.

"Susan loves me. The last thing she would do is fire me. But I gotta say, Rose made me look really bad."

"I don't know why she freaked out like this. You think it was because I didn't hook up with her again."

I smile a little. "No, it's probably something else."

"Because she was like begging. I don't want to say anything bad about her, but she was acting all pathetic. She was like saying like 'please Chip, please' and then she kind of went down on me in my car, but I stopped her."

"This was yesterday?" I asked, not recognizing Rose anywhere in his description.

"Yeah, this was right after you left."

'Oh fuck, I'm fired.' The thought hit me like a barbell on the chest. Rose was fuckin' pissed. She was humiliated by me not talking to her after what we had done, and then she was humiliated by Chip. What all that meant was that she was out for blood and she was at corporate in search of it.

The phone in my office rang, breaking my thought. I looked at Chip who was looking back at me. Chip looked as scared as I felt. And as horrible as I felt, it kind of felt good to have someone there who was going through it with me. It made me feel a little less alone.

I left Chip standing there and went into my office and closed the door.

"Hello?" I answered.

"Ben, this is Susan. Rose has left."

"Is everything ok?" I asked, hoping that it was.

"It is. She has agreed not to sue."

"What would she sue for?" I asked, not realizing how far Rose would go.

"Sexual harassment."

"But she was the one who kept coming on to me. I almost didn't want to do it."

"So, you didn't want to have sex with her?" Susan asked with a glimmer of hope.

"Almost," I said, hoping that it changed everything.

"Almost? No, once you put yourself in that position you opened the company up to a lawsuit. We have a very strict policy about management becoming sexually involved with the people they manage, and this is why."

"But I didn't sexually harass her."

"Maybe, but by admitting that you two had sex, and because of the awful bet you made up, you gave her ammunition. And with that ammunition she could at least get it to trial. It is simply cheaper for us to settle."

"Rose is not the suing type. I'm sure she'll settle," I added, a little excited that it could all soon be over.

"She already did. She only wanted one thing. She wanted you to be fired."

When Susan said that, my heart sunk. My face began to feel very hot, and a lump developed in my throat. "So what are you gonna do?" I asked Susan, praying that she could make all of this go away.

"I'm going to let you go. We have a very strict policy about this, and you signed a contract that stated that you wouldn't get involved with any of your employees. So on that basis, we have to let you go."

There was an emptiness that consumed me when she told me that I was going to be fired. It was an awful feeling. And without realizing it my chin began to twitch uncontrollably. I was beginning to lose my composure.

All of the friends that I ever had in Orlando I got because of this job. Everything good that I thought about myself was because of this job. This job was my reason for getting up in the morning. It was all I had. I managed a sports store. It wasn't impressive. It wasn't flashy. But it was what I was good at.

"Did you hear me, Ben?" Susan asked in a very flat voice.

The first time I tried to reply the sound of my voice betrayed me. My voice was high and it hurt to speak. I quickly cleared my voice and tried again. "Yes, I heard you. When do you want me to leave?"

"I think that it would be best if you left now. You will be paid for an extra two weeks as long as everything goes well."

I recognized what she was doing. This was my reward for not stealing anything on the way out. That is what she meant by 'everything going well.' It ripped my heart out to know that after all of these years Susan thought so little of me. I felt like falling down onto my knees right there in my office and throwing up. But I wasn't going to let that happen.

"So you just want me to go?" I asked, trying to imagine how they could survive without all of my experience.

"You can just go. Don't worry about anything."

"Ok," I said in a voice that cracked again.

"I'm sorry. Bye Ben," Susan said with a hint of compassion.

"Should I come in to pick up my check?"

"We'll mail it to you."

"Ok." I tried to say bye but nothing came out. Instead I simply hung up the phone.

Susan had made it very clear that she wanted me out, but I had to stay in my office for a bit. I didn't move, I just stood there. It was all happening too fast. Too many changes were happening too fast. It was all too much. I felt the vomit pushing to my throat again and it took a lot to hold it back. It took a lot to hold the tears back. It took a lot to just keep standing. And I almost let go of all of it at once when someone knocked on the door.

After a moment Chip popped his head in. "Are you ok?" he asked.

I couldn't reply. I couldn't speak without everything pouring out.

"Susan just called me. She told me what happened. She wanted me to collect your key. It's not right Ben. You shouldn't be fired. Who's gonna train me? I don't think I can do this without you."

I looked at Chip and knew that he wasn't just saying words. He really didn't know if he could do it without me. I got the real sense that he needed my support. He needed me to say something to him, because what he was doing was a lot harder than what I was. My entire life had just fallen apart. But I got the sense that Chip had real problems.

I made sure that my voice sounded strong before I spoke. "No, you'll do fine."

"I don't know what I'm doing," Chip admitted.

"They'll send someone down to train you. And who knows maybe one day you'll be the manager here."

I was glad that I had promoted Chip before things started happening. I liked Chip. Chip was a good guy. I wanted him to do well. So instead of falling apart there in the office I reached for my keys and handed them to Chip.

"Are we going to stay in touch?" Chip asked.

"Absolutely," I said with the same tone that I had used with Brian.

Chip smiled a smile of relief. But the truth was that I never expected to see Chip again. It wasn't like I was going to avoid him. I just knew that we would never cross paths again.

"So, should I call you or something?" he asked.

"Sure, or I'll call you. Either one."

I collected my stuff out of the drawers and piled it on the desk. I emptied out the ledgers from a box and replaced it with my years of workplace items. It was amazing just how little of my stuff I kept here, in spite of the fact that it felt like this job was all I was.

On the way out the door, I called out Justin and Tammy's names and waved bye to them. They obviously didn't know what was going on because they just stared back stunned.

Chip walked me all the way to my car. Even after I got in, it felt like he didn't want to let go of me. It felt good to feel wanted, even if it would be for just a short while more. I started the car and drove away, and Chip followed behind me a little. But once I got onto the street, he was just a person standing alone in the parking lot.

I was sure to hold it together until I was far enough away that no one from work would ever see me. And I almost held it together longer than that. But unfortunately, the brotha decided to speak up for the first time in days and said, "did you sleep with Rose because you thought that I wanted you to?"

"No, I..." I thought about what he asked, and the truth was that I kinda did. And with that thought everything came out. I pulled the car onto the side of the road and dry heaved as I leaned outside the car. And when the moisture rolled down my chin I thought it was spit, but I was crying. That fuckin' job was everything to me. It was fuckin' everything. And now it was gone. I wondered what I had left.

Chapter 13
How to Be Happy

Days passed as I waited for Susan to call me and tell me that the place had fallen apart without me. What I expected was that after a day or two of being short-staffed, the company would be brought to its knees. I did a great job there and I kept their trains running on time. But in spite of that fact, Susan didn't call.

I also waited for Rose to call me, upset with herself, begging for my forgiveness for doing what she did. Certainly everyone does things in a heated moment that they might not do otherwise. And once the fog clears we have regrets. Rose had to have had regrets about what she did. I assumed that she would be so overwhelmed with guilt that she would call me. But she didn't call either.

In fact, as those few days had passed, my phone hadn't rung at all. My mom hadn't called, Brian hadn't called, and not even Chip had called. There was no one reaching out to me trying to find out how I was or what I was going to do next. It was painful to accept this while the sun was still shining through the windows.

At night after the gym I found it easy to flip on the television and let the noise fill the space. The sounds the TV made were comforting. The dialog between the characters on the shows made me feel like there was more life in the house than my own.

But during the day, when all that was on were reruns and talk shows, I was starting to feel a little pathetic. How did I go so long like this? How did I live the past twelve plus years in a city where the only person that I spoke to out of work was a borderline alcoholic penis? How could this be my life?

Without work I moved everything on my schedule up. I woke as usual, had breakfast, but instead of work I headed to the gym. I did one extra rep of everything and then took an extra-long time in the steam room.

In the days since leaving work there was almost never anyone in the steam room with me. In the one day that there was, I was kind of hoping that the brotha would try something or say something, but that didn't happen either.

What I experienced instead was silence. And the other thing I experienced was loneliness. As the dark cloud set upon me I wondered if these were new feelings or feelings that I had been experiencing all along. And to my surprise, the answer that came out of nowhere was yes, the feelings that I was having were nothing new. And once I heard that unknown voice speak to me I began to wonder what else I may have missed all of this time. What other things could I have brushed over in all of my hours at work?

As soon as I asked I remembered my father. He wasn't a person that I thought about much, but for some reason over the last two weeks he had come up at least three times. My dad was a buried thought. I didn't allow myself to think about him. He was a man that stayed just long enough to be able to say that he did his obligation. I didn't hate him because at least he stayed that long, but he wasn't a person that deserved my time either.

'Was that it?' I wondered. 'Is that all there was to me?'

That wasn't it however. Without thinking about it I remembered when I was 14 and my friends had left me in the pit and taken my clothes. I remembered how the brotha had treated me ever since. I remembered how Tommy had left me in Orlando. And after that it hit me that Susan wasn't going to call. I wasn't going to hear from Rose and I was sitting in my house alone. That's when I raced for a drink.

Speed was important for this process because it all was beginning to weigh down on me. And the weight was actually beginning to make my knees buckle. And unless I wanted to be trapped on the ground under the weight of it all, I needed to get drunk fast.

The first thing I could grab from the liquor cabinet was vodka. I didn't like vodka. It was more of the brotha's drink, but it had the benefit of already being in my hand and time was of the essence. I was pulled down onto my knees as I unscrewed the cap. My back was already starting to bend under the weight when I tried to lift the bottle to my mouth.

I found that my head was already too weighed down to pour the vodka in it so I let my body fall onto the ground and then poured the vodka in from the side. It was a messy way of doing it. I mostly missed my mouth but I soaked up what hit the floor with my clothes. After a few gulps I knew that I had enough. All I had to do next was wait. It usually took fifteen minutes before my thoughts began to scatter, so I just had to lay there and wait it out.

"Do you hate me?" I heard from somewhere below. My mind was beginning to drift so it took a second to recognize the voice of the brotha.

"I don't fuckin' hate you. I hate me. You know why I hate me?"

"Why?" the brotha asked in a very sad voice.

"Because you're attached to me. You're a fuckin' destroyer of lives. But I let you do it. I'm a fuckin' weak ass pussy son of a bitch, and I let you destroy my life."

"So are you going to blame me for everything? Is that it?" the brotha asked in a tone unchanged from the sadness he'd expressed earlier.

"Yeah, I'm fuckin' blamin' you. I was gonna be normal. I was gonna be like everyone else, but then you opened your fuckin' mouth and turned me into a fuckin' loner. You hear me. I'm a fuckin' loser loner."

"Are you happy?" the brotha asked me in a way that made it seem like there could be more than one answer.

"Am I happy? You're asking me if I'm fuckin' happy? I fuck some woman because I knew you wanted me to. And then that causes me to get fired from the one thing that matters to me and you're asking me if I'm happy? What the fuck?"

"You blame me for the way your life turned out?" the brotha asked, still in the calm, sad tone.

"Who the fuck else's fault could it be?" I yell back, feeling the effects of the vodka.

"It could be yours," the brotha calmly replied.

"Mine?"

"I feel bad about what happened to you. And you could even say that's my fault in a way."

"The fuck you say?"

"But Rose didn't fuck you over because you screwed her. She fucked you over because you fucked her over. You screwed her and then didn't talk to her again even though you worked in the same room with each other. How do you think that might have made her feel?"

"So you're gonna talk to me about etiquette? Oh that's rich. That's fuckin' hilarious. You are a funny motha fucka, my brotha."

"Yeah, I know. But the truth remains that she fucked you because you fucked her," the brotha replied.

"Hmm. So what do you want me to say to that?"

"I want you to admit to it. I want you to admit that what's happening to you now is because of you and not me."

"Ah fuck off," I say, feeling the relief that allowed me to roll over onto my back.

"And I want you to admit to the fact that the reason you have no friends is because you never call anyone back."

"You're getting fucking annoying now."

"Think about it. You fuckin' cried like a little pussy when Brian left. But have you bothered to pick up the phone and call him? Chip wanted you to call him. He could have been a friend, but have you done that either? Kelly's got the fuckin' hots for you, but you won't even pick up the phone and call her."

"Get to your fuckin' point," I say, hating the brotha for showing me my ass.

"My fuckin' point is 'are you happy?'"

"No I'm not fuckin' happy!" I yell back.

"Then why the fuck do you think that is?" the brotha says back, raising his voice for the first time. "Do you think that's because of me? Or do you think it's because your father fucked you up in the head and now you don't call anybody back?"

"You fuckin' dick."

"Well, you're a fuckin' asshole!" the brotha says with fire.

"You're a fuckin' dick. You piece of shit fuckin' dick."

"God made me a dick. What's your excuse you fuckin' turd?"

"So what do you want from me? Huh?"

"I want you to get off your ass and call someone."

"Is that what you want? Is that what you want?"

"Yes, that's what I want," the brotha replied without backing off.

"Ok, fine. I'll call someone. I'll call someone you fuckin' fuck." I'm really wasted and it's very hard for me to get up to my knees but I do. And after that I can't muster up the strength to make it to my feet so I crawl into my bedroom.

As I feel my knees drag across the carpet I think about who I'm going to call. And in my drunken state, only one person comes to mind. Kelly. She was the only one I wanted to talk to. In fact, I think that she was the only person that I could talk to. There was something about her eyes and about her face that said to me that she wanted to listen and that I was safe. So after the weight of all of the vodka made it to my legs I continued by dragging them along.

When I made it to the bedroom with the phone in my hand I did my best to remember the number but I couldn't. Then I tried to remember how to find her number on the phone and that didn't work either.

'Her name's not Kelly," I thought. 'It's under something else.'

I scroll through the numbers but it's tough because my focus was becoming really bad. But when I finally recognize a name I stop and dial it. It rings for a bit and a less than enthusiastic voice on the other end replies.

"Hello?"

'This isn't right,' I think. But I'm not thinking straight so I do my best to continue. "It's Ben. I'm sorry. I should have called you. I don't know why I didn't call you. I know why I didn't call you. It's because I'm fucked in the head. I am. I'm fucked in the head and I'm sorry about that.

But I need to talk to you. I need to see you. Will you meet me? I want you to meet me, will you meet me?"

"Where do you want to meet?"

"I don't know. That's how fucked I am. No wait, I know." There was only one place that I knew about where people went to meet others. "Do you know the Grand Hotel?"

"Yeah."

"Will you meet me there?"

"What time?"

This was a hard question. I knew I couldn't drive now. I couldn't even see, but I had to figure out when I could. 'It must be one o'clock,' I guessed. "Eight".

"Ok, eight."

"Are you gonna be there? Are you gonna be there at eight?" I asked.

"I'll be there."

"Ok, bye."

She hung up without a bye and even in my drunken state I questioned if she would be there. But even if she wasn't I knew that I had to be. I looked at the time display on the phone. It looked like it was two-something. I wasn't sure where the time went from when I was just talking to her to it being two o'clock, but it had. Instead of thinking about the passage of time, I rolled over and threw up on the carpet. It was alcohol filled puke, so I knew that having thrown up would help me to sober up.

'I'm gonna have to take a shower,' I thought. But that was in the future, right then the vomit made the carpet warm. And I had to admit it felt kind of nice. It stunk to high hell, but it felt good.

I woke up four hours later still lying on the carpet. All I could perceive was the most god-awful smell imaginable. The smell alone made me want to vomit, but I choked it back and opened my eyes instead.

I didn't rush to get up. I knew that I had been lying in puke for the last however long so a few seconds more wouldn't change anything. I slowly sat up and looked at the clock. It was 6:30. I still had an hour and a half before I had to meet Kelly, so I had enough time to clean up.

When I made it to my feet I couldn't help but notice that I was still pretty drunk. I wasn't stumbling anymore and my head wasn't spinning, but my head felt like it was on a slide. All of my moments felt like they were happening on a doll that I was attached to but wasn't me. That was the way I always felt when I was drunk and this was the same.

I looked down at the carpet. The vomit didn't cover too large of an area. I knew how to clean it up and in a few days there wouldn't even be a smell anymore. But the first thing on the list would be to shower off the chunks that had stuck to my hair and had attached itself to my face.

The warm water felt good when I got there. I always liked being drunk in the shower because I felt the feeling of the droplets even more. And when I looked down to let the water hit my neck, it felt good to see the brotha right where he was supposed to be. The two of us didn't exchange any words. The truth was that I didn't know what to say to him. I remembered everything that he said to me and now that I was a little more sober the words were beginning to sting.

I didn't bother to get dressed to clean up the carpet. I knew whatever I put on would just smell like puke and cleaning supplies afterwards so what would be the point. Instead I mixed a capful of lilac floor cleaner into some water in the sink and deposited a rag. When the smell of lilacs diluted in the water I added more. The scent of lilacs had to be as overwhelming as the puke. And when I was done the carpet smelt like flowers as well. I then pointed the fan onto the spot to help it dry.

It was now forty-five minutes away from my meeting and I still felt too drunk to drive. So I hopped in the shower for another quick rinse and then found something to eat. The left over fried chicken was good, but didn't settle in my stomach very well.

'I'm a mess,' I thought. 'I'm a fuckin' mess.'

With twenty minutes left I got dressed and headed out the door. Outside I smelled myself again to make sure that all of the recent smells were gone. And when I was assured I hopped in the car and left. Driving there I still felt drunk, but I didn't feel too drunk to drive.

Driving there I thought about it and relaxed into the idea that Kelly was my dream. When I was a kid I once had a dream about a naked blonde girl standing in the docking area of an empty warehouse. I found her so perfect and beautiful that I never forgot her. But as beautiful as she was, what struck me most about here was her innocence.

I was worried about this naked girl because the warehouse wasn't in a safe neighborhood. But she knew where she was and she never felt worried. For some reason she felt that she would be safe. Even as a kid I knew that I would do everything I could do to allow this girl to remain naked while also feeling safe. And now I was sure that in spite of the fact that the dream girl was fair and blonde, and Kelly was dark-haired and tanned, I knew my dream girl was Kelly.

I crossed the Grand Hotel lobby not caring who was looking at me. I was in a march of destiny. I stepped through the restaurant doors and found the tables half-filled with people.

'Oh, she's going to have a hard time finding me,' I thought. 'I should sit at the bar.'

I crossed the room toward the bar and my pace slowed the closer I got. I wasn't sure, but sitting at the bar at the same spot that I had seen him before looked like Chip. Chip looked out and spotted me, and then immediately spun back around hoping I hadn't seen him.

I was disappointed to see Chip there. This was the place where Chip picked up his clients and he had promised me that this part of his life was over. As I thought about it, as tragic as my firing was, one of the things that gave me some relief was the thought that I had changed Chip's life. It seems that wasn't true either.

I walked over to Chip and sat down next to him. "Hey man," I said, trying to hide my disappointment.

"Hey," he said without looking me in the eyes.

"I didn't expect to see you here," I added, hoping it would inspire him to explain why he was there.

"Yeah," he replied, not saying any more.

"How's it going at work? You still there?"

"It's rough, man. They have me working all these hours and I don't know what I'm doing. It sucks that you're not there, man. I can't handle it all."

"You been coming here often?" I asked, trying to not seem judgmental.

"No."

"No?" I asked, hoping he would explain.

"No, this is the first time since you left. I've been too busy."

The bartender approaches me, and although I wasn't planning on drinking, the sight of Chip makes me want a drink. "Amaretto sour, please."

"I thought you said that you weren't going to do this anymore?" I ask trying my best to not spook him.

"Yeah, that's when I thought you were going to be working there with me. But you left."

"I didn't leave on purpose. Believe me, if I could, I would still be there."

"But you still left and I'm in way over my head, man. I can't do this. Why'd they have to fire you, man. I can't do this by myself. They're expecting me to do stuff. Why'd you leave, man?"

A person wants to be missed when they leave a job. You want the person who fired you to feel screwed for doing it. But I didn't consider the impact that it would have on Chip. I didn't realize to what extent Chip would miss me being there. I'm sure that he would have been content to just keep doing what he was doing. I was the one that made him consider more. And just like that I left him when he needed my help most.

It didn't matter to him whether I was fired or I quit. All he knew was that he trusted me to help him through the most difficult transition of his life and then I disappeared. My heart broke for him in that moment.

When the bartender arrived with my drink I was happy to get it down. The glass was half empty before it touched the bar again and I encouraged the feeling that would follow.

"I'm sorry, man," I said with as much sincerity as I could produce. "I let you down. I should have been there to help you."

"You got fired, man. You didn't want to leave," he said, trying to give me comfort.

"But I didn't call you to help you through it. I should have called you, man. I don't know why I didn't call you."

Chip silently stirred his drink with his finger. That silence spoke a mouthful. He agreed that I should have called him. And it was now even harder on me knowing that he thought it too.

I returned to my glass and considered finishing off my drink. "You know, nothing they're going to ask you to do is that hard to learn."

"Yeah, but how am I supposed to learn it?" Chip said, breaking his silence.

"I could help you?" I said, surprised that it came out of my mouth.

"Yeah, but you don't work there anymore," he said, turning to me.

"I could call you and walk you through stuff."

"You mean like that thing with having to fill the till in the morning? I don't know how much of anything I'm supposed to put in there. I figured out that I was supposed to deposit the money at the end of the day, but I didn't realize that I was supposed to get change in the morning as well."

"These are all just simple things that you don't know. But I could tell you these things and once I do, you'll know it. These are all easy problems to solve."

"So you're gonna help me?" Chip asked me with a look of vulnerability that I had never seen in him before.

"Yeah, I'm gonna help you. And when I'm done, you're going to be the best manager they've ever had. Because you are going to have all of my knowledge and you won't sleep with any of your employees, right?" I ask with a smile.

"Right," Chip replied with a knowing smile back. "So you slept with Rose too, huh?"

"Yep, she was hot."

"Yeah, she was. A little boring in bed though," Chip said with a smile.

I laughed aloud at that and then remembered to look around for Kelly. As I scanned the room I didn't see Kelly, but to my surprise I saw Rose walk in.

"Fuck!" I exclaimed under my breath.

"What?"

"Rose just walked in, and I'm supposed to meet Kelly here."

"Fuck."

"She's gonna make a scene if she sees us talking together," I said to Chip.

"I'm gonna go," Chip said, knocking back his drink.

"Thanks. I'll call you tomorrow at 7:45 am. Got it?"

"Got it boss."

"Talk to you then."

Chip subtly got up and crossed the room in the opposite direction. After he's gone I look back at Rose. This time when I look back she sees me and starts walking towards me.

"Fuck," I said under my breath.

"I almost didn't come," she said.

'Almost didn't come?' I thought. 'What does she mean by that?'

"But you sounded pretty bad so I thought I should."

'Fuck, I called Rose instead of Kelly! Crap, what did I say?'

I stared at Rose blankly and with my mouth hanging open. I was at a loss for words.

"Ummm, I was pretty drunk when I called you."

"You sounded like it. That's why I almost didn't come. I didn't know if you would really be here."

"I'm here."

"I can see that," Rose said, with an edge in her voice.

My again drunk mind raced through all of the things that I could say or should say. And then it raced through all of the things that she would want me to say.
But after that it stopped racing and I didn't know what to say.

"So you wanted me to come here so you could continue to not say anything to me?"

"Rose, I didn't mean to ignore you like that."

"Then why did you?" Rose said angrily.

"Because I'm fucked up Rose. I am one fucked up guy."

"Yeah you are," she replied with venom.

"I am. But I never meant anything to be hurtful. I liked you. I really liked you. And I invited you by my place because I really wanted to make something real happen between the two of us."

"That's what I wanted too," she said, lowering her mask a little. "That's why I was so pissed when you acted like such an asshole afterwards."

"I get it. I was an asshole. But I was an asshole because I'm screwed up, not because I'm a dick. I just didn't know what to say because I didn't want to hurt you."

"Oh," Rose said, understanding how I felt about our time together. "So you didn't like me and you didn't want to hurt me by telling me."

"I guess."

"So instead you hurt me by not telling me."

"I guess. Did I mention that I was fucked up?"

"Yeah you are. You're also an asshole for telling me this. I could have just gone on hating you. You didn't have to invite me here to reject me properly."

"That's another thing. I didn't know what to say to you because after we were together, I met someone else. And the thing was that I didn't know how to handle that with you."

"You asshole!" Rose said, a little too loud for the space.

"What was I supposed to do? Put yourself in my position. I didn't go out to meet someone else, I just did. It was surprising. And say what you want, but with you the sex was awkward. It was awkward, right?"

"Yeah, it was a little off."

"With her it wasn't. I just had chemistry with her that we didn't have. We were really great work buddies, but it didn't translate. I wanted it to translate. I'm sure you wanted it to, but it didn't. Am I wrong?"

"No, you're right. I wish you would have told me this before though."

I turned back to my drink and finished it off. "I have a hard time talking about stuff sometimes." I turn back to my empty glass and stare at it.

After a long moment of silence I felt a hand slide across my back. No words followed. Instead we stayed like that for a while. After a few minutes Rose removed her hand and got up to go.

"I'm sorry I got you fired," Rose said. "I'll ask them to take you back if that will help."

"No, it won't," I say, accepting my new life the way it is.

"Ok."

Rose takes a few steps away and then walks back to me. I turn around and look at her.

"You can call me if you ever want to talk about anything. I liked talking to you. I know we're both screwed up, but maybe we could get past it."

I look at Rose's softened eyes. "Maybe we can. I'll call you." And this time when I say it, unlike with Brian and Chip, I meant it.

Rose walks off and I watch her go. She really did have a smokin' hot little body. It was too bad the way things turned out.

I spun around and looked at my empty glass again. I lifted my hand to see how much my joints floated. They floated a little. I was definitely buzzed. I considered what I should do next. I thought about buying another drink but that meant that I would be stuck on the stool for at least another hour.

'No, I want to go,' I thought.

I then started doing the math. 'The DMV says that at my body weight I could handle three drinks per hour and still be under the legal limit. I had one drink in thirty minutes plus an unknown amount that left me buzzed seven hours later. So that meant unless I had the equivalent of twenty-two drinks I should be fine to drive.'

I pay my bill and leave. I get into my car and consider my conversations between Chip and Rose. They both felt really good. It felt good to talk, and it felt good to help Chip. With those thoughts I began to look forward to the next morning when I would start to mentor him. It would feel great to help him do well. In fact, I began to think that helping Chip succeed could be my greatest accomplishment. That thought was exciting to me.

But as good as I was starting to feel, I knew that there was still one thing that was left undone. And after I pulled into my driveway, I sat there thinking about it.

"Are you awake, brotha?" I asked.

"I'm awake."

"I'm thinking about calling Kelly," I admitted to him.

"You mean, again?" the brotha added in a light-hearted way.

"Yeah, I guess. What do you think?"

"I was into you doing it the first time. I feel the same way now," the brotha replies as a matter of fact.

"But now, I am sober enough to realize why I shouldn't. I'm a no one who has nothing now. Who would want to be with a no one?"

"You have me, man, so that's more than nothing. And who knows, she may think that you have more than you think. Now, hurry up and call her before you completely sober up."

"Yeah, you're right."

I pull out my phone, find her number and press send. Two rings go by before she picks up.

"Hello?"

"Hey Kelly, this is Ben. Remember me?" I said, immediately regretting it.

"Umm, yeah, I remember you Ben," she said, laughing at me a little bit.

"I'm sorry that I haven't called you before."

"Yeah, I was starting to wonder, but that's ok, you called now."

"Listen, I was wondering if…" I didn't know what I was going to say. So without thinking I said, "if you wanted to come by my place tonight. There is something that I want to show you."

Kelly remained quiet. My mind was moving too slowly to figure out why she wasn't talking. Did I say something offensive? Was I being too forward? Was it ok for us to have sex at her place, but inappropriate to invite her to talk at mine?

"Umm, I wasn't inviting you to come over for sex or anything, I just wanted to talk," I said, trying to encourage her to speak.

"No, it's not that. I just wanted you to know that I was looking around online and I found exercises that I can do that would help me take you. I just wanted you to know that."

"Ok. That's fine."

"Just in case that is why you didn't call," Kelly said.

"No, it's not that. Could you come by? I really want to show you something," I persisted.

"Ok, where do you live?" she asked.

I gave her my address and she said that she would be over in an hour. My plan was that I would show her that even though I didn't have a job or a lot of money, I had a house. But the soberer that I got waiting for her, the stupider the idea felt.

Fifteen minutes before she arrived I was at a loss about what I was going to say to her. There was nothing unique about me. I had nothing that could convince this beautiful, dream girl that I was worth her time. I considered having another drink, but I had had enough at that point, so for good or bad, I was going to face this moment sober.

When the doorbell rang my chest hurt. It felt like someone had reached in and squeezed my heart and I didn't like it. Walking to the door I still didn't know what I was going to say. And looking into her beautiful face didn't help.

"Hi," was the only thing I could get out of my mouth. I liked this girl so much that I was struck dumb.

"Hi," she replied.

"Come in."

She walked in and looked around. "So, this is your place? I can't help but notice a surprising lack of shoes."

I laughed and when I did I could feel my voice return to me.

"These are nice though. Did you take these?" she asked, referring to the pictures on the wall.

"Yep, I took these when I visited the Bahamas. Have you ever been?"

"No, but I want to," she said, making her way from picture to picture. "What is this?" she asked stopping on the photos of a marsh.

"There's a national park in Grand Bahama called Lucaya National Park. One part of the park is a marsh and it leads to this incredible beach. In fact, this is it here."

I lead her over to the picture of the beaches that I often stared at; the three that hung in a row at the entrance of the kitchen.

"The two outer photos are of Gold Rock Creek beach, the beach attached to the park. And the middle picture is the same beach from a different angle," said, watching her as she looked at the photos.

"These are beautiful. I like this middle one."

I looked at the middle beach picture again. It was the photo of the beach from behind the thick web of mangrove tree roots. It was a darker picture. It always saddened me to look at that photo.

"The middle one is me," I said without thinking. "That's the way I see life."

Kelly looked at me for a moment staring deep into my eyes. She then turned back to get a better look at the photo. "How so?"

"To me life seems so beautiful. The sun is out, the water's warm and the sand is white and cool. But I can't touch it. All I can do is look at it from the darkness, blocked in by all of the things that are stopping me. I want to get out from under everything but I can't."

Kelly turns back to me and again looks deep into my eyes. I notice how she began to breathe harder, and it looked like she wanted to speak, but couldn't.

"I have something I need to tell you. I'm not a rich man. In fact, a couple of days ago I was fired from the job that I did have. I don't have much. And I'm kind of broken. You're so beautiful and so great that I can't think of any reason why you would want to be with me. But I still want you."

Kelly fights for a couple of seconds and then pushes the words out. "I never asked you to be rich. I never cared about what type of job you had. I know those types of guys, but I don't want to be with any of them. I want to be with you.

You make me laugh. And I like the way you speak. It's hard to meet a guy that knows how to speak, and the way you speak makes me feel good."

With those words my heart started to race. I wasn't sure what was happening or who she was describing, but I liked that she was saying it to me. I looked closer at her eyes and they began to shine in the light. If I wasn't mistaken, she was beginning to cry.

"But I'm just scared," she continued, with the tears rolling down her face. "I'm scared that I won't be able to please you and you're going to leave me."

My heart ached for her as she fell onto my chest and reached her arms around me. I wanted to pull her into my body and protect her, never letting her go. I loved her; her beauty, her humor, her incredible innocence and her acceptance of me. I loved her and wanted her. And the thought of her leaving my house and not seeing her began to feel unbearable to me. I wanted to protect her, I wanted to care for her. And I knew whatever it took to keep her, I would do.

Sex wasn't important. The size of the brotha wasn't important. What I did to earn money wasn't important. What was important was that she was someone I could talk to. She was someone that I could share with. Intimacy is what people called it. And she was my intimate.

In that moment I realized that I had now lost everything that once mattered to me. But I also began to realize that I had gained a few things in return. I had lost my job and the powerful feeling that came with being the boss. But in Chip I had gained someone I could actually help. As the boss I helped myself. But from what I could tell so far, it felt even better helping someone who truly needed it.

I had lost someone I could feel good flirting with in Rose. But what I instead gained with Rose was someone that I could be honest with. There was a rush that came when she and I flirted. But the idea of having a friend felt even better. It felt more real somehow. It felt like the difference between being asleep and being awake.

And most importantly I had lost my bubble, my protective shell where I could hide when things got too hard. But with Kelly, that was now gone too. I couldn't seem to hide myself from Kelly. Somehow Kelly had a way of making all of the things that I locked inside of me come out.

It was involuntarily. And because I couldn't control it, it felt scary. But if I were truly honest with myself, I knew that even if I had a year to think about it, there was nothing else that I could possibly want. It was scary, but somehow it felt like I was returning home.

All of these thoughts were new to me, but the feelings that they made me feel were familiar. It felt good. I was happy. And as I looked down into Kelly's tearful eyes, I had no question what she was thinking. She was happy too and she wanted, or even needed me to kiss her.

So with a final breath of what felt like my old life, I stepped back a little. I placed my hand on her face, bent down, and touched her lips to mine. It felt good. And with all of that, with everything that had happened, I could say it without having to think about it. My life was better. I was happy! And I knew that the brotha was happy too.

The End.

Buy the Sequel Available Fall 2010:

Happiness thru the Art of...
Having Sex like a Porn Star:
A 'Novel Guide' to Sexual Positions, Multiple Orgasms, <u>Increasing Your Sex Drive & Other Sexual Secrets</u>*

'Happiness thru the Art of... Having Sex like a Porn Star' is the sequel to 'Happiness thru the Art of... Penis Enlargement'. Follow the further adventures of Ben and his talking penis 'the Brotha,' as the Brotha tries to stop drinking, and Ben attempts to make his new relationship work.

*Go to RateABull.com to check release dates and availability.

Buy these Books Now from author Cristian YoungMiller:

Everybody Masturbates

'Everybody Masturbates' is the perfect gift idea for anyone from ages 8 to 42 yrs old. In the style of the classic book 'Everyone Poops,' 'Everybody Masturbates' is designed to make boys and girls of all ages feel comfortable about masturbation. (It also makes a great party gift for adults.)

Everybody Masturbates *for Girls*

'Everybody Masturbates *for Girls*' is the perfect gift idea for girls between the ages of 7 to 38 yrs old. Also, in the style of the classic book 'Everyone Poops,' 'Everybody Masturbates *for Girls*' addresses the specific issues that girls have accepting their emerging sexuality. (It also makes a great party gift for adults.)

*Go to RateABull.com to check release dates and availability.

Buy Winter 2010 from author Cristian YoungMiller:

The First Day After Life:
A Spiritual Adventure about Why Bad Things Happen & How to Shape your Future*

'The First Day After Life is a story about a psychic who dies, tours the afterlife like he's backstage at a theme park, and as a result, discovers the real explanation for why God lets bad things happen to good people.

The Story Synopsis:

In the story, Tian is a young psychic with overwhelming personal demons and a strong sense of purpose. When he dies unexpectedly he arrives in the afterlife to find that the new world is nothing like he read in books or that his psychic abilities led him to expect. Irabell, a guide, shows Tian that the afterlife is a repository for more than just humans, and explains to him the mystery that created his psychic abilities and the afterworld. Disturbed by what he learns, Tian escapes his spiritual guide and breaks into heaven. There Tian meets a 1500 year old, discontented, heavenly resident who shares with him the secret of heaven and god.

Tian's otherworldly journey is cut short when he is forced to make the most important decision of his life; whether to stay knowing the secrets he's uncovered about the afterlife, or to forget everything and return to his broken, earthly body to complete what he now understands was his life's mission. The story alternates between the unfolding drama of the man's earthly life, and the evolving journey of his afterlife. And it uses the interaction between each to reveal how to use the universal laws to shape your own destiny, and why god lets bad things happen to good people.

*Go to RateABull.com to check release dates and availability.

Join the Free Online Community at RateABull.com

RateABull.com is an online community created by author Cristian YoungMiller. Cristian created the website so that members can give and get advice from each other on all topics. Because you may not know the answer to your problems, but there's a world of people that do. Connect with them and make your life better.

Here's what you can do there:

- Communicate with the author Cristian YoungMiller and ask him questions about the book
- Connect with others that are following Cristian Jelqing technique
- Ask for and give advice about sex, relationships and life
- Watch the videos and read the conversations that inspired this book
- Find out about upcoming seminars, webinars and appearances by author Cristian YoungMiller

Take a Trip to The Bahamas Online at RememberTheBahamas.com

Author Cristian YoungMiller was born in the Bahamas. Go to his popular online store to purchase the most popular products from the Bahamas and take a trip without even leaving home.

- Rent a beach house on one of the most beautiful, secluded beaches in the world
- Purchase the popular pineapple flavored soda Goombay Punch
- Buy the colognes made and sold only in the Bahamas
- Connect with others that have visited the Bahamas

www.ingramcontent.com/pod-product-compliance
Lightning Source LLC
LaVergne TN
LVHW091537060526
838200LV00036B/645